Life, Slightly

Life, Slightly

Nigel Jay Cooper

ROUNDFIRE
BOOKS

Winchester, UK
Washington, USA

JOHN HUNT PUBLISHING

First published by Roundfire Books, 2022
Roundfire Books is an imprint of John Hunt Publishing Ltd., No. 3 East St., Alresford,
Hampshire SO24 9EE, UK
office@jhpbooks.com
www.johnhuntpublishing.com
www.roundfire-books.com

For distributor details and how to order please visit the 'Ordering' section on our website.

Text copyright: Nigel Jay Cooper 2021

ISBN: 978 1 78535 963 7
978 1 78535 964 4 (ebook)
Library of Congress Control Number: 2021942793

A CIP catalogue record for this book is available from the British Library.

Design: Stuart Davies

UK: Printed and bound by CPI Group (UK) Ltd, Croydon, CR0 4YY
Printed in North America by CPI GPS partners

We operate a distinctive and ethical publishing philosophy in
all areas of our business, from our global network of authors to
production and worldwide distribution.

Praise for Life, Slightly

Compulsively readable like a thriller and beautifully written like a Sally Rooney novel, this is a story I won't soon forget. Heartwarming and heartbreaking at the same time, this book is certainly going places!
—Awais Khan

I was deeply moved by this beautifully told story of love, forgiveness, and finding your way. The characters really shone and I couldn't stop turning the pages.
–Laura Pearson

Praise for Nigel Jay Cooper

Semi-finalist, Best Debut Author, Goodreads Choice Awards.
Finalist, The People's Book Prize for Fiction.
Longlisted, *The Guardian's* Not The Booker Prize.
An author with a truly compelling insight into the human condition.
—Siobhan Kennedy, *Channel 4 News*
Cooper has a rare knack for presenting flawed characters in a way that makes the reader care about them.
—*Love Reading UK*
A new voice. Fresh and different.
—Maha Diwan

With love, for anyone who needs it.

Part 1

Strangers on a Bench

~ Chapter 1 ~

She finds them on benches. The broken ones, the lonely ones, the ones who don't know they're broken. She tries to mend them and although she isn't always successful, sometimes she is and that's enough. Most of the time.

She leans back against her wooden bench and surveys the park. The sun is low in the sky for this time of year, casting a yellow-orange light that makes everything seem slightly displaced and unreal around her. Overgrown bamboo rustles lightly in the breeze as birds play on the stone waterfall that rises from the back of a small, ornate pond. They splash themselves, bathing or drinking or doing whatever it is birds do when they find themselves ankle deep in water.

She's been sitting here for over an hour now, singing to herself quietly as families drift in and out, children on scooters, mothers showing infant babies the pond, searching for fish. They aren't her type, not today at least. This one has to be special and while she can't put her finger on exactly who she's looking for, she trusts the process. Someone *right* will come along, they always do. It's still early, she has all day. No rush. Perhaps she'll nip to the café to get a take-away coffee while she waits.

No.

Her heart pulses, again, again, again.

There he is.

Late thirties, early forties, maybe? Wearing jeans and white trainers. A blue T-shirt with the words 'I see you' written in small white letters to the left of his chest.

Gavin.

Her song dies in her throat, dried by recognition and excitement. He leans on the low railings by the pond with his back to her, about a metre in front of the bench she's sitting on.

'Nina Simone,' the man says, jolting her back to reality. His voice is low, gravelly but reassuring, the type of voice she immediately wants to hear more of. It's him, she's sure of it.

'What?' Jackie replies, chalk dust in her throat. Nobody speaks to her first, that's not how this works. She always does the introductions.

'The song you were singing. It was Nina Simone,' he says, turning around to look at her, breeze ruffling his dark hair.

'Oh,' she replies. He can't know her, at most he might have seen her in Louise's café but even then—

Get up and leave, the voice in her head says. It used to be confined to her dreams but it invades her waking life more frequently by the day.

It's fine, she replies internally. He doesn't know who I am.

But you know him.

He doesn't know that.

Stop lying to yourself.

'I didn't mean to disturb you,' the man continues quickly. 'You have a nice voice, that's all.'

'Thank you,' she replies, attempting to return his smile, deliberately slowing her breath down.

Okay, this is okay. He doesn't know who she is, how could he? She's being silly. He's being friendly, that's all.

He looks away from her, clearly losing himself in his thoughts as the surface of the pond undulates in the wind. Eventually, she gets up and walks to stand next to him, staring into the murky water silently, chest thrashing and kicking beneath her rain mac.

'What happened to the fish?' she asks clumsily.

'Dead, I imagine,' he replies. 'Since they did the refurb.'

'It looks exactly the same as before, why did they refurbish it?'

'It probably had cracks underneath,' he says quietly, almost to himself.

'Maybe,' Jackie replies, African drummers on her temples. There's an energy about him, something *electric*. The air between them is fizzing. The voice in her head is right, she should walk away but she already knows she won't. She can't.

'I'm Gavin,' he says with a wide smile, extending his hand.

'Call me Jackie,' she says quietly, taking his hand as her cheeks flush.

'If you like,' he replies, shrugging his shoulders. The park around them descends into quiet, save for the distant sound of children in the playground. For a moment, Jackie and Gavin stand side by side in each other's company, strangers at the start of something.

You're not at the start of anything. You never are.

Shut up.

He's nothing to do with you. They're never anything to do with you.

That's not true.

Name one of them that mattered.

Adam.

He killed himself.

I tried to help him.

Stalking someone isn't the same as helping them.

That's not fair.

You're supposed to be moving on.

What do you think I'm doing?

Talking to Adam's friend.

They were hardly friends.

Are you sure about that?

What's that supposed to mean?

Jackie shuts her eyes tightly behind her sunglasses, centring herself, refusing to let the negative thoughts take hold. It isn't her voice, she knows it isn't. Breathe deeply. Focus. She doesn't have to listen to it, not right now.

Besides, he's different, it's not like it was with Adam, she can feel it. When she looks at Gavin, it's like the future is reaching back for her, grabbing her tightly and pulling her gently towards it. If she wants to, she can resist any time, but why should she?

'What's your story then?' Jackie asks, waving her hand towards Gavin's jeans and T-shirt. 'Day off work?'

'Sort of,' he replies quietly. 'I'm a photographer, at least I'm trying to be. Long story.'

'Now you've got my interest,' she says with a playfulness she doesn't feel. If anything, she feels inexplicably nervous, like events are moving out of her control.

'I had your interest the moment I walked in here,' he replies, an infectious smile crossing his face.

'You started talking to me, remember?'

'Yeah, sorry, I'll leave you to it, I didn't mean to interrupt your singing.'

'You don't have to go,' she says quickly. 'You didn't disturb me, honestly.'

He shrugs his shoulders again and turns around, stepping back towards the bench behind them, sitting down where Jackie had been moments before.

'You've stolen my seat,' Jackie continues with forced levity.

'Have I?'

'Yes.' She nods towards him. 'I was just sitting there, you saw me.'

'The seats don't have names on them.'

'They do actually.'

He stands up, looking to where she's pointing, at a brass plaque and inscription which reads:

Christopher Baker

Elsie Winterbottom

'I've always wondered who they were,' Jackie says, ashamed that in reality, she's never given them a second thought. As Gavin squints at the plaques in the sunlight, Jackie moves in front of him and sits down, obscuring them and smiling up at him widely.

'You don't care about poor Elsie and Christopher at all, do you?'

'No, I just wanted my seat back.'

He smiles amiably and sits down next to her, putting one ankle up on his knee.

'So,' she continues gently. 'Long story, you said.'

'Oh, it's nothing,' he replies, waving her off.

'Humour me,' she says, forcing a smile. 'I'd like to hear it, if you've got time.'

'Honestly,' he replies, shifting uncomfortably. 'I wouldn't know where to start.'

'At the beginning?'

'Too dull,' Gavin says. '*Your* story is probably much more interesting. How did you get to be sitting in the park talking to strange men?'

Jackie shuts her eyes against the sunshine, enjoying the warmth on her face for a moment, concentrating on her breathing.

'Are you strange?' she says finally.

'Nah,' he says amiably. 'I'd be more interesting if I was.'

She stares at him for a long while, holding his gaze and realising for the first time that while his grin isn't false, it's also hiding something, an inner turmoil or sadness his dark eyes can't quite contain. Emotion emanates from him in waves, undulating towards her and enveloping her, wrapping her in its complexity until she loses herself, just for a moment.

'I think you're very interesting, Gavin.'

'I'm pretty bog standard,' he continues. 'But you? There's

something special about you...'

'You're deflecting,' she says, blushing, glad not for the first time that her mother's sunglasses cover so much of her face.

'I'm just a ghost.'

'You look real to me.'

'Most shadows do,' she replies quietly.

'Shadows?'

'I don't know,' she waves him off again, looking away. 'Sorry, ignore me, I'm talking rubbish.'

'Don't apologise,' he says gently. 'You say whatever you like.'

'God, no,' Jackie laughs. 'If I started, I'd never stop. You can help take my mind of things by telling me *your* story, though.'

This is the moment. Usually at this point, they'll either walk or start talking, commit to opening up or panic and clam up. The men usually panic and run but she can already tell that he's different. He's holding eye contact with her, happy to talk, she can sense it.

'Pushy, aren't you?' he says, smiling.

'I don't mean to be,' Jackie replies, holding his face to hers with her gaze.

'I never got over my first love,' he says eventually, turning away from her and staring blindly at a pair of magpies. He pauses for a long time before turning back towards Jackie and miming a bomb exploding with his hands in front of his face.

'Married?' Jackie asks, already knowing the answer, knowing full well he's married to a woman called Imogen with long dark hair, a moneyed accent and a withering stare.

'It's complicated,' he replies quietly, rubbing his jaw.

'Who is she?' Jackie asks, mirroring his own hushed tone. 'Your first love, I mean? Not your wife, I assume?'

He laughs, emitting a hint of sadness before he expertly masks it again.

'Like I said, it's complicated. We used to be happy, we

really did,' Gavin says as Jackie studies his face intently. He's handsome, certainly, but not in a traditional sense. It's more that there's something… compelling about him.

'We?' Jackie whispers, a breeze, not loud enough to distract him, gentle enough to guide him.

'Me and Imogen.'

'Your wife?'

Gavin takes a deep breath, unconsciously running his hand over the skin of his neck as he speaks.

'We needed to find a way back…' he pauses again, hand still stroking his chin, part self-comfort, part self-flagellation. 'It's a long story.'

'I've got time,' Jackie coerces.

'I don't know where to start.'

'At the beginning,' she repeats quietly, leaning back into Elsie and Christopher's epitaphs and removing her sunglasses. 'Tell me about her. Your first love.'

'Him,' Gavin says slowly, eyeing her warily as he speaks. Jackie nods lightly as her heart speeds up a notch, careful not to speak, not to take him out of the reverie he's falling into.

'We met when I was 17,' he continues quietly. 'Back in the '90s…'

~ Chapter 2 ~

Gavin's dad walked into the living room, topless beer belly swelling over his dusty, mud and cement-covered jeans.

'You all right lad?'

'Yeah,' Gavin answered, knowing there was only one acceptable answer.

'It's just your mum...' his dad faltered uncomfortably. 'She's worried about you. Don't you have *any* friends to knock about with?'

Gavin wasn't sure what his dad's point was. It wasn't like he had enemies. He wasn't bullied at school like Matt Edwards. Last week, Carl Rogers had warmed a two pence piece on the wall heater in the English hut and spammed it onto Matt's forehead, burning an effigy of the queen there like a fucked-up Bindi. Gavin never got hassle like that. Mostly he was ignored and that was fine by him.

'I've got friends,' Gavin lied, ushering his dad out of the way of the television so he didn't miss any of *Live and Kicking*.

'We never see you with anyone. What happened to you and Jamie? You used to be mates.'

'When we were 8, Dad. I'm 17.'

'Still.'

'Still what?' Gavin frowned, flicking his dad the smallest of glances before turning his attention back to the TV.

'At least turn this shit off and get out in the garden,' his dad grumbled, walking over to the TV and switching it off.

'I was watching that.'

'It's lovely out, I'm not having you sitting in here in the dark all day.'

It *was* dark in their living room. Ornate, oversized chandeliers hung from their living room ceiling, ignorant of the fact they were designed for a much grander home than their 1930s semi. Far from casting too much light, they somehow managed to throw their faint orange glow upwards, creating shadows on the ceiling where polystyrene strips laced back and forth, exhausted from their effort to masquerade as traditional oak beams.

The darkness was exacerbated by the extension his father had built at the end of the living room. He'd birthed a new room, Siamese-twin-like, between it and the garden, stealing all the natural light in its wake. His parents called this extension the *Sun Lounge* and because of it, the living room had become a long, dusky cave.

'Come on,' his dad said a little more softly, still standing between Gavin and the blank television screen. 'Get in the garden and get some sun.'

'I was watching TV,' Gavin countered weakly, knowing already this wasn't a battle he was going to win.

'You're 17 for God's sake, you never go out, you never *do* anything.'

'Don't start, Dad, I'm fine,' Gavin continued defensively.

'Don't you have *any* friends?' his dad repeated. 'Your mum said all the other kids walk home from school with someone, they have girlfriends, they even go to the pub. You're *always* on your own.'

Somehow these conversations always left Gavin feeling that his dad's concern was more about how it reflected on him rather than genuine concern.

'Come on, get outside' his dad said, grabbing Gavin playfully, trying to wrestle his T-shirt from him.

'Get off,' Gavin said, half-laughing and batting his dad off.

'Go on, get some sun on you.'

'Is there any sun cream?' Gavin asked, standing up from the sofa and pulling his T-shirt off.

'Don't be a big girl's blouse.'

'He's got pale skin,' his mum said, walking in from the kitchen, cup of tea in hand.

'Don't you start,' his dad said. 'You were the one that wanted me to get him out there.'

'I'm just saying he should put some sun cream on, that's all. Little Bobbie down the road got terribly burned last summer, do you remember? He was all purple, bless him. All because his mum was on the wine with her friend in the garden. I'm not one to gossip, you know I'm not, but what kind of mother sits drinking wine with her friends while her 6-year-old goes purple in the sun?'

'Gavin's 17, not 6,' his dad replied.

'Still, he should put some sun cream on, that's all I'm saying.'

'No wonder he hasn't got any friends,' his dad said, turning to leave the room. 'You baby him too much.'

At school a few days later, Gavin tried to hide as he changed for Games, pulling his shirt off quickly and trying to get his PE top on before any of his classmates noticed the burnt skin falling from his torso or the blisters on his chest.

'What the fuck is that?' Jamie said, spotting the sun damage and grabbing at Gavin's T-shirt.

'Fuck off,' Gavin squirmed self-consciously. 'It's just sunburn.'

'Sunburn? Looks like someone threw chip pan oil over you,' Jamie said, trying to pull the T-shirt out of Gavin's hands again to get a better look.

'I said fuck off,' Gavin shouted, grabbing his trainers from the wooden bench and moving away, sitting down next to another boy at the end of the changing rooms.

'He's such a weirdo,' Jamie said to his mate Trevor, turning his back on Gavin.

'Why do you even talk to him?' Trevor countered, sneering over Jamie's shoulder at Gavin.

'Ignore them,' said a soft voice to Gavin's left. Gavin glanced over to see he'd sat down next to the new boy, Steve. As his gaze settled on the boy's gentle smile, a calmness washed over him.

'I'm Gavin,' he said quietly, pulling his PE top on fully and leaning down to sort his trainers out.

'I know who you are,' the new boy said, standing up and walking away.

Word was, Steve had been asked to leave his A-Level college but nobody knew exactly what for. Rumours, of course, ran rife. Depending on who you spoke to he'd slept with his English tutor or he'd set fire to the Art room, but Steve wasn't even taking art A-Level so Gavin couldn't imagine how that could be true.

Gavin hadn't spoken a word to Steve since he'd joined, even though his form teacher had asked him to 'look after' Steve. Thing was, it didn't look like Steve needed 'looking after' to Gavin. He seemed remarkably self-sufficient. At lunch and break time, he would be found with his head in a book on a bench somewhere, alone but seemingly happy. Gavin could see that, like him, it wasn't an affectation; Steve was genuinely okay with his own company.

During their lunch break after Games, Gavin plucked up the courage to go and sit next to Steve, who had his head lodged firmly in one of their English Literature books.

'You a boffin, then?' Gavin asked nervously. Steve didn't look at him, but instead held a finger up, asking him to wait a moment. Gavin sat awkwardly for what felt like minutes, glancing around to make sure none of their classmates were watching because the last thing he needed was to give them something to take the piss out of him for.

'Sorry,' Steve said eventually, looking at Gavin and grinning widely. 'Just finishing the chapter.'

'No worries.'

'You read it yet?' Steve continued, holding the book up so

Gavin could see the cover.

'Nah, not yet. Not sure I'll bother.'

'It's a set text.'

'Looks boring.'

'It's not,' Steve replied confidently, turning his attention back to the book, turning the page and starting to read again. They sat in silence next to one another for the rest of lunch break and to Gavin's surprise, it felt comfortable, like he didn't need to speak but he didn't have to get up and leave, either.

'People say you had sex with your English tutor,' Gavin said eventually.

'People say a lot of things,' Steve laughed.

'Well?' Gavin asked. 'Did you?'

'Come on,' Steve said quickly, ignoring the question and grabbing Gavin's arm to pull him up from the bench. 'We'd better get to class.'

After school, they went to the park. Steve said he'd help Gavin to revise for their English exam given that Gavin wasn't reading half the books they were supposed to. As Gavin sat on the park bench, arms outstretched along the grainy, damp wood either side of him, Steve sat down at the other end of the bench, book in hand, and slung his legs up over the armrest to lay down backwards, resting his head on Gavin's lap.

'Bit weird,' Gavin said, looking down at Steve but not attempting to move him. Steve didn't reply, neither did he move. Instead, he opened the book in his hands and leafed through it urgently.

'Listen to this and tell me it's boring. Tell me it doesn't give you goose bumps.'

Gavin already had goose bumps from the weight of Steve's head in his lap. As Steve read, his voice was low and passionate, filled with life. Without meaning to, Gavin found himself absently stroking his new friend's hair. It wasn't premeditated, it was natural, like taking a breath. Steve's hair was thinner than Gavin's, silkier. His fingers could move through it with ease.

'I sometimes have a queer feeling with regard to you,' Steve read, glancing up with a sparkle in his eyes. 'Especially when you are near me, as now: it is as if I had a string somewhere under my left ribs, tightly and inextricably knotted to a similar string situated in the corresponding quarter of your little frame. And if that boisterous Channel, and two hundred miles or so of land come broad between us, I am afraid that cord of communion will be snapt; and then I've a nervous notion I should take to bleeding inwardly.'

Steve gently shut the book and closed his eyes, head pressing ever so gently down into Gavin's lap, only imperceptibly more than was necessary.

'Bleeding inwardly,' he repeated, more to himself than to Gavin. 'That's how I feel sometimes, you know what I mean?'

I feel like I've got a string in my *stomach,* Gavin thought but didn't say, *knotted and connected to you.*

Before that day in the park, Gavin had never thought about boys sexually. Mostly, he'd fantasised about Mrs Rankin, the French teacher. But after that day, he noticed he was thinking about Steve and before long, Mrs Rankin was a fantasy of the past and the only body that filled his mind was Steve's. He'd never felt so physical in anyone's presence before, every part of him alive and breathing. His skin felt like it was being pricked gently with needles whenever Steve brushed against him. Sometimes, at school, if they were sitting next to each other, he'd gently push his leg out until it touched Steve's under the table. Steve would return the pressure and they'd glance at each other, grinning, locked in their own secret world that none of their classmates knew anything about. For a long while, that was all it was: two boys finding subtle ways to be alone together, to brush against each other's skin, to be that little more tactile than they'd be with anyone else. If they were alone, they'd lie as they had on the bench that day, one nestled into the other's lap, chatting, laughing, reading. Sometimes, on deserted, leaf-lined narrow lanes, far away from prying eyes, they'd hold hands. At no point did they discuss what their friendship was. It was unsaid, unnecessary. Gavin suspected verbalising it would ruin it, change things and destroy their bubble.

'Why don't we ever go around to your house?' Gavin said one day.

'We don't go to yours either,' Steve replied.

'Wouldn't want to give them the satisfaction of seeing me with a friend,' Gavin said, grinning.

Steve stared at the pavement as they walked, not replying. They'd been to the cinema, a date by any other name. As they walked home, the streets were dark but the warmth of the early summer evening held them tightly, caressing their skin and producing the lightest of sweats.

'Okay,' Steve said simply.

'What?'

'My house. Let's go.'

'Now?'

'If you want to?'

Gavin nodded and they walked on in silence. Steve never mentioned his family, his mother or father. At first this hadn't seemed strange to Gavin, but then he realised everyone mentioned their parents in passing sometimes, even if it was to moan about how embarrassing they were, how they wouldn't let them go to so and so's party, how they wouldn't pick them up from bowling. But Steve? Nothing. It was like they didn't exist at all.

When they got to Steve's house, the smell hit them before he'd opened the front door.

'It'll be Rosie,' Steve said, pushing his key into the lock and looking back over his shoulder and smiling sadly. 'The dog,' he clarified, seeing Gavin's confused look.

They walked into the small, cluttered hallway and Gavin could hear the television blaring from the room to the right of them. As they walked past it towards the kitchen, Steve glanced in and said 'hi, Mum' quietly. The figure on the sofa didn't move. Neither did the two bottles of wine on the table beside her.

'She'll be out cold until morning,' Steve said, nodding his head backwards towards his mum and carrying on to the kitchen. Gavin followed closely behind, uncomfortable and unsure what to say. Was this how Steve lived? He didn't seem phased at all, like it was normal for him. Gavin wanted to grab and hold him and tell him it wasn't normal, family life wasn't supposed to be like this. As they reached the kitchen, the stench became unbearable. A child gate was across the open doorway and a scruffy white dog was whimpering and wagging its tail, jumping up and down for Steve's attention. Its fur was covered in smears of faeces and damp patches which Gavin assumed to be piss. Behind it, the kitchen lino was covered in poo and wee, puddles and smears trodden all over every inch of the kitchen.

'Hey, girl,' Steve said gently, reaching over and stroking her head. 'Mum hasn't taken you out again, has she?' He pursed his lips together and looked back at Gavin. 'She's old now, a bit incontinent. I don't think she's got long left. Mum can't look after herself, let alone Rosie. I took her out before school but Mum just locks her in here and... well, you can see.'

'Steve, I...' Gavin started, but Steve shirked him off and turned around.

'No,' he said, shaking his head. Gavin knew implicitly what he meant. He didn't want their friendship, their relationship, to be based on pity. That wasn't what they were about, wasn't who they were for each other.

'I'd better go and rinse her off, shampoo her. There's a hose in the back garden.'

He turned to Gavin and lifted his shirt up and pulled it over his head before quickly stepping out of his trousers, standing in only his underwear and socks.

'Bit weird,' Gavin said, unable to stop himself looking Steve up and down.

'Don't want to get my clothes covered in shit, do I?'

He smiled. That smile. Gavin could have grabbed him right then and kissed him but before he could act on it, the moment passed and Steve hopped over the child gate and picked the dog up, running and jumping towards the back door of the kitchen, avoiding puddles and smears and lumps of poo as he went.

'You got a mop?' Gavin called after him. 'I'll clean this mess up.'

'Under the stairs,' he called back over his shoulder. 'Floor cleaner is under the sink.'

After Steve had cleaned the dog up, he went for a shower while Gavin finished mopping the kitchen floor.

'Thanks for that,' Steve said, appearing in the kitchen doorway, towel around his waist.

'No worries. The dog all right?' he said, indicating to the dog sitting soggily in its bed in the hallway, staring at them both nervously.

'Yeah, she's fine.'

'And your mum?'

'Yeah, she's always like that.'

'Right,' Gavin said quietly.

'Right,' Steve responded, eyes locked onto Gavin's.

They stood awkwardly, not speaking, Gavin aware of Steve's near nakedness, trying not to make it obvious that he was aware of it.

'Why don't you come and stay at mine? If your mum's going to be out cold all night anyway?'

'Can't leave Rosie, can I?' Steve said. 'She'll need feeding and a walk in the morning and Mum will be in no state.'

'Bring her along, my parents won't mind? Well, my dad might, but he'll be okay.'

'Nah, best not.'

'Right.'

Silence. Steve shivered, goose bumps covering his pale flesh.

'I'd better go,' Gavin said eventually, desperate for Steve to stop him, to suggest something, anything.

'Right.' Steve nodded.

Gavin moved to step past Steve so he could pass him in the hallway and get to the front door, brushing against him as he did so. As his arm touched Steve's chest, he stopped dead, turning his head towards his friend and, in a moment of bravery, he leaned in and kissed him lightly on the lips. A peck, nothing more, but enough. Enough to leave no doubt as to his feelings. His heart sped, fear gripping him as he searched Steve's eyes to judge his reaction.

'Bit weird,' Steve said, grabbing Gavin's T-shirt and pulling him close to kiss him back, this time more passionately. 'Now fuck off home,' he said, breaking away from the kiss and pushing Gavin down the hall.

~ Chapter 3 ~

The flag for homophobic abuse at Gavin's school was less to do with who you were having sexual contact with and everything to do with how *masculine* you appeared to be. For example, Gavin's classmate Charlie wanked at school all the time. Under the table in English while Mrs Goddard taught at the front, face flushed, pretending she hadn't noticed. Or at the back of the room in Maths while old man Spencer sweated crusty yellow patches under his armpits as he wrote equations on the chalkboard. Charlie's behaviour had never been considered gay by his classmates, it had been considered rebellious. Funny, even. Even when Charlie and his friend Mark wanked together in the games changing rooms, egging each other on, having a race to see who could climax first, nobody said a word. Nobody called them gay. Conversely, Shane, skinny, emotional and prone to crying, was mercilessly called a gay boy. He was bullied and abused, beaten and humiliated. In fact, all the kids who were teased for being gay were the wimpy kids, the effeminate kids, the late bloomers whose voices hadn't broken until two years after everyone else's. Nobody knew if these boys were actually gay or not, of course. It didn't really matter. Their obvious *difference* mattered. Their lack of perceived *masculinity* had undone them and made them open targets. On the positive side, for Gavin and Steve at least, these rules meant their budding romance passed unnoticed. Neither of them was particularly effeminate and whilst they weren't *blokes* by any stretch, they passed well enough on the masculinity scale to fall under the radar.

Their first kiss in Steve's dank hallway went undiscussed like everything else. They both knew it had happened, of course, but for a while, they carried on like before: more than friends, less than lovers. They created situations where they could be alone together, but the kiss remained unrepeated. They enjoyed reading and chatting together, brushing against each other's skin as they walked next to each other in the park, teenage hormones raging beneath the surface. Their relationship was hidden from the outside world but more than that, it was hidden from themselves. If anything, after the kiss, Gavin made a point of talking about girls a bit more often.

'Ursula Kilmarten is well fit,' Gavin said, leaning lightly against Steve as they sat on the school bench. Not obviously, not as much as he would have if they'd been alone in the park, but a gentle lean for the contact, so he could get *the tingle*. Steve shrugged, not looking up from his book but gently sliding his leg away from Gavin's.

'What?' Gavin said, shoving him playfully. 'You don't think she's fit? Everyone thinks she's fit. Even Skinny Shane said he likes her.'

'Skinny Shane says whatever he has to so the gang doesn't torment him.'

'They're not so bad,' Gavin started. Recently, Jamie and *the gang* had begun to give Gavin a little leeway, a nod here, an 'all right, Gav' there. Before that, Jamie had ignored him for years and the rest of them hadn't ever paid him the slightest attention. He didn't know why he wanted to be accepted by them, in fact he hadn't thought he had wanted to be, but once they'd started talking to him, it had become addictive. He *wanted* their approval.

'Not so bad? Really?' Steve said, flipping his book shut with a *snap* and pushing himself to his feet.

'What's up with you?' Gavin said, irritated. 'You can be really intense sometimes, you know that?'

'Whatever,' Steve said, walking away and leaving Gavin feeling confused.

After that, Gavin didn't know what to say or how to act around

Steve. Things weren't exactly awkward, but Steve was being weird with him and Gavin couldn't work out why.

'Look, mate,' Gavin said one day as they walked into the park after school. 'I think things went a bit far the other week, don't you?'

'Not really,' Steve said bluntly.

'I meant... you know. The kiss,' Gavin clarified, mentioning the unmentionable for the first time, heart pumping so hard a little sick rose in his throat.

'I know what you meant,' Steve said, not looking at Gavin, careful not to make eye contact.

'So, let's just forget about it, shall we? Put it behind us.'

'If that's what you want?' Steve said, still walking by Gavin's side, not looking at him.

'I thought that's what you wanted?' Gavin said carefully.

'No,' Steve said slowly. 'But you're into Ursula Kilmarten, aren't you?'

'Ursula?' Gavin stopped dead. 'Is that what this is about?'

'What *what's* about?'

'Your weird mood. You've been funny with me for days and I thought you were regretting the kiss, thought you were...'

'*My* weird mood,' Steve exclaimed. 'You've done nothing but talk about girls you want to get off with ever since.'

'You're jealous!' Gavin said, his heart speeding up a gear, so much so he felt giddy. 'You're jealous!'

'Fuck off.'

'You *so* are.' Gavin punched Steve playfully on his arm, chasing after him into the park until he finally caught Steve in the shadow of a large oak tree. Despite the fact it was still light and there were people in the park, he pushed Steve back against the trunk, hand firmly against his chest and leaned in to kiss him.

'You boys!' an older male voice shouted.

'Shit,' Steve said, grabbing his school bag from the ground

with one hand and Gavin's hand with the other. 'Run.'

They ran and ran, out of the park, across the bridge on the dual carriageway and back towards Gavin's neighbourhood and the chippy near his house. He couldn't remember when they dropped their clasped hands, probably before they got out of the park, but Gavin could still feel the sweaty warmth where Steve's hand had been and longed to feel it again, just for a moment. But they were back in the real world now where builders were picking up fish and chips for their families. When they finally stopped running, they were both panting and Gavin had a rusty blood taste in his mouth from running too hard, too fast.

'Do you think he saw us?' Gavin said eventually, bent over, breathing hard, hands on his knees.

'Of course he saw us.' Steve laughed. 'He wasn't fucking blind.'

'Who was he?'

'I don't know, some crusty in the park, does it matter?'

'Of course it matters,' Gavin started.

'Why? What would he do?'

'Report us to the police?'

'We were only kissing.' Steve laughed, putting his hand on Gavin's shoulder. 'I wasn't bum fucking you over a bench.'

'Don't,' Gavin said, shirking Steve's hand off his shoulder and looking behind him to see who was in the local chippy. 'Someone will see.'

'Oh come off it,' Steve said. 'It's nothing.'

'It's not nothing, what if it got back to my dad?'

'What if it did?'

'Are you kidding me? He already thinks there's something weird about you, he'd kill me. And Mum... she'd have a breakdown.'

'So melodramatic,' Steve muttered.

'Doesn't anything bother you?' Gavin shouted. 'Is this all a game to you?'

'Lots of things bother me, Gav,' Steve said, sounding irritated. 'Who I kiss isn't one of them.'

'Well, it should be,' Gavin started. 'It's not a game. Nobody can know, do you understand?'

'Heaven forbid,' Steve said sarcastically.

'What's that supposed to mean?'

'You're scared.'

'About what?'

'About us.'

'Us?' Gavin spat. 'There isn't an us,' he flicked a glance towards the chip shop again, feeling the hurt in Steve's face as keenly as if it were his own pain. He'd gone too far.

'There *is* an us,' Steve said quietly. 'You know there is.'

'It's not that simple,' Gavin whispered, every inch of his skin aware he was standing outside his local chip shop where friends and neighbours might hear anything and everything they were saying.

'I love you,' Steve said loudly. 'That simple enough?'

'Don't be stupid,' Gavin looked around frantically. They stood staring at each other in silence, Gavin shaking his head but not speaking, unsure what he could possibly say, scared of Steve staying, even more scared of him walking away.

'We're friends,' Gavin said eventually. 'Can't that be enough? Things were fine when we didn't talk about it.'

'No, they weren't, Gav.'

'Look, I don't know what you think this can be, Steve, but I can't, I...'

'It doesn't matter,' Steve turned his back. 'I'm going home.'

'Steve, don't,' Gavin said, grabbing his shoulder. 'That's not fair. I'm not like you, I *do* like girls, too.'

'Then go and find one and stop shoving your tongue down *my* throat,' Steve said, shirking his hand off his shoulder.

'Fine,' Gavin shouted after him.

As Steve disappeared into the distance, Gavin leaned back against the brick wall outside the chippy and did something he hadn't done since he was a kid, something he'd been trained not to do. He cried, swallowing the deep, soulful sobs into silence so nobody in the chip shop would hear him.

With their A-Level exams fast approaching, it was relatively easy for Gavin to avoid Steve. At least, that's what he told himself but it was clear that in reality, Steve was avoiding him. Their exams came and went with barely a nod of acknowledgement passing between them.

After his last exam, freedom from school beckoned but there was no feeling of euphoria or achievement, just emptiness. Nothing had any sheen without Steve. He walked down the local high street, hands sunk deep into his pockets, rucksack double-strapped on his back, head low.

'We're going camping!' an excitable voice behind him said, startling him. He turned to see Olyvia with a 'Y', a girl from the local girl's school they sometimes did joint classes with. She grabbed him by the shoulder, eyes beaming. 'Just for two days. Say you'll come!'

'I don't know,' Gavin said, 'camping's not really my thing...'

'A-Levels are over, Gav! We've got to mark it somehow.'

'Thanks, Olyvia but...'

'No buts. There's a bunch of us going and I'm trying to convince Nat to come.'

She said 'Nat' as if it should mean something to him, as if it might entice him to go, except Gavin wasn't even sure who Nat was, let alone why he might want to go camping with her.

'Honestly, I...'

'Steve will be there too,' she said breathlessly, staring at him with wide, pleading eyes.

'We aren't really friends anymore,' Gavin said awkwardly, looking over his shoulder, hoping someone else might arrive and rescue him.

'Then come camping and sort it out. You're off to Uni soon, aren't you? If you don't make up with him before then, you never will.'

'Did he put you up to this?' Gavin asked, eyeing her warily.

'Steve? Why would he put me up to it?'

'No reason,' Gavin said awkwardly. 'I mean, I just...'

'He misses you, Gav,' Olyvia said, forcing Gavin's heart to stop beating. 'Everyone needs their best mate, I'd be lost without Nat,' she continued meaningfully.

He exhaled slowly as she eyed him with excitement.

'All right,' he said quickly, holding both palms face out in submission. 'I'll come. But I don't have a tent and...'

'That's okay, you can share with me, Steve and Nat. My parents have got one of those tents that's like Southfork Ranch, you know? It's massive, we'll all fit in easily.'

~ Chapter 4 ~

Olyvia's tent wasn't like Southfork Ranch. It wasn't like a small, terraced house. It wasn't like a Mini Metro.

'I remember it being bigger,' Olyvia said unconvincingly, the mid-summer air ruffling her hair as they all stood in a line, staring at the newly erected tent. 'But I haven't been camping since I was about 6.'

'Will we all even fit in there?' her friend Nat said nervously.

'Of course we will,' Olyvia replied. 'It'll be a bit of a squeeze but we'll be fine. 'We can sleep boy, girl, boy, girl,' she continued brightly, eyes shining as she turned to look at Steve, who stood next to Nat, staring down at the yellowing grass of the campsite in front of the tent and refusing Olyvia eye contact.

'I can sleep next to Steve!' Olyvia continued breathlessly, immune to his disinterest. Gavin instinctively covered his mouth to cover the smile that appeared, threatening to become a full-blown laugh. Now he understood what this whole camping trip was about.

'Wait,' he said, not able to contain the laugh. 'Who else is coming?'

'What do you mean?' Olyvia said breezily.

'You said loads of us were coming. How will everyone else know where we've pitched the tent?'

'Oh, it's just us,' Olyvia shouted over her shoulder as she climbed in the tent, sleeping bag in hand. 'I thought I'd told you.'

'No,' Gavin replied quietly, glancing over at Steve's awkwardness and chuckling. 'You really didn't.'

After squeezing their sleeping bags into a sleeping area designed for three stick thin people who were four feet tall, Gavin walked to the toilet and shower block with Steve. They hadn't spoken since the day of their kiss in the park, apart from a nod and an awkward hello at school. Polite. No drama. Gavin's mouth was dry and he wasn't sure how to open the conversation. Luckily, Steve did.

'I don't know what you find so funny,' Steve said, deadpan. 'You know she's got Nat lined up for you as well, right?'

Gavin laughed, smiling at Steve, heart swelling, filling every inch of his veins with love.

I've missed you, Gavin wanted to say, but the words died in his throat. Instead, he shrugged, trying to affect a nonchalant, couldn't-care-less attitude.

'Nat's pretty,' he replied. 'There are worse things.'

Steve glanced at him as they walked and continued looking until Gavin looked back, feeling sheepish, ashamed.

'You're such a dick, Gavin,' Steve said quietly, less an accusation, more a statement of fact.

'Right, boys. Be quick,' Olyvia said, running up behind them, dressed up in a short skirt and tight T-shirt, ready for their first night out. 'We're headed for the Treble B disco in a bit. It's not far, we'll be able to stumble back to our tent after,' she said, touching Steve's elbow meaningfully as she spoke.

'Where's Nat?' Gavin asked, looking over Olyvia's shoulder.

'She's just nipped to the loo. She'll be pleased to know you're asking after her, though.'

'Everybody's happy then,' Steve muttered, shirking Olyvia off and walking into the toilet block.

The Treble B disco was the campsite's own disco, a couple of fields away from their tent. From the outside, it looked like it was a converted barn with breezeblock extensions and a corrugated iron roof.

'Okay, look, it's not quite what I had in mind, but...'

'Is anything on this holiday *quite* what you had in mind?' Gavin said, grinning wildly. Despite all expectations, he was really enjoying himself.

'Fuck off, Gav,' she said, shoving him and walking in through the dirty white doorway into the disco.

'It'll be fun,' Nat said, not sounding at all convinced as she followed her friend.

At the bar, they stood and surveyed the clientele. Other campers, certainly. Locals from the surrounding villages, young guys from the local school or college, eager for some fresh meat.

'You've caught their eye already,' Gavin said to Nat, noticing a group of lads elbowing each other and looking her way from the other end of the bar.

'Shut up,' she said coyly, glancing back at them, then to Gavin, unable to hide a small smile of satisfaction as she did so.

'Snakebite and blacks all round?' Olyvia said, slapping the bar. 'Or do you want a vodka or something, Nat?'

'No, it's fine, I'll have one,' Nat said.

'Snakebite's fine for me,' Gavin said.

'Yup,' Steve agreed. 'And how about a chaser to get us started? I reckon we're going to need it.'

'Are you trying to get me drunk?' Olyvia said breathlessly, lifting her hand to get the barman's attention.

The night progressed in a sea of multicoloured disco lights and badly mixed music but none of them cared as they were quickly too drunk to notice. At some point, Gavin collapsed into a chair in the corner, watching his friends as they continued to dance stupidly, alive in every pore of their bodies. Olyvia was getting closer and closer to Steve, mouthing the words to Hadaway's 'Please Don't Go' with ever more intimate dance moves. Eventually, as the tune turned to Opus III's 'It's a Fine Day', Nat also left the dance floor and flopped down next to Gavin.

'I feel like a spare part up there with those two,' she said.

'You think they're going to get it on?' Gavin asked.

'Olyvia's giving it her best shot,' Natalie said, slurring

slightly. 'Not sure Steve's into her though? Has he said anything to you?'

'Me? Nah, Steve wouldn't confide in me, we're... I don't know. We kind of fell out.'

'You're all right now though? You've been talking tonight.'

'Yeah, we're okay,' Gavin said, shaking his head.

'I'm not used to drinking pints,' Nat slurred. 'What even is a snakebite and black? I didn't want to ask.'

'Lager, cider, blackcurrant.'

'It's very purple.'

Gavin looked at Nat as she leaned her head back and stared at the ceiling lights, multicoloured and swirling. She was pretty. Long dark hair, very little makeup. He did like her, he realised, he hadn't just said that for Steve's benefit.

'That guy has been following you around all night,' Gavin said, nodding to one of the lads they'd seen earlier when they came in. 'I think you've got a fan.'

'You jealous?' she said, a hand moving to rest on his thigh lightly.

'What makes you think I'm into you?' he said, grinning.

'I didn't, I mean...' she fumbled, removing her hand from his thigh.

'I'm joking,' he said quickly. 'You're lovely.'

She smiled and leaned towards him, only to be interrupted by Olyvia running towards them, whooping on the dancefloor, arms in the air.

'More drinks, whose round is it?'

'Steve's?' Gavin said, looking across the room to see where Steve had got to.

'He's in the loo. I think it's my round anyway,' she said. 'Same again?'

'Okay,' Gavin said, standing up. 'Just nipping to the loo myself.'

Gavin used the urinal and washed his hands, noting that all the stalls were empty and Steve wasn't in the toilet at all. Leaving the loos, he walked outside to find Steve leaning against the wall, pint in hand, staring at the sky.

'You can see so many stars here, can't you? You never see this many at home,' he said, without looking at Gavin.

Gavin didn't respond but instead took the pint from Steve's hand and sipped it.

'Get your own,' Steve said, taking it back, the threat of a smile on his face.

'Olyvia's getting another round in.'

'She can be a bit full on, eh?'

'She likes you a lot.'

'Yeah, well, she's barking up the wrong tree, isn't she.'

'Never say never, she's really pretty.'

'Gavin, stop,' Steve said.

'Stop what?'

'You know what.'

They stood side by side quietly for a while, both looking up at the sky.

'Why did you come then? You knew Olyvia was into you, you knew it would be awkward...'

'I'm supposed to avoid going away with my friends, now?'

'Since when was Olyvia with a Y your friend anyway?'

'Since you stopped talking to me.'

'You're the one who couldn't leave things as they were!' Gavin erupted.

'It's wasn't about keeping us a secret,' Steve said calmly, swigging his pint. 'You didn't even want to talk about us in private. You could only cope with it if you pretended it wasn't happening.'

'I can't have this conversation,' Gavin said, leaning back against the cold breeze block walls and staring across the fields beyond, Steve's plastic pint dewy in his hand.

'What conversation?'

'*This one.*'

'Nobody's asking you to.'

'You totally are,' Gavin said, leaning ever-so-slightly into Steve, unable to focus on anything but his lips.

'Fuck sake, Gavin, stop messing with my head. You've been after Natalie all night and now you're flirting with me?'

'I'm not flirting,' Gavin replied unconvincingly, leaning back against the wall and sighing. They passed Steve's purple pint back and forth to each other in silence until it was drained. Olyvia and Nat would realise they weren't inside soon enough, Gavin knew. And what about later on? When they all headed back to that tiny tent to squeeze into it for the night. He wasn't averse to something happening with Nat but he knew it wasn't the same for Steve with Olyvia.

'We shouldn't have come,' Gavin said quietly. 'It's not fair on Olyvia and Nat.'

'It's not fair on us, either,' Steve said, maudlin, swigging the remainder of his drink. 'You get that don't you? This isn't fair.'

'Do we have to do this? Why do you want to *talk* about things all the time? Why can't things just *be*?'

'Get back inside to Nat,' Steve snapped. 'That'll be easier for you, right?'

'She's nice,' Gavin started. 'I'm allowed to like her. Just because you and me are... whatever we are... it doesn't mean I can't have normal...'

'Stop, Gavin,' Steve said, raising his voice a little.

'I can't be your boyfriend!' Gavin snapped, knocking the empty pint glass out of Steve's hands onto the ground.

'And I can't be your friend,' Steve responded angrily.

'Can't you?' Gavin said, grabbing Steve by the T-shirt with both hands, pulling him close until their faces were only millimetres apart.

'No,' Steve said quietly, lips brushing against Gavin's.

'Fighting again?' Olyvia's voice jarred from behind. 'We wondered where you'd got to. Can't you guys stop falling out for two minutes? You're supposed to be friends.'

'We're okay,' Gavin said, letting go of Steve and adjusting his jeans to disguise his hard on before turning to face Olyvia, hands hovering awkwardly over his crotch.

'Don't lose your chance,' she said, nodding her head towards the door of the Treble B disco. 'One of the locals is chatting Nat up in there and it looks like she's well into him.'

Gavin didn't move as Olyvia stared at him pointedly, eyes darting to Steve in an obvious plea for Gavin to leave them alone.

'Right,' he said, stepping past Olyvia and walking back into the disco without looking back.

Nat was still sitting in the seat Gavin had left her in, except this time she was flanked by the lad who'd been following her around all evening. Both he and Nat were downing a shot in unison and slapping the table before slamming their glasses down. There were four more empty shot glasses on the table in front of them.

'Jesus, Nat, I've only been gone ten minutes, how many shots have you had?'

'Do us a favour, mate and leave us alone,' the guy with Nat said. Her head was lolling forward and she didn't look at all well.

'She's my friend,' Gavin said, holding his hand out to shake the guy's hand.

'I don't give a fuck if she's your sister,' the guy said aggressively. 'We're having a drink, here.'

'Okay,' Gavin said, to Nat, not the guy. 'Come on, I think it's time to go.'

'She's old enough to decide when it's time to go.'

'Nat,' Gavin said, continuing to ignore the guy. 'You okay?

You don't look great.'

'I fucking told you to do one,' the guy said, moving to stand up. At that moment, Nat looked at him and began to vomit, heaving a bucket load of bright purple sick from her mouth in one exorcist moment, covering the guy's shirt, trousers and hands.

'Fuck sake,' he shouted, stepping back in horror, lumpy sputum everywhere.

'Jesus Christ, Nat,' Gavin said, moving in to grab her as she crumpled on the table. He grabbed her by the arm and hoisted her up as the guy retreated backwards, not offering to help. Gavin put Nat's arm over his shoulder and walked towards the back of the dancefloor where there was an open door out to the back of the club.

'Okay, let's get some fresh air,' Gavin said, leaning her against the wall. 'Shall I get you some water?'

'Nahamokahy,' she slurred, dropping immediately to her knees on the flagstones and throwing up again.

Gavin crouched down, holding her hair back until her vomiting became a dry heave. There were purple stains all over the back patio and halfway up the wall. Try as he might, he couldn't manage to stop Nat from kneeling in her puke, so her knees were covered in purple bile as well. At least she'd been wearing shorts, he thought. He could probably help rinse her down under the water tap on the campsite.

'Have you got a hairband or anything?' he asked, left hand gripping her hair behind her head as she crouched on all fours, hands either side of the puddle of vomit.

'Iwannaslee,' she slurred, semi-conscious.

'How many shots did he buy you?' Gavin asked. 'Was that your first or...?'

'Iduon... Ijuswann...'

'Okay, it's okay, I've got you. Can you stand?'

Nat didn't reply, but moved, trying to push him off her so

she could lie down on the floor to sleep. He managed to grab her before she lay down in a pool of sick.

'Come on, Nat, you can't sleep here. I'll get you back to the tent, okay?'

'Nah, Ijustwanna...'

'Okay, I'm going to put your arm over my shoulder, okay? And we'll walk you back.'

While Nat was slim, she was still a dead weight and Gavin felt he was more dragging her than walking her as they circled from the back of the disco around to the front. As they rounded the corner, he could see Steve and Olyvia sitting with their backs against the breeze block walls, chatting happily.

'Why didn't you tell me before?' Olyvia was saying. 'I feel like such an idiot.'

'Don't be stupid, I'm flattered but...'

Steve stopped speaking as he saw Gavin and Nat approaching over Olyvia's shoulder.

'Shit, what happened?'

'That prick was plying her with shots, fuck knows how many. She's been sick,' Gavin said as Steve pushed himself up and came to take Nat's other arm over his shoulder.

'Shit, Nat,' Olyvia said, running to her friend and lifting her head and face up to see if she was still conscious. 'Don't worry, we're here.'

Gavin and Steve supported her as they walked her back and Olyvia cleaned as much sick off Nat as possible with the water tap. That seemed to wake her up a little and back at the tent, Olyvia was even able to coax Nat into some water before putting her on her side in the tent and draping a sleeping bag over her.

'I'm just going to the loo,' Steve said to Olyvia. 'You okay with her?'

'Yeah, she's asleep already, she'll be okay,' Olyvia said, lying down next to her friend so she could keep an eye on her.

'I'll come with you... you're the only one with a torch,' Gavin said to Steve, crawling out of the tent after him and standing up straight, zipping it closed behind them.

They walked quietly towards the toilet block, the light from Steve's flashlight creating patterns on the grass as they avoided other people's guy ropes.

'That was eventful,' Steve said.

'Yeah,' Gavin replied.

They reached the toilet block and Steve stopped.

'I told Olyvia,' Steve said abruptly.

Gavin's veins stopped pumping blood. For a moment, he was nothing but a statue, coagulating, solidifying, unable to speak or respond.

'Not about you,' Steve continued hastily. 'I didn't mention you at all, but she was really coming on to me and it was really awkward and I didn't want to lead her on so I... well. I told her.'

'Told her what?' Gavin said hoarsely.

'Oh come on, Gavin,' Steve said dismissively.

'Told her what?' Gavin said angrily.

'That I like knitting, Gavin, what do you think?'

'Do you?' Gavin asked, heart thumping, refusing to hear what Steve was telling him.

'Do I what?'

'Like knitting?'

'Fuck's sake, Gav. I told her I'm gay.'

'Why?' Gavin said, dry throat.

'I just told you...'

'It's your business, Steve, nobody else's. Why do you have to label it? Why do you want to go on and on about it all the time?'

'I'm not going on about it, I'm not labelling it, I'm just...'

'What's gay if not a label? She's going to put two and two together about me and you and...'

'And what?' It was Steve's turn to get angry now. 'We kissed, that's it, Gavin. It's hardly the affair of the century.'

'You don't have to tell everyone,' Gavin continued. 'That's all I'm saying. Why can't you just get on with being gay in private if that's what you want to do?'

'Fuck sake, Gavin, you need to sort your head out,' Steve said, turning to walk into the toilet block.

'I'm not the one who needs to sort my head out,' Gavin shouted after him. 'You're the one who can't stop telling everyone!'

The next morning, Olyvia pulled her cardigan close around her in the cool morning sunlight.

'I can't spend another night squeezed in there with you lot,' she said.

'Besides,' Steve muttered, 'it stinks of sick now.'

'Don't,' Nat said, dropping her head down in shame. 'I'm so embarrassed.'

'Don't be silly,' Gavin said gently. 'It could have been any of us, you don't need to feel embarrassed.'

'Thanks for looking after me,' she said, glancing up at him coyly.

'You're welcome,' Gavin replied, returning her smile and trying to ignore Steve's hurt face looking away in the background.

'Don't worry,' Olyvia said, pushing Nat playfully. 'You'll have sobered up before Ursula's party.'

'You're kidding, I'm never drinking again,' Nat said seriously.

'Don't be ridiculous, it's our final hurrah before we go off to Uni. Everyone will be there.'

~ Chapter 5 ~

Days stacked up against each other, their weight hammering them into weeks, into months. Gavin's exam results came and along with them, the knowledge he'd secured a university place at the University of Sussex. Then, just two weeks before he was due to move to Brighton, Olyvia called. Ursula Kilmarten's party. *Everyone* was going. Surely, he wouldn't miss the event of the summer?

Against his better judgement, Gavin decided to go. The night arrived and he leaned nervously against the side in Ursula's kitchen, watching as Olyvia and Nat arrived, shrugging their jackets off and throwing them onto a pile on the stairs before walking into the kitchen. Nat looked stunning in a slim fitting black dress as she smiled shyly at him, pushing her long dark hair behind her ear.

'She's into you,' Jamie said, nudging Gavin in the ribs.

'No, she's not,' Gavin replied, embarrassed. Jamie and the gang had been talking to him as if they were old friends since he'd arrived. In spite of himself, he couldn't help feeling included. Wanted.

'You a virgin?' Mike said, pouring another cider into the plastic cup in Gavin's hand.

'What?'

'You look like a virgin,' Trevor jumped in, smirking at his mates.

'I...' Gavin had no idea how to respond. Would it be cool to admit he was? No. He should lie.

'Ursula's way out of your league anyway, mate,' Trevor said. 'Michael's going to have a crack at her later, aren't you Mike?'

Gavin swigged back some of his cider and stared desperately around the room. There, in the corner of the kitchen, stood

Steve, wearing black jeans and a white T-shirt, understated, handsome. For a moment, he couldn't move, couldn't breathe, couldn't hear a sound.

'Who are you going to have a crack at?' Jamie's voice floated in from somewhere but Gavin couldn't listen, couldn't answer.

'Hold on,' Gavin said, walking across the room to Steve, heart thumping loudly, dreaded drumbeats, uneven, punchy.

'I knew you'd be here.'

'Leave me alone,' Steve replied, looking over Gavin's shoulder, feigning disinterest so obviously that Gavin wanted to laugh.

'Like you didn't know I'd be here.'

'Leave me alone.'

'You don't really want that,' Gavin said, unsure where his confidence was coming from. Perhaps just seeing Steve, being near him again was enough.

'You seen Olyvia?' Steve asked, ignoring him.

'Olyvia?'

'Yes, Olyvia.'

'Has she said anything?' Gavin said, his confidence disappearing as soon as it had arrived.

'Who?' Steve said deliberately.

'Olyvia.'

'Has she said anything about what?'

'You *know* what!'

'I didn't ask her to keep it a secret, Gav.'

'Well, you should have done,' Gavin snapped.

'And this is why we aren't friends,' Steve snapped. 'You'll never change, will you?'

'I shouldn't have to,' Gavin started. 'Stop being a dick, will you? I miss you,' Gavin continued quietly, his unconscious mind taking over, doing the work for him in case his conscious self wasn't up to the job.

'I'm not interested, Gav. I just want to find Olyvia. Gemma

said she's got some vodka.'

'Can't we at least talk?' Gavin whispered. 'Please?'

Steve looked at him slowly, opening his mouth to respond just as Jamie, Trevor and the gang appeared behind Gavin.

'What's up gaylords?' Trevor laughed, glancing at Mike and Jamie for support as he spoke. 'Had a lover's tiff?'

'Fuck off, Trev,' Steve shot back.

'Funny, now I think of it, I never see you with any girls, Steve. Or you, Gav. You talk the talk, but there's never any action.'

'What are you talking about?' Gavin blustered, shoving Trevor as if it was larks, all a bit of fun. 'I've had loads of girlfriends.'

'Oh really,' Steve said sarcastically.

'Fuck off, Steve,' Gavin whispered, his shoulders stiffening. 'It's not funny.'

'All right, calm down gay boy.' Trevor glanced at Jamie and Michael, a glint in his eye before turning his attention onto Gavin. 'I'm just saying. That Nat's been giving you the eye since she got here and you haven't looked at her twice.'

'Nat?' Gavin glanced over his shoulder to see her across the room, still smiling at him.

'Well?'

'Well what?'

'You going to do anything about it?'

'I bet you a fiver you can't get to third base with her,' Michael said.

'Are you for real?' Steve said, making eye contact with Gavin and shaking his head. That was the moment Gavin could have changed everything. He could have grabbed Steve's hand and ran. Instead, he ignored Steve's glare and turned and walked towards Nat as she stood near the toilet at the back of the kitchen. Music played loudly and people stood around, not quite dancing, drinking from plastic cups and talking loudly. When he got to her, he reached out his arm and touched her

Chapter 5

lightly, smiling.

'I've been waiting for you to notice me,' she flirted. 'I haven't been near a shot or a snakebite tonight, I promise.'

Gavin laughed, feeling the gang's stares on his back like insects crawling and scratching and nipping.

'How's your summer been?' he asked, aware of Steve out of the corner of his eyes, stock still and staring.

'I've been meaning to talk to you,' Gavin lied, reaching out and tucking her dark hair behind her ear, fake smile spread across his face.

'Really?' she said, blushing. Without thinking, Gavin leaned in and kissed her, waiting to see if she accepted it before putting his arms around her waist and continuing more passionately. After a few moments, he broke off the kiss and held her, looking directly into her eyes.

'You look amazing tonight,' he said honestly.

'I don't,' she replied coyly, straightening her black dress down her legs a little, an adorable nervous tic that made him want to grab and kiss her again. Steve could fuck off. If he wanted to tell everyone he was gay that was his call, but he had no right making everyone think Gavin was gay, too.

He and Nat kissed in the corner of the kitchen for a long time. At some point Michael wandered past and tapped his nose cryptically.

'What was that all about?' Nat asked, glancing over her shoulder as someone left the small toilet at the back of the kitchen, walking between the two of them as he did so.

'Nothing,' Gavin said, grabbing her by the waist and pulling her in for another kiss. As they kissed, he shuffled them backwards into the small toilet, shutting the door behind them as they entered, his tongue never leaving her mouth as they did so. Her black dress rode naturally up her legs so it was easy for his hand to explore from her knee upwards, slowly at first, then more urgently.

'Don't,' she said, pushing his hand down a little, without conviction as she continued to kiss him. He moved his hand up again, over her knickers, under them, feeling her warmth, feeling inside her.

Third base. Bet you a fiver you can't do it.

'Gavin, no,' she said, pushing him off her and grappling with the toilet door.

'Natalie, I...' he said as she flung it open to reveal the kitchen, complete with Jamie, Michael and Trevor, all standing applauding.

'What?' Nat whispered, tears in her eyes as she looked over her shoulder at Gavin, then back to *the gang.*

'Did I win the fiver?' Michael sneered.

'Course not,' Gavin said, glancing at Nat as she made her way hurriedly across the room. 'Didn't get any further than third base though, I think she's frigid,' he continued, lowering his voice and hoping she wouldn't hear him.

'Oh, top lad!' Trevor shouted, slapping him on the back and grinning.

Gavin had never felt more ashamed of himself as he leaned back against the kitchen side, watching Natalie bolt out of the room, clearly devastated. To make matters worse, as his eyes refocused in the dim light of the kitchen, Gavin saw Steve staring at him in disgust before turning on his heel and running. He couldn't go after both Natalie and Steve and without thinking, Gavin chose Steve. He ran through the living room, dodging the circle of stoners doing a bong in the hallway and diving out of the front door. Steve was already halfway up the road when Gavin caught up with him, grabbing his arm and spinning him around.

'When did you turn into such a wanker?' Steve snapped angrily.

'What's got into you?'

'What's got into *me*?'

'I'm allowed other friends,' Gavin said uselessly.

'Aren't you too old to want the approval of arseholes?'

'They're all right!'

'Fuck's sake, they're wankers, Gavin. You know they are.'

They stood facing each other in the warm night air, time slowing around them.

'I miss you,' Gavin said again, more desperately than earlier. 'I need you.'

'Is that why you had your tongue down Nat's throat?'

Gavin glanced over his shoulder to check there was nobody else on the street around them and leaned in so he could kiss Steve.

'Don't!' Steve said, pushing him off.

'What's your problem?' Gavin said.

'I saw how you treated Nat.'

'I didn't... I mean, I...'

'That was brutal. It's not you, it's not normal...'

'Normal? *This* isn't normal!' Gavin shouted, indicating first to himself, then to Steve.

'Yes, it is!'

'You think we can just date like anyone else?' Gavin countered angrily. 'That it wouldn't have consequences?'

'*Life* has consequences!'

'There's no point anyway,' Gavin replied, the anger dissipating as he spoke, replaced by resignation. 'I'm going to university in a few weeks.'

'So?'

'So? What's the point? You're staying here, I'm moving south. We can't have a relationship... I can't put a bomb under my life for nothing. What's the point?'

'Love?'

'Grow up, Steve, we're not in love.'

'Why are you being like this?'

'I'm being honest.'

'Bullshit.' Steve shook his head and started to undo his belt, walking around the other side of a phone box to have a piss as he spoke.

'You need to sort your head out, Gav,' he said. 'It's nothing to do with me. Leave me behind, forget about me, whatever. It won't go away.'

'I like girls, I'm not like you.'

'We were happy, weren't we?' Steve said, buttoning his flies up, anger flashing across his face.

'We were mates!' Gavin repeated.

'We weren't mates!'

'Why are you being so needy?' Gavin shouted.

'What's needy about loving you?'

'You don't love me! Besides, I'm moving away, you'll forget all about me.'

'I'll never forget you!' Steve grabbed his arm, squeezing it hard and pulling him closer. 'You're under my skin, you know that.'

Gavin stood opposite Steve on the dark street and clarity flooded in. He knew Steve was right but he also knew he wouldn't – couldn't – do anything about it.

'Don't throw us away,' Steve said more quietly, releasing Gavin's arm.

'There's nothing to throw away,' Gavin said coldly, his discomfort forcing his emotion deeper, into the dark crevices where he wouldn't see or feel them anymore.

'Why *did* you humiliate Natalie like that?'

'I was a dick,' Gavin said quietly, shame heating his face. 'Michael wound me up, you wanted to tell the world I was gay and… I don't know. She was there.'

'She didn't deserve that.'

'I didn't mean it.'

'It was ugly. That's not who you are.'

'Maybe it is, though? Maybe that's exactly who I am.'

Steve reached out and touched Gavin's cheek lightly, shaking his head.

'It's not, Gavin. Trust yourself. Stop trying to please people you'll never please.'

'I'll apologise to her,' Gavin said, eyes on the floor. 'I'll make it right somehow.'

'Good,' Steve said, pursing his lips together. 'Make sure you do.'

They stood in silence, a metre apart, neither reaching out for the other.

'This is it, isn't it?' Steve said eventually.

More silence. Awkward, nothing like things used to be.

'I can't give you what you want,' Gavin said eventually.

'I know,' Steve replied, nodding solemnly.

The darkness stroked Gavin's skin, offering no comfort as the breeze picked up, pushing leaves down the road, the rustling filling Gavin's ears as if it were magnified.

'Right then,' he said, nodding firmly and shoving his hands into his jean pockets.

'Right then,' Steve mirrored. 'Be happy, Gavin. Or at least try to be.'

'You too,' Gavin said, wanting more than anything to lean forward and kiss him so he could feel safe, just for a moment longer. Something to take with him, to remember in the days to come when he was feeling lonely or confused. Instead, he turned around quickly and walked back along the road, opting to walk home instead of heading back to the party. As he walked, his entire body was alive with possibility, hoping Steve was going to come after him and grab him and spin him around to kiss him hard and hold him tight, turning his life into a romantic movie with a happy ending. As he entered the cool, dusky high street, he glanced back. Steve hadn't followed. His life wasn't a film. It was over.

~ Chapter 6 ~

'You just let him go?' Jackie says breathlessly, heart beating rapidly in her chest.

'I said it was complicated,' Gavin replies. He's standing with his back to her staring at the pond again while she sits on the bench, totally absorbed in his tale.

'You have a wife, so...'

'That means nothing.'

'Clearly,' Jackie says, mind racing. 'I can't believe you let him go. Please tell me that wasn't the end of it?'

'No,' Gavin says, turning around and leaning back against the railings. 'It wasn't the end of it.'

'So?'

'It got complicated.'

'How?' Jackie says urgently. 'Come on, I need to know what happened next.'

'Why am I telling you all of this?'

'I'm a good listener,' she replies, a natural smile spreading across her face.

'That you are, Jackie,' he says, returning her grin.

You're a liar.
I'm not lying.
You're withholding information, that's the same thing.
It hasn't come up.
You think he'd be talking to you if it had?

'Well?' Jackie perseveres, shaking her head to rid herself of her critical inner voice. She hasn't done anything wrong. There's no real reason she shouldn't talk to him. Besides, she likes him a lot. He's charming, funny. More than that, he's interesting, so much more interesting than she'd have imagined from watching

46

his wife, Imogen, talk with Louise in the café.

'Well what?' he says, glancing at his watch.

'What happened next?'

'I should probably get off,' he says. 'I've blathered on enough; you must be sick of me already.'

'No!' she says, patting the seat next to her on the bench. 'I've got all day.'

'Okay,' he replies, walking over and sitting down next to her again, putting his left ankle on top of his right knee. 'I guess the next important thing that happened was meeting Imogen.'

'Your wife?' Jackie asks, picturing Imogen's long dark hair and disdainful smile, already fascinated by their obvious mismatch, wondering how on Earth they got together.

'My wife.' Gavin nodded. 'We met at university. I always wonder what would have happened if I'd got a place in the Halls of Residence instead of moving into that house share. Things would have been *so* different...'

* * *

'For god's sake, just go,' Gavin said, grinning and pushing his mum out of the door of his new bedroom.

'I don't like leaving you here all on your own,' his mum replied. 'Look at the state of this place! Ellie Farnborough's boy caught scabies when he moved away to university, I bet he lived somewhere filthy like this. Let me have a word with the university, I'm sure there will be people who were in Halls that have dropped out already.'

'Mum, it's fine, 'Gavin said firmly, squeezing her arm.

'At least let me give it the once over,' she continued. 'It's disgusting.'

She wasn't wrong. The house was dirty in a *ground-in* way and it was obvious that a hoover and cloth would never shift it. The décor was outdated, clinging on, years past its prime.

The living room ceiling had signs of damp, most likely a leak from the bathroom above, and one of the bedrooms had mushrooms growing in the corner. Luckily, Gavin was the first of his housemates to arrive, so got to choose the largest double bedroom on the third floor.

'You'll catch something if you stay here,' his mum continued dramatically as he ushered her back downstairs to his father, who was standing jangling his keys in the living room. 'Mark my words. You remember what happened to Sally Jenkins when she went travelling.'

'She got dysentery, yes.'

'Well, we don't want...'

'Mum, it's fine!' Gavin said. 'I imagine it's what all the houses are like.'

'Then they're all a pile of shit,' his father said bluntly. 'Come on love,' he said, turning his attention to Gavin's mother. 'He doesn't need us prattling around him. Let him get on.'

'Shouldn't we wait until someone else arrives, at least?' his mum said nervously, putting her arm around Gavin's waist.

'Christ sake, woman, he's fine,' his dad said. 'You're all right, aren't you lad?'

It wasn't a question. They all knew it wasn't a question.

'I'm fine,' Gavin said. In truth, he couldn't wait for them both to go so he could unpack and get settled. For once, he and his dad were on the same page.

'Right, work hard lad. First one in our family to go to university.'

With that, his father turned and walked about the living room, leaving Gavin slightly dumbfounded.

'Don't look so shocked,' his mum said gently, taking him and hugging him hard one last time. 'You know he's proud of you.'

'Have a safe trip home, Mum,' Gavin said, holding her tight for a moment longer before letting her go. 'Thanks for bringing me down.'

'Don't be silly, love. What were we going to do, send you on the train with all your belongings?'

With that she turned and followed his father out of the front door, closing it behind her without turning around, unsuccessfully trying to hide her tears.

There were five bedrooms in his new student house, along with a shared bathroom, living room and kitchen. There was only a small back yard, barely two metres square, which Gavin later learned was common for properties in central Brighton. It was over an hour before the first of his housemates arrived, giving him time to unpack his clothes and sort his computer out on the desk in his bedroom. He was sitting in the living room drinking a cup of coffee when he heard voices.

'Imogen, you are *not* staying here.'

'Mum, it's fine. This is what university is like.'

Their voices were southern. Posh. Cut glass.

'Squalor and decay? It certainly wasn't like that for me. Or your father. You're so wilful, Imogen. You had other offers; you could have gone anywhere. Fashion and Textiles, Imogen. Of all the subjects.'

'Mum, leave it will you? We've been through this a thousand times, I enjoy it. People make careers out of it.'

'I'll never understand you, Imogen,' her mother countered as she opened the living room door. Gavin sat smiling on the sofa, coffee cupped in his hand.

'Hi,' he said, standing up out of politeness. 'I'm Gavin.'

Imogen's mother was tall and thin, her body crafted into a tailored blue-grey suit, small handbag crooked in her right elbow. Immaculate dark hair hung in a bob just below her chin line. Behind her, stood Imogen. The same height and build as her mother, but wearing a long, floating dress, open at the neck. Immediately she gave the sense of being a younger, freer version of her mother.

'I'm Imogen,' she said, extending her hand.

'I heard,' Gavin said awkwardly. 'Sorry, that sounded weird. I just meant I heard your mum calling you Imogen. I mean, I assume she's your mum, she might not be, she could be...' he trailed off, looking at the floor and taking a deep breath.

'Sorry,' he said, extending his hand to take hers and shake it.

'This is all a bit much, isn't it?'

'Just a bit.'

'You're the second to arrive. I got here about an hour ago,' he said. 'I'd grab a bedroom quickly. Avoid the one at the back, it's got mushrooms growing in it.'

'Imogen! That's it, you can't stay here!' Imogen's mother exclaimed.

'Mum, enough,' she said firmly, looking back at Gavin with a cheeky grin. 'Help me unpack the car, will you? Mum is next to useless. Worried she'll break a nail.'

'Of course,' Gavin said, returning her grin and putting his cup down on the coffee table.

'What's your name, by the way?' Imogen asked as they walked towards the front door, leaving her mother to inspect the kitchen, bathroom and toilet in disgust.

'Gavin,' he replied. 'I'm doing a photography degree.'

'I didn't ask,' she said, glancing back over her shoulder at him, eyes shining with mischief.

Gavin's next housemate was a foreign student from Spain called Paco. He arrived a couple of hours after Imogen, followed by another new arrival around 6pm.

'Pub?' the girl said, forsaking introductions as she dropped her cases in the hall. Gavin and Imogen looked at each other and smiled.

'Pub,' Gavin nodded.

'Pub,' Imogen repeated.

'Should one of us ask Paco?' Imogen said, looking at Gavin.

'He hasn't come out of his room since he got here.'

'I'll get him,' Gavin said. 'You show...' he paused, glancing at the new girl. 'What's your name again?'

'Susie,' she said, smiling and offering her hand.

'Gavin,' he responded. Then: 'Imogen can show you the last two rooms, then we can get going.'

'Fuck that, I'll look later, let's get a drink,' Susie replied in a broad Scottish accent.

'One of the rooms has mushrooms growing in it,' Imogen said quickly. 'You might want to grab the other one before we go.'

'Shouldn't we wait for whoever's got mushroom room?' Gavin said, pausing on the stairs on his way to get Paco.

'We can leave him or her a note. If we just go to the student union, they'll be able to find us.'

Of course, they'd forgotten one key fact: mushroom room housemate had no idea what the rest of them looked like, so wouldn't be able to find any of them, even if he or she had wanted to.

'Are we arseholes?' Gavin asked when he finally realised this, leaning against the bar in the SU bar.

'They'll live,' Susie said, grabbing Paco's arm and dragging him away to the dancefloor. 'There'll be plenty of other nights.'

Gavin leaned against the bar and downed a triple vodka, lemonade and lime, glancing at Imogen as she did the same.

'Another?' he asked.

'Definitely,' she replied.

Later, as their new friends dissolved into the smoke and disco lights around them, Gavin and Imogen leaned into one another, slurring.

'Never? Shut up!' Imogen said, clearly dumbfounded enough to make Gavin wish he hadn't been so open or honest.

'Yeah, so what?'

'You've never had a girlfriend before?'

Gavin shrugged, as if it was nothing, not important.

'You've never...' Imogen paused, as if unsure how to phrase it. 'You know.'

'No,' he said slowly. 'I've never... you know.'

'That's ridiculous, you can't be a virgin,' she said, twirling the straw in her drink as she spoke. 'Look at you.'

He laughed nervously, not quite sure what she meant. Did she fancy him?

'Do you want to change that?' she asked, lifting the straw to her lips and taking a slow drag on it.

'Change it?' he frowned, gulping down another shot followed by a sip of lager.

'Being a virgin?'

'Oh, oh shit. I see.'

'Well?' she asked again, putting her drink down and picking her small clutch bag up from the counter.

'Fuck yes,' he replied, summoning all of his courage. Imogen grabbed his hand and dragged him out of the Student Union, almost running over to the cab stop to get back to their new house.

When they got home, they discovered that mushroom room housemate was a guy called Ross. He was in the living room watching TV so they stopped to say hello quickly before decamping to Imogen's room.

After that, Ross never did gel with them, he never became part of their group. Gavin always wondered after if it was because they'd already excluded him before he'd arrived but more likely, it was because they'd paired up around him. Living with them must have been a nightmare because not only had Gavin and Imogen become an item that night, so had Susie and Paco. Ross was outsider before he'd had the chance to become anything else. Whatever the reason, Ross quicky began to avoid them and spent his time out of the house or in his room. He didn't join in with the joint cooking, didn't watch TV with the rest of them and barely spoke two words to any of them. He was polite enough but that was it.

'Don't you think he's a bit strange?' Susie said one evening, curled up in Paco's lap, drinking a bottled beer.

'Ross?' Gavin said. 'Nah, I think he's okay. Must be hard for him, living with two couples.'

'Is that what we are?' Imogen said, looking at him coyly. 'I thought we were just having sex; I didn't realise we were a thing.'

'Sorry,' Gavin said, heart in his throat. 'I didn't mean... I just thought. Shit, I mean...'

'Oh, you're definitely a couple,' Susie said, laughing.

'I've never seen two people so...' Paco squished his hands together in a charades type manner, clearly trying to find the English word for what he wanted to say. 'Squished,' he finished eventually.

'Squished?' Imogen replied, frowning.

'I think he means tight?' Susie said, glancing at Paco and nodding, continuing to laugh. 'Or together?'

'No,' Paco said confidently. 'I mean squished. You know, never leaving each other alone.'

'What do you mean?' Imogen said, sitting up straight, indignant. 'We aren't squished!'

'Of course we aren't,' Gavin said, squeezing Imogen's hand and glaring at Paco.

'You are,' Paco continued. 'I'd feel, how do you say... suffocated.'

'So, I'm suffocating now?' Imogen said indignantly.

'Nobody said *you* were suffocating,' Susie said, touching Paco's arm, a clear signal to tell him to stop talking.

'We can't help being in love!' Imogen snapped, face red with anger.

'Gavin's as bad,' Paco said, doubling down. 'When you're not here, he doesn't stop talking about you, Imogen.'

'Christ, am I really boring?' Gavin asked.

'No, it's sweet,' Susie said, full on squeezing Paco's arm. 'And I'm sure Paco talks about me just as much!'

'He never talks about you,' Imogen snapped, standing up and grabbing Gavin's hand. 'Come on Gavin, let's go to bed.'

Later that night, lying in bed as Imogen absently stroked his chest, Gavin couldn't help feeling troubled.

'I'm sick of those two,' Gavin said irritably. 'Who do they think they are?'

'Totally,' Imogen replied. 'We could move out? Get a place together, just the two of us?'

'We could never afford that...'

'I can ask my parents. Tell them some sob story about why I can't stay here anymore.'

Gavin was about to argue with her, tell her it was ridiculous, but stopped himself. Everything with Imogen was easy, she was so... in control. He liked that about her. She knew what she wanted, when she wanted it, how she wanted it. He never felt like that. He could barely work out what he wanted to eat for dinner let alone anything else so being with someone so confident was refreshing. Why not move in with her?

'Okay, let's do it,' he said.

'Yes?' Imogen replied, leaning up on her elbow and staring into his eyes.

'Yeah, why not?'

~ Chapter 7 ~

Gavin didn't visit home at all in his first year at university. His parents came down for a couple of weekend visits, staying in a local hotel, but he didn't go home and didn't tell them he'd moved in with Imogen, they'd think it was too much, too soon. His first summer came and went and he got a part-time job in the local supermarket so he could afford his half of their flat's rent.

It wasn't until Christmas of their second year that Gavin first brought Imogen home to meet his parents. Despite his nerves, he was surprised to realise that he *wanted* to show her off to them. Mainly to his dad, if he was honest. He needn't have worried. Imogen's beauty drew his father in just as her posh accent and impeccable manners drew his mother in. The excitement dripped off them like sweat from a runner as they fussed over her, laying an extra place at the dinner table, cooing and chatting like they'd never seen a teenage girl before. Gavin couldn't pretend it didn't make him feel pleased, proud even. It was the first time he could remember making his father happy. Imogen was funny and charming. Everything was so very *normal*.

After dinner, he and Imogen went to the local pub. Future Gavin would look back and realise this was the moment the true damage began, when he started to etch away at her, creating the first whispers of future Imogen in the air, coalescing around his girlfriend, becoming the foundation of the woman she'd become, burying this Imogen – young and happy – inside, trapping her, mute, unable to scream.

'Take me to some of your old haunts,' she asked, clutching his arm tightly and staring at him, filled with love and excitement. 'I've never been this far north before, is everyone as friendly as people say?'

'Some of them.'

He smiled, leaning in to kiss her on the mouth.

'I want to know what your life was like before university, before you met me.'

I don't think you do, he thought but didn't say, pushing thoughts of Steve out of his mind. If he didn't think of him, he wasn't real. The new life he'd created for himself was real. Look at how happy his parents were with Imogen coming for Christmas. Would they have beamed so brightly if he'd turned up with Steve in tow? Of course not.

As they entered the pub and walked towards the bar, Gavin stopped dead. There he was. It was a small town with limited pubs but he'd put the possibility of bumping into him to the back of his mind and hadn't prepared himself. As it was, seeing Steve was a body blow and for a moment he thought he was going to vomit. Steve was standing at the bar, leaning and chatting to a guy with his back to Gavin. A boyfriend? Surely, he wouldn't have a boyfriend? Not in their hometown, he'd get lynched. Gavin stood still, not sure what to do. Everything seemed different to when he'd left home a year ago. The pub seemed less friendly than it once had, no longer familiar. Perhaps the real truth of it was that Gavin had changed, not the pub or the people. But Steve had changed too, Gavin could tell. He looked more self-assured. Still handsome, magnetic in a way few people genuinely are, but more confident than before. Maybe Gavin leaving had been good for him, too?

'You okay?' Imogen said, unhooking her arm and smiling at him.

'Yeah,' he replied, manufacturing a smile in return.

'Come on then,' she walked towards the bar, completely oblivious to the stress she was putting him under. 'Let's get a drink.'

'I'll get these,' he said, grabbing Imogen's arm. 'You go and find us a table. What you having? Large dry white?'

'Yes, please,' Imogen said. 'I'll see if there's anywhere near the window, shall I?'

Gavin held his breath as he approached the bar. It was already quite busy with only a few gaps to get in and order drinks. A gap opened up next to Steve and Gavin knew he had no choice, he'd have to say hello because Steve would notice him any moment, so he braced himself and walked up next to him, not looking at Steve but at the bar staff instead, trying to get their attention.

'Gavin!'

'Oh, hey,' Gavin said, fake-nonchalantly. Steve's smile, his warmth, wrapped itself around Gavin instantly, so much so he had to grab the bar with his hand to steady himself. He made eye contact and they both stood, lost in each other. Nothing had changed. They both knew it, both saw it in each other instantly. Gavin wanted to kiss him, to grab him and hold him and tell him he was sorry, that he never should have left him but he'd been scared, he hadn't known what to do so he'd run, he'd run as far away as he could and he hadn't looked back. Instead, he said 'Steve,' and nodded, leaning on the bar next to him and looking away, motioning the barman for his attention.

'Gavin?' Steve repeated, sounding less sure of himself.

'How you doing? All right?' Gavin said awkwardly, glancing to his left.

'Yeah, good,' Steve said. 'You remember Jamie, of course?' he indicated the guy on the other side of him, the one he'd been chatting with.

'Jamie?' Gavin said, focusing on Steve's companion. Jamie. From the gang. What was Steve doing with Jamie? Were Trevor and Michael here? He frowned at Steve before offering Jamie a handshake.

'Back for Christmas?' Jamie asked. 'Haven't seen you since Ursula's party. First time back?'

Gavin didn't answer because the barman arrived at that moment to take his order. After paying and picking up his pint and glass of wine, he said: 'Good to see you both again,' and walked back over to the table for two in the window where Imogen sat, not looking back over his shoulder, scared of what he might do if he did.

'Hey,' he said to Imogen, heart visibly reaching out of his chest.

'Hey handsome,' she replied, leaning over and clutching his hand. 'Is it weird being back?'

'What do you mean?'

'You seem a little edgy. Is it weird being back? When I went home last week it felt really weird. Like another life, one I'd left behind. Nothing felt the same. Strange isn't it, we've only been at university a year but everything's different.'

'Yeah,' he replied, glancing over to Steve. 'Everything's different.'

Two more pints and he and Imogen chatted freely. The drink had loosened Gavin up a little and he hadn't seen Steve for a while so he assumed he and Jamie might have left. Probably for the best. No need to open old wounds. Focus on Imogen, forget it all.

'I'll get another drink on the way back from the toilet,' he said and Imogen nodded, leaning back in her chair and looking around the pub to people-watch in his absence. Turning a corner towards the toilet, he saw Steve heading back along the corridor. He stopped, almost tripping up over his own feet, not sure what to do as Steve moved towards him.

'It's good to see you, Gavin,' Steve said, stopping just before him. Gavin faced Steve but refused eye contact, looking towards the floor instead.

'I'm sorry for how things ended,' he said. *Shit. Don't get into it, there's no need to dredge over the past.*

'It's okay.' Steve reached out and touched his arm, forcing Gavin to look up at him. 'We've both moved on. It all feels like a million years ago, doesn't it?'

'Longer.'

'We had fun though, didn't we?'

'Yeah, Christ yeah, the best of times.'

Steve nodded.

'So, Jamie?' Gavin said. 'Is he? I mean, you're not?'

Steve laughed. 'Ha, God no. Although, I *would*, actually... but I don't think he's... anyway. He's on the same training course I'm doing. Animal welfare.'

'Animal welfare? That's amazing. You were always so good with Rosie.'

'God rest her soul.'

'Oh shit, is she gone? You okay?'

'She was in pain. She's gone to a better place, eh?'

'Ha,' Gavin said, leaning against the side of the hallway to let another guy past to go to the toilet. 'Have you found religion since I left?'

'Oh, fuck off,' Steve replied light-heartedly.

'When does your course finish?' Gavin asked. 'Will you get a qualification? I'm really proud of you, especially having to look after your mum and everything.'

'Careful,' Steve grinned. 'It's almost like you still care.'

Gavin could feel the draw, the need to grab Steve and hold him tight but he resisted and remained motionless as silence wrapped its hands around his throat, squeezing gently.

'You left me behind,' Steve said finally.

'Yes.'

Breathing. Nothing but eye contact, beating heart and —

'Can I ask you something?'

'Of course.'

'Do you love her? The girl you're with?'

Not like I love you, Gavin wanted to blurt out. Instead, he nodded in guilty affirmation.

'And you?' Gavin asked, his whole body beating, clammy, as if a sickness was overtaking him. 'Has there been anyone?'

'A couple of guys,' Steve said. 'None of them were you.'

'Don't,' Gavin said, taking a step forward to pass Steve, desperately looking away from his eyes, fearful he'd get lost in that hopeful sea of blue, aware they could convince him of anything.

'I'm glad you're happy.'

'You're always so nice, Steve.' Gavin said. 'I treated you like shit, you should be angry.'

'It's okay, I...'

'What you wanted was impossible,' Gavin cut in, desperately needing to explain himself, to absolve himself. 'I couldn't live like that.'

'Like what? We could have been happy!'

'I'm happy now.'

'Like I said, I'm glad.'

'It wasn't simple, you and me. You know it wasn't. I'm not like you, Steve. I do like girls. I like Imogen.'

'So you keep saying,' Steve retorted.

Gavin leaned forward, not in control, not able to do anything else but grab Steve by the scruff of his shirt, pulling him close and kissing him. Steve barely fought it before kissing him back, electricity ran through every part of Gavin, making him feel completely alive. Their hands were all over each other and Gavin was so lost in the moment, he even forgot they were in public, in a local bar where anyone could see them or catch them or—

'What are you doing?' Imogen shouted, the shock twisting her vocal cords from wail to whimper. Gavin spun around to see her standing behind them in the corridor. He pushed Steve off him, looking away from Imogen in shame.

'Nothing,' Gavin said, flustered. 'I mean, this is Steve. He's my. Was my...'

'Hi,' Steve said awkwardly.

'Fuck off,' she said, grabbing Gavin and pulling him away from the corridor towards the door.

'What the hell was that?' Imogen said, dragging him into the cold night air.

'It's not what you think,' he said. 'Don't get stressed out.'

'You were just kissing a guy,' Imogen shrieked. 'What the fuck is going on?'

'It's not what you think,' Gavin repeated, trying desperately to think of a lie that would convince her it wasn't *exactly* what she thought it was.

They got a cab back to Gavin's parents' house in silence, then made polite chat with his mum, who still waited up for him to get in when he was at home.

'You'll always be my little boy,' she said, hugging him tightly. 'I couldn't sleep without knowing you were both home safely.'

Gavin and Imogen said their goodnights, got glasses of water and went upstairs to his bedroom, shutting the door behind them.

'It's disgusting,' Imogen spat eventually, eyes wild.

'No,' Gavin countered angrily. 'I know what I did was wrong, but...'

'You know it was *wrong*?' she sneered.

'Look,' Gavin took a step towards her again, trying to remain calm. 'I know you're upset, it's clearly shocked you. But nothing's changed.'

'Everything's changed!' Imogen spat, her anger turning momentarily to something else. Fear? Desperation? Gavin couldn't tell.

'How? You had loads of boyfriends before me...'

'Yes, but I didn't expect you had too,' she screamed, grabbing a hairbrush from the side next to her and throwing it across the room at Gavin.

'It was just Steve.'

'Oh, that's okay then!'

Gavin ducked out of the way as another missile hit the bedroom door behind him with a loud bang.

'You had boyfriends before me,' he tried desperately.

'But I wasn't kissing them by the gents' toilets tonight, was I?'

'Look I know…'

'And I'm not secretly gay,' she continued, fresh tears coming. 'I don't understand how you can be gay.'

'I'm not,' he said. 'Come on, our sex life is good. You know I'm not gay.'

'I wouldn't say it's good, Gavin,' she hissed. 'Kind of makes sense why, now. None of this makes sense.'

Imogen sat down on the edge of the bed and ran her hands through her hair.

'We had a thing,' Gavin said. 'When we were younger, that's all. It ended but tonight when we saw each other… I don't know, it just happened. It doesn't change how I feel about you.' He walked over to Imogen and kneeled down before her. 'Don't make it complicated.'

'*Me* make it complicated?'

'I love you, Imogen,' Gavin said softly. 'I shouldn't have kissed him, it was wrong,' he paused, sensing a slight change in her demeanour, her anger. 'Tonight was just, I don't know. He got under my skin.'

'So, it was his fault?' she eyed him warily.

'He didn't know about you,' Gavin said, not quite willing to throw Steve under the bus. 'We just… it just happened. It's over, that's all you need to know.'

'It didn't look over,' Imogen said, but the fire in her voice had gone, not yet replaced by softness, but Gavin could already hear a creeping resignation. 'Why didn't you tell me before?'

'I don't know, it didn't seem important, that's all,' Gavin

started, faltering only for a millisecond. 'We just... it was *ours*, that's all. Nobody knew. Nothing ever really happened between us, we kissed once before, that's all. It was nothing.'

'The more you say nothing the less it sounds like nothing. I can't deal with this,' Imogen shook her head. 'I can't.'

'Come on, Imogen,' Gavin said, still kneeling before her and putting a hand on each of her thighs as she sat on the bed in front of him. 'I love you, you know that.'

'Did you love him?' She asked desperately, clearly wanting a lie, needing a lie.

'Yes,' he replied, unable to give her one. 'He was important to me, what we had was... I don't know. It was what it was, but it's over, in the past.'

'It didn't look in the past,' Imogen repeated. 'It looked very much in the present.'

Silence. Gavin squeezed her thighs ever so gently before rubbing them up and down.

'I love you Imogen,' he said. 'Nothing's changed. Tonight was a mistake, it was all a long time ago, before I met you.'

'But it's,' she squeezed her shoulders up to her ears and grimaced. 'I can't stop picturing the two of you, it's disgusting.'

'We didn't sleep together.'

'I don't understand. What was it, then? If you didn't even have sex, then what was it all about?'

'Stop winding yourself up,' Gavin said, standing up and turning his back. 'It's in the past.'

'Winding *myself* up?' she snapped. 'I can't get rid of the image of you kissing him.'

'I don't spend my days picturing you screwing your exes, do I?'

'None of them were women!'

Silence enveloped his old bedroom again and for a moment Gavin wondered if they'd disturbed his parents with their arguing.

'Look,' he said, taking a deep calming breath. 'You know I love you, right?' he made eye contact and reached out his hands, waiting for her to take them. After what seemed like hours, she held her own hands out and lightly squeezed his, nodding. 'I should have told you, but I didn't know we'd bump into him.'

'Would you ever have told me if we hadn't?' she asked.

'Probably not,' he replied. 'Like I said, we didn't tell anyone. We were teenagers, it was a thing, then it was over. It's not a big deal.'

'I think it is,' Imogen started.

'Oh look, I can't spend the rest of our lives apologising for loving someone before I met you.'

'I'm so sorry for being upset!'

'Imogen,' Gavin said, staring at her steadily. 'You're not listening. I can't spend *the rest of our lives* apologising.'

'The rest of our lives?' Imogen said, panda eyes finally making contact with his, flitting back and forth in her head desperately.

'Can you move past this or not?' he said slowly.

'You have to give me time,' she said. 'It's a lot, Gavin.'

'I told you.' He reached up and touched her cheek lightly. 'I'll give you the rest of our lives if you want it?'

'The rest of our lives?' she said again, her eyes locked onto him, searching his face desperately.

'Yeah, why not? If you'll have me?' Gavin said.

Imogen snorted, a lump of snot shooting out of her nose and resting on her upper lip.

'Do you mean it?' she half laughed, half cried, wiping the snot away with the back of her hand.

'I hadn't planned it, I'll grant you,' Gavin said, taking both of her hands in his and holding her gaze. 'But yeah, I mean it. What do you say?'

She squeezed her jaw together, eyes narrow.

'You can't see him again. Can't see him, can't talk to him. Not ever.'

'Okay.' He nodded.

'Promise me?' she reiterated.

'I promise.'

'Right then.' She nodded, hugging him tightly. 'You'll need to get me a ring.'

That was it, they were engaged. As they squeezed each other tightly, Gavin stared at the bedroom wall behind her, all curls of '70s wallpaper that should have been redecorated years ago, yellow and purple and brown. Bruised, swirling and uncertain.

~ Chapter 8 ~

'That's the worst marriage proposal I've ever heard,' Jackie says, wide eyed, connected.

'Don't,' Gavin laughs. 'I'm so fucking embarrassed.'

They are still sitting next to each other on Christopher and Elsie's bench in the pond enclosure. Gavin's throat sounds hoarse from talking but Jackie doesn't want him to stop, it's been years since she's found anyone this interesting.

'I panicked,' he continues. 'I don't know what I was thinking.'

'And she married you? After that proposal?'

'Yeah.'

'Bloody hell,' Jackie says in genuine wonderment. 'I'm not a relationship expert but that's all kinds of fucked up.'

'I *did* love her,' Gavin starts, defensively.

'I'm not judging,' Jackie says, holding her hands up and smiling. 'Really I'm not...'

'Okay,' he replies, returning her smile coyly. 'I could have done things differently, I get that. But believe it or not, we were happy. At first at least.'

'And Steve? Did you do what Imogen asked and keep your distance?'

'I didn't say that,' Gavin replies guiltily, eyes to the floor, lost in his own memories again.

'I knew it,' Jackie says, leaning forwards, desperate to hear the rest of his story. 'So, what happened?'

'I *did* love her,' he repeats, more to himself that to her. 'I do love her. It's complicated, that's all.'

'You're still together? You and Imogen?'

'I told you, it's complicated.'

'Not that complicated, either you're still married or you aren't, there's no in-between.'

'There's always an in-between, Jackie.'

'I'm starting to wonder if that's your problem, Gavin. All this in-between-ness.'

'Who said I have a problem?'

He falls into silence but she isn't sure if he's contemplating what she said or is simply lost in his own memories again.

You're judging again.
No, I'm not, I'm just...
Judging.
Leave me alone.
Truth hurts.

'I think we were okay until she got pregnant,' Gavin says, not looking at her.

'So, it's your child's fault now?' Jackie says slowly. The voice is right, she *is* judging, breaking her cardinal rule in the process. Also, she's clearly pushing her luck. If she continues down this path, she'll make him defensive or angry but she can't help herself. In her experience, men always have someone else to blame, never themselves.

'Tim? No, he's amazing,' Gavin says, his face lighting up at the mere mention of his son's name. 'I could never regret him, that's not what I meant.'

Jackie's cheeks burn with shame and embarrassment, not only because she's judged him but because she's so clearly *misjudged* him.

More listening, less judging.
When did you get so wise?
I've always been wise, you just never listen to me.
Why would I? You try and kill me in my sleep every night.

'It changed us, you know?' Gavin continues. 'The cracks we'd papered over for years started getting bigger after he was born.

We stopped bothering to repair them. I guess that happens to a lot of parents, right?'

'I wouldn't know, I don't have kids,' Jackie says, instinctively touching her stomach. 'I've never even had a relationship. Besides, it's all night sweats and brittle hair for me nowadays.'

'Your hair's lovely.'

'You can't even see it, I'm wearing a head scarf,' Jackie says.

'Well, I'm sure it's not brittle.' he continues, a cheeky smile spreading across his face.

'You're really not good at the compliments, are you?' Jackie says, mirroring his grin in spite of herself.

'They aren't my forte,' he says. 'But at least I tried.'

'Carry on, then,' Jackie says, using the most soothing voice she can find. 'What happened next?'

'You must be bored of hearing me speak by now.'

'On the contrary,' Jackie replies lightly. 'I want to hear all of it.'

'Okay then, where was I? I can't remember…'

'The moment it all started to go wrong?' Jackie says. 'When Imogen got pregnant with Tim.'

'Okay.' Gavin nods, taking a deep breath and closing his eyes. 'It was about ten years after we'd graduated. We were still living in Brighton and I'd been true to my word, I'd never contacted Steve again after that night in the pub…'

* * *

'Virginia Woolfe was from Sussex, you know,' Imogen said, absently flicking through a magazine. 'She killed herself… weighed her pockets down with stones and walked into the River Ouse.'

'That's cheery,' Gavin replied, leaning on the side of the sofa and slipping a hand on her knee, gently letting it creep up her leg to her inner thigh.

'She must have been so unhappy,' she continued absently.

'Why are you so maudlin?' Gavin said, hand pausing.

'I'm not, I'm just saying. Happiness is a funny thing, isn't it?'

'You're a funny thing,' he said, half ignoring her as his fingers spidered up her leg again, exploring.

'Look at you,' she said, a small smile on her face as she glanced down at his hand on her thigh.

'What?' he asked, frowning.

'Don't take this the wrong way,' she said slowly, pulling him close so that his face was close to hers. 'Because you're very good in bed...'

'Okay,' he said hesitantly, leaning closer and kissing her on the lips. 'I'm glad to hear it.'

'But you never instigate it, it's always me.'

'I'm instigating it now,' he said, pulling back from her slightly.

'I know, I know, it's just,' she held his T-shirt so he had to remain close. 'I'd like more of that. You don't need to be so passive all the time.'

'Okay,' he repeated, not sure how to respond. 'I wouldn't call myself passive, I mean...'

'I don't mind *you* being in control sometimes,' she said, leaning into him again, lips brushing against his, the previous sexual excitement in her eyes evaporating as she spoke, replaced by discomfort. 'In the bedroom, I mean. That's all I'm saying.'

'I get it,' he said, trying to reassure her, mind racing.

'Not all the time, not every time, but sometimes,' she clarified quickly, awkwardly.

'I get the point,' Gavin said, grabbing the back of her hair and twirling it around his hand before tugging it backwards and kissing her again, pushing her back onto the sofa.

After, lying into one another on the couch.

'I'm happy in Brighton,' Imogen said. 'I want to stay here.'

'Of course, why would we move?'

'I mean, even if one of us had to commute to London or something... I wouldn't want to move there. I like it here.'

'So do I,' Gavin said, shifting a little, forcing Imogen to sit up. 'What's this all about?'

'We can't go on living like students anymore, Gavin, living in a pokey rented flat. We're in our thirties, for Christ's sake.'

'We're happy, aren't we? I know I don't make much money but...'

'What if we had kids? I'd want them to have more than this.'

'More than what?'

'More than what we have. I had everything growing up, everything. What do we have to offer a kid?'

'Love, Imogen. They don't need a massive house and lots of things. That didn't do you any good, did it? Where has this all come from?'

'I'm just saying. I don't want to move to London.'

'Jesus, nobody said anything about moving to London. My photography studio is here in Brighton, our lives are here. What's going on, Imogen?'

'I spoke to my uncle earlier,' she said tentatively, glancing at Gavin nervously.

'Oh, I get it,' Gavin said, standing up and pulling his underwear and jeans back on. 'The rich relatives have been telling you I'm not good enough for you again, haven't they?'

'It's not like that! We have other options, Gavin, that's all. We don't have to live in poverty.'

'Poverty? We're hardly poor. What's wrong with our life? We do jobs we love, we're by the sea *and* the Downs! What more do you want?'

'I *don't* love my job. I don't even like it. But that's not the point, I'm talking about getting a place of our own, Gavin? Is that too much to ask?'

'We can't afford it, you know that.'

'We could though, if you'd…'

'Oh fuck,' Gavin said, slapping his forehead in mock amazement. 'Uncle fucking banker, right? What's he offering this time?'

'A job, Gavin. Is that so bad?'

'I can hear him now… *you'll never make any money in fashion, Imogen. Sell your soul to my bank.*'

'I don't work in fashion, I work in a department store, it's hardly what I dreamed of, is it.'

'You're not over the hill, Imogen, you've got time to change career path,' Gavin said.

'I'm not good enough. I was never good enough.'

'I hate it when you talk like that,' Gavin said softly. 'That's your dad's voice, not yours. You can do anything you set your mind to, you know you can.'

'I'm sick of living like this, Gavin. My uncle…'

'What?' Gavin interrupted snappily. 'What does he want you to do? He's asked you to go and work for him again, hasn't he?'

'Not me.'

'Oh, you're fucking kidding me. Me? What does he want *me* to do?'

'You know what.'

'You've turned down every offer he's ever made.'

'This is different.'

'Why?'

'Because I'm pregnant!'

'What?' Gavin stuttered, pausing half in, half out of his T-shirt as he pulled it over his head.

'Yes,' she nodded over and over, studying him for a reaction.

'We're going to have a kid?' he said, pulling his T-shirt down and staring at his wife, eyes darting back and forth in his head.

'Yes.'

'Oh my God.' Gavin leaned down and grabbed her off the sofa in one movement, cradling her in his arms like she was herself an overgrown baby, lifting her up and spinning her around and around. He dropped her back onto the sofa and collapsed next to her, grabbing her hand as he did so.

'Couldn't you have found a better way than that to tell me?' he asked, smiling at her widely.

'I didn't mean it to come out that way. I just... I don't know. I did the test yesterday...'

'And you only told me now?'

'I didn't know how you'd react.'

'What?' he grabbed her other hand, holding them both firmly in his. 'We're having a baby!' he repeated, 'I'm happy, why would you think I wouldn't be?'

'We live hand to mouth, Gavin.'

'Hardly. We aren't raking it in, but...'

'Come on, Gavin. Be honest.'

'We're okay.'

'Gavin, I work in a department store, you're a photographer, we barely make ends meet. Why won't you let my family help us?'

'You've never wanted them involved before! Neither of us want their handouts.'

'It's not a handout, it's a job. A really well-paid job.'

'Oh Imogen...'

'We need the money, Gavin.'

'But I don't know anything about Investment banking, I'm not trained...'

'They'll train you, that's the point. We'll need the money, you know we will. I'll have to stop work, for a while at least.'

'You'll get maternity leave...'

'That's peanuts and you know it. Think of the baby.'

'I thought we agreed not to make decisions based on money?'

'We haven't only got ourselves to think about now,' she said, hand resting on her stomach.

'We *agreed* Imogen. Look at your family...'

'What's wrong with them?' she said tersely.

'Where should I start?'

'I never went without for anything, though, did I?'

'Except attention, Imogen. And love.'

'What about your family?' Imogen snapped.

'Don't start, I'm not being unkind, I just...'

'Look,' she said, in a quieter, more reasonable tone. 'I don't want to argue...'

'Then stop pushing me. Christ Imogen, investment banking? Really?'

'We've got a child on the way Gavin,' she said. 'You need to grow up.'

'What about the photography studio? I'll never have time for it if...'

'You can keep it as a hobby,' Imogen said, reaching over and squeezing his hand. 'It's not like it makes ends meet anyway. Can you really turn down the chance to earn this much money when you're about to be a father?'

Gavin didn't respond, he didn't know how to. His wife's hands felt cold in his, alien. He pulled them free, turning away from Imogen and standing to stare out the window onto the street below.

'It doesn't have to be forever, does it?' Imogen said reasonably, like logic itself had possessed her and was using her as a mouthpiece. 'Just for a while, to earn some cash and get us and the baby set up.'

He remained silent, watching an old woman walk slowly down the street below him, hunched over, unsure on her feet but persevering, half-empty shopping bags gripped in her gnarled knuckles.

'We need a place of our own, Gavin,' Imogen said, moving to stand behind him and taking his arm gently, pulling him around to focus on her.

'I suppose,' he sighed, pursing his lips together tightly. 'I mean, for a while. Just to help us get set up for the baby.'

Imogen smiled, leaning in and kissing him.

'It'll mean me commuting to London every day, you know that, right?'

'You won't regret it,' she said, ignoring him. 'You'll see. This is the start of our future. Our family.' She took his hand and placed it on her belly. He nodded and his mouth smiled convincingly enough for her to turn and walk away.

'Fancy a cup of tea?' she asked as she left the room.

'No, you're all right,' he replied, turning back to window and staring out blindly.

Gavin took the job, steeling himself for a new life, providing for his family. His mum was proud, his dad, too, in his way. They'd always wanted him to earn more money, to set himself up. They'd never understood the photography, his need to create, to document, to breathe.

Eight months later, their son was born. Gavin cradled him to his bare chest as he sat next to Imogen's hospital bed and she whispered: 'We're a team, Gavin. We'll do this together.'

In that moment, he felt invincible, like the three of them could and would take on the world.

'I'd like to call him Timothy,' Imogen said, touching him lightly on the arm.

'After your dad?' Gavin frowned, not pulling his gaze away from the baby in his arms. 'Really?'

'It's tradition,' she replied. Gavin was lost in his son's puffy, red, new-born face. He stroked his cheek, pausing before he replied.

'Okay,' he said, aware he'd lose the argument if he tried to have it. 'Tim it is.'

'Timothy,' Imogen said.

'You can put Timothy on the birth certificate, but I'm calling him Tim.'

'Just don't call him it in front of my dad, okay? You know how he hates to be called Tim.'

'Yeah, well, this isn't his son, is it?' Gavin said, staring down into his boy's face. 'He's mine.'

As Tim grew from baby to toddler, from toddler to pre-schooler, from pre-schooler to primary school child, endless commuting meant Gavin felt further and further removed from both his wife and son.

'You could go back to work?' Gavin said to Imogen one day, after Tim had started school. 'It's not too late to restart your career.'

'Who would pick up Tim from school? You're in London until all hours.'

'We could work it out. We could at least explore the options, see what's possible?'

'Why are you so desperate to get me back to work again?' she snapped.

'I'm not, I just... I want you to be happy.'

'I *am* happy,' she said unconvincingly. 'I want to be there for Tim, you know? Make sure he knows he's our number one priority.'

'Of course, but...'

'But what? What's this about, Gavin?'

'Nothing, honestly,' he said, manufacturing a smile. 'I thought you might want something else in your life, that's all. You're on your own with him a lot, with commuting and the hours I work.'

'So why would you want to put more pressure on me?'

'That wasn't... I wasn't. Look, it doesn't matter.'

'If you're feeling guilty because you don't spend enough time with Tim, don't take it out on me,' she snapped, not making eye contact.

'That's not fair, I do my best, you know I do.'

'Do you?'

'You were the one who wanted to send him to private school, not me,' Gavin started. 'The money's got to come from somewhere.'

'I know,' she said, 'I'm not saying you don't work hard. It's just... you're never here. Even when you are, it's like you're not mentally in the room.'

He stared at his wife. She still resembled the woman he'd met all those years ago. He supposed he still resembled the man she'd met as well. Funny things, resemblances. By definition, they're likenesses, facsimiles of the real thing.

'Hey,' he said softly, moving towards her and hugging her tightly. 'We'll work through it, won't we?'

'Your mum rang earlier,' she said, awkwardly extracting herself from his arms and walking over to the kitchen taps, picking up a cloth and wiping down the granite surfaces with her back to him.

'Right,' he said, arms limply dangling by his sides.

'I said you'd call her back.'

'Right,' he repeated.

As Imogen went upstairs, Gavin walked thoughtfully through to the living room where Tim was slouched on the sofa, head down in his Nintendo Switch.

'You okay, sweet boy?' he asked.

'Yeah,' Tim said, glancing up and holding an arm out for a cuddle without taking his other hand off his console. Gavin leaned down and hugged his son tightly, picking his mobile phone up off the side table by the sofa.

'Just going to call Grandma back,' he said, waving the phone at Tim by way of explanation. Tim's attention was already fully back in his games console as he muttered 'okay' in response.

Gavin hit the dial button for his parents' landline – they were the only people he knew who still had one – and wandered into the hallway, leaning against the wall near the front door opposite the large circular mirror that hung there. As the phone at the other end rung, he stared at his reflection, at the dark rings under his eyes.

'Hello?'

'Hey Mum,' he said, trying to sound relaxed and happy because he knew his mother was easily stressed. Besides, things were fine, really, weren't they? Nothing had changed. Tim was happy, he had friends and was doing well at school. He and Imogen had a lovely house and could afford to go on nice holidays. Things were amazing. They had the perfect life. Nothing was wrong.

'Faye Killingbeck died yesterday,' his mum said salaciously. 'The drink finally caught up with her, I think. I knew she'd been ill, poor Steve was always so good with her, wasn't he, he'll be devastated.'

'Have you seen him?' Gavin said, still holding his reflection in the mirror, watching the colour drain from his face as his heart stopped pumping blood.

'Steve? No, but I saw Mariella at the supermarket, you remember Mariella, the one with the black gums and stained yellow teeth? Anyway, she said he was with her at the end. He was always such a good boy. I never understood what went on with you two, you used to be such good friends.'

'We just drifted apart, Mum, that's all. It happens.'

'You shouldn't drift from people, Gavin, not the important ones, anyway.'

'I've got to go, Mum,' Gavin said, clenching his jaw tightly and squeezing his eyes shut.

'The funeral is next week. I can't go, I didn't know her, not really. But you two were always such good friends. It would be nice if you went, don't you think? And you knew her, back in the day, didn't you? Wouldn't you like to pay your respects?'

'I can't go, Mum,' Gavin said, swallowing hard.

'I'll Facebook you the details, okay? In case you change your mind?'

Gavin hung up, wiping tears from his eyes with the back of his jumper. He wasn't crying for Steve's mum, he'd barely known her and what he had known, he hadn't liked. He was crying for Steve. She'd been his world, he'd given up so much to care for her and now she was gone. He'd be bereft, cut loose to float through the world with nothing to ground him.

'You okay?' Imogen said, walking into the hall from the kitchen.

'Yeah, fine,' Gavin said hastily, wiping his face and pushing himself back to his feet.

'You're not, you've been crying. What's happened?'

Imogen moved towards him, putting her arms around him and holding him for a moment. He wanted to push her off him and run away. Instead, he stood limply, not returning her embrace until she finally let him go.

'What happened?' she asked again. 'It's not your dad, is it?'

'No, no, nothing like that,' Gavin said, mind racing. 'An old family friend died, that's all. Mum wants me to go to the funeral next week.'

'An old family friend?'

'Yeah, silly really, don't know why I'm so upset. Haven't seen her for years and it's not like she was family or anything. I just... I don't know. It's always sad when someone dies, isn't it?'

'Who was she, one of your mum's friends?'

'One of the mums from school, that's all.'

'You okay?' she said, rubbing his arm lightly and staring at him compassionately.

'Yeah, I'm fine. Like I said, silly. I think I'll go to the funeral, though. If that's alright with you?'

'Will they give you time off work?'

'I'm sure they will.'

'We can all come,' Imogen started.

'No, no... Tim will have school. Besides, you didn't know her. I'll go up for the night, that's all. Just to pay my respects.'

'You sure?' she said, eyeing him warily.

'Of course,' he replied, shaking his shoulders out and managing a smile. 'Right, think I'll go for a run, blow some cobwebs away.'

'Okay, babe,' Imogen said. 'You sure you're okay?'

He leaned in to kiss her on the lips.

'I'm fine,' he said firmly. 'You don't need to worry. Everything's going to be okay.'

~ Chapter 9 ~

Jackie's knees are pushed up to her chest and she's leaning forward on the bench towards Gavin, completely enraptured.

'Did you go?'

'To the funeral? Yeah.'

'And you met Steve again?'

'Well, yeah… it was his mum's funeral.'

'And did you? You know?' Jackie says, nodding her head sideways, unsure how to phrase her question.

'Shag?' Gavin laughs. 'What, on his mother's grave?'

'No,' Jackie replies, instantly embarrassed. 'I didn't mean… well, I… anyway. You saw him?'

'Of course I saw him.' Gavin smiled, running a hand lightly through his hair. 'What bit of *it was his mum's funeral* are you finding challenging?'

'All right, smart arse… excuse me for being interested.'

'Do you want to hear this or not?'

'Yes, carry on.'

'Right, where was I?'

'You'd just lied to Imogen so you could go to the funeral.'

'Do you have to put it like that?'

'How else would you like me to put it?'

* * *

Gavin remembered the churchyard well. As a teenager, he'd used it as a cut-through from the main high street to the market area of town. Legend had it that Gwen Chamberlain and Thomas Duncan shagged on one of the gravestones on his sixteenth birthday, something she was vilified for while he got unlimited kudos.

Gavin shifted uncomfortably in his suit, loosening his tie slightly. He wasn't sure of the protocol for funerals. Was he was supposed to wear a suit or would an all-black outfit suffice? He'd opted for the suit, to be safe. Once he arrived, he was pleased he had, it seemed appropriate and others were doing the same. Besides—

There he was.

Standing outside the large church doors, shaking hands with some elderly relative or other, smiling through the grief and anxiety made obvious to Gavin through the tension in Steve's shoulders and forehead, his clenched jaw.

Gavin stopped dead on the path, throat dry as Steve turned and looked towards him.

'Steve,' Gavin said, feet moving of their own volition, breaking into a run as if independent of his conscious mind, doing whatever they could to get close to Steve. He grabbed him in a tight embrace and held him, feeling Steve return the embrace feverishly. They stood holding each other, more tightly than any embrace Gavin could remember before.

'I'm so sorry,' Gavin whispered in Steve's ear. 'I'm sorry I wasn't here.'

'You're here now,' Steve whispered back, finally loosening his arms and leaning back, placing his own forehead on Gavin's, his nose lightly touching Gavin's own. 'You're here now,' he repeated.

For a moment they stood still, the rest of the funeral-goers and churchyard dissolving around them, pixelated, unreal. Then a voice interrupted, breaking the spell.

'She'll be missed,' a man's voice said. 'She was the life and soul down at the Rose and Crown.'

Gavin stood back and Steve straightened his jacket, holding his hand out to shake the man's hand.

'Yeah, life and soul,' Steve said quietly as the man walked past him into the church. Gavin pursed his lips and touched Steve gently on the arm as he walked into the coolness of the church.

After the service, mourners littered the graveyard again and their chatter turned to the wake at the Rose and Crown. Gavin stood alone, shoulders hunched, wondering whether to leave or go along to the pub. Should he give Steve some distance? It had been more than a decade since they'd seen each other and it wasn't like things had ended well so there was no reason to think he'd want or need Gavin around.

'Fancy a smoke?' Steve said, coming up behind Gavin and putting his hand on Gavin's waist, whispering into his ear conspiratorially, close enough that he could feel the moistness of his breath.

'A smoke?' Gavin replied, not moving. Steve let go of his hip and walked around to face Gavin, holding up a rolled joint in his hand and smiling before walking away from the funeral-goers towards the other side of the church.

'Don't you have to go to the wake?' Gavin said, shuffling after him. 'People will expect you there.'

'I'll go in a bit. Most of my family hadn't seen her in years, they'd all washed their hands of her. Fucking hypocrites. The only other ones here are her mates from the pub. They won't care if I'm there or not as long as the beer's flowing.'

At the back of the churchyard there was a large, above ground, stone tomb – probably the same one Gwen and Thomas had sex on. Steve slunk behind it and sat down out of view of the church. Gavin followed, sitting down next to him and resting his back against the cold stone.

'Your eulogy was beautiful,' Gavin said, glancing sideways at Steve. He hadn't changed, not really. His widow's peaks were a little more pronounced, perhaps, but he still looked youthful. Still handsome. His eyes were puffy from tears and his skin was blotchy where he'd been rubbing his eyes but he had the same openness about him he'd always had.

'Thanks.' Steve fished a lighter out of his pocket and bit the end of his joint off. 'I didn't mean a word of it.'

'What?'

Steve lit the joint and inhaled.

'I loved her, don't get me wrong, you know I did.' Steve looked awkward, guilty, even. 'But she wasn't mum of the year. Let's face it, she wasn't mum of the decade. But you can't be honest in a eulogy, can you? You can't stand up there and say she was an alcoholic, borderline abusive. You can't stand up there and say she neglected me.'

'Oh Steve,' Gavin started.

'No,' Steve said, shaking his head. 'Don't do that.'

Gavin nodded, wanting to reach out and touch Steve's leg but not feeling confident enough to do so. Those days were past, that intimacy was from another life, another history.

'Okay,' he said instead. 'But whatever her faults, she was still your mum.'

'I know,' Steve said sadly. 'But do you want the honest truth? I don't miss her. Does that make me an arsehole?'

'No,' Gavin whispered softly. 'You've never been an arsehole. I don't think you ever will be.'

They fell into silence for a while and Steve handed Gavin the joint.

'It was complicated,' Gavin continued. 'You and your mum. I mean, it *was* abusive. She took your childhood, so how you're feeling makes sense.'

'She didn't mean to.'

'People hurt you without meaning to. They do it all the time.'

Gavin handed the joint back to Steve, holding the smoke in his lungs as he did so.

'I did love her,' Steve repeated. 'But I can't help feeling that her dying has given me... I don't know. Freedom, I suppose.'

'Don't beat yourself up,' Gavin leaned over and touched Steve's leg, the weed giving him confidence he lacked moments ago. 'Grief isn't one-size-fits-all.'

Steve looked at Gavin's hand on his thigh but didn't move

his leg away, didn't take Gavin's hand off.

'Thanks for coming, Gav. I didn't know how much I needed to see you until I saw you standing there.'

Gavin didn't reply, he didn't need to. He leaned his shoulder into Steve's a little, pressing against him lightly.

'You should be all kinds of fucked up, given your childhood,' Gavin said quietly. 'But you're not. How's that?'

'I had you,' Steve said eventually. 'For a while, at least. Besides, you haven't seen me for years, you've no idea how fucked up I am.'

'Doesn't matter how many years it's been, though, does it? Things are still the same between us.'

'I don't know, are they?'

'As soon as I saw you, I felt like I always did, like I'd never stopped feeling it, you know?'

'And how does that feel?' Steve said, steel in his voice.

'What's up?' Gavin said, frowning. 'I just meant... it's good to see you, that's all. I didn't mean anything by it.'

'You never mean anything by it, Gavin, that's the problem.'

'I don't know what you mean.'

'You left me, Gavin. Cut me out of your life.'

'I know,' Gavin replied, shame colouring his cheeks. Nothing he said would be enough, Gavin knew, there was no way of explaining himself because his betrayal snaked back into their past, venomous and hissing, connecting them to this moment, irreparably, irrevocably.

'Imogen made me promise I'd never see you again,' he said eventually. 'That's not a good enough excuse, I know that. I just... I thought it was for the best.'

'No, you didn't,' Steve said, taking another drag on the joint. 'You thought it was easiest, that's not the same thing at all. Did you ever learn that lesson, Gavin? That the easiest route doesn't necessarily end up being easier? You hurt me.'

'Things were different back then and...'

'And what?'

'I was scared.'

'Scared of what?'

'How I felt about you.'

'Were you? Or were you just scared people might find out?'

'That too, but I couldn't...' Gavin reached out and took the end of the joint back from Steve, inhaling deeply before flicking it away, holding his breath against the words he wanted to say. 'I couldn't admit it, how I felt, who I was.'

'And now?' Steve said, his voice softer again, tinged with the smallest amount of hope.

'Doesn't it scare you?' Gavin said, smoke signals escaping his mouth as the words poured out. 'Us, I mean. It scared me then and it scares me now. We can't get away from it, can we? No matter how long we stay apart.'

'It never scared me,' Steve said calmly, reaching over and taking Gavin's hand in his, squeezing it lightly. 'I think it's beautiful. Most people would kill to feel like we do.'

'It fucking terrifies me.'

'You were always scared of your own emotions.' Steve flicked him a playful glance. 'You're a bigger pansy than me.'

'Shut it,' Gavin smiled, letting go of Steve's hand and leaning his head over onto Steve's shoulder.

Time passed and at some point, Steve lay back on the grass, staring up at the sky.

'Your mum told my mum when you got married. She was so proud.'

'Yeah, Mum likes Imogen.'

'And you? Do you like her?'

'She's my wife.'

'That's not what I asked.'

'It's a life,' Gavin said. 'It's a family. We used to love each other, I think, it wasn't a lie. Nowadays we chip away at each other, destroying the things we might have once liked, you know what I mean? Do all relationships go like that?'

'No idea,' Steve said simply. 'I've never had a relationship that lasted, not really. I only ever fall for straight men.'

'A psychologist would have a field day with you,' Gavin said, lying down perpendicular to Steve so his head rested on his lap. 'Only falling in love with unavailable men.'

'Man. I've only ever fallen in love once.'

'You said men,' Gavin persevered. 'There must be someone else, it can't only be me.'

'I didn't say I was in love with you, did I?' Steve said, hand gently stroking Gavin's hair as he spoke.

'Fuck off,' Gavin said, smiling. He hadn't felt this relaxed for years. He could blame the weed but he knew that had nothing to do with it. It was Steve. Just being near him had a calming effect, made him feel things would be all right. Could be all right.

'I had a thing with Jamie,' Steve continued. 'He was just like you, though. Everything had to be behind closed doors. I thought for a while he might make the leap from just sex and have an actual relationship with me. I never learn though, do I? He's got a girlfriend and three-year-old twins now.'

'Jamie? I knew you were trying to shag him that night in the pub! I didn't think he was gay, though.'

'Oh, come on, don't you remember the way he used to look at you in the changing rooms at school? He was always finding ways to rib you, to take the piss. He always had a thing for you.'

'No, he didn't, don't talk rubbish.'

'There was a lot you didn't see, Gav. Still is.'

They drifted into silence again, staring up at the clouds and blue-grey sky.

'I mean it. I've never loved anyone else,' Steve repeated.

Calm cradled Gavin as he lay with his head on Steve's lap.

He existed only in the moment, he had no past, no future. There was only now, together.

Eventually:

'Did you ever tell your mum you were gay?'

'Yeah. She didn't care.'

'Didn't care or *didn't care*?'

'Bit of both. It was always a bit of both with her, wasn't it?'

'Yeah.'

The wind rustled, the birds sang, the sounds of other people's lives carried on in the distance, opaque and unreal.

'When did you know?' Gavin asked. 'That you were gay, I mean.'

'I don't know. Young. I don't really remember a moment of realisation, it was just who I was,' Steve replied thoughtfully. 'I remember starting secondary school and there was this graffiti in the toilets... Got Aids Yet. And I knew... I knew the kind of sex I wanted could kill me. Fucking terrifying. Do you remember how scary it was to realise you were gay in the middle of that plague?'

'It was different for me,' Gavin said quietly. 'I wasn't gay, it wasn't something I thought about.'

'When did you know, then?'

'Know what?'

'That you liked guys as well.'

'When I met you, I suppose. I'd never thought about it before.'

'You saying I made you bi?' Steve said, laughing lightly.

'Yeah, if I'd never met you, I'd be straight as a die,' Gavin chuckled.

'I mean, I can understand it, I *am* fit,' Steve said, a broad grin on his face.

'Seriously though, you were the first guy I fantasised about... you weren't the last, obviously.'

'There's me thinking I was special.'

'You were special. You know that.'

'Don't,' Steve said, his smile disappearing.

'I'm sorry, I didn't...'

'It took me a long time to get over you,' Steve said.

'I know,' Gavin said, the past and possible future flooding back in, drowning him, making it difficult to breathe. He sat up, tucking his knees to his chest and resting his chin on them, staring down at Steve's face intently. 'I'm so sorry.'

'I thought I had you out of my system,' Steve said. 'I've made a life without you.'

'I shouldn't have come,' Gavin said, heart beating hard in his chest. 'I didn't mean to make things worse for you.'

'You've got a wife,' Steve said. 'A son.'

'I wanted to be here for you, that's all. I didn't come to reopen old wounds.'

'Tell me about him,' Steve said.

'Who?'

'Your son.'

'Tim? He's 8 already, I can't believe it. He's a great kid, so kind and funny.'

'I bet you make a great dad.'

'I don't think Imogen would agree with you.'

'Then she doesn't know you,' Steve said. 'I mean, you lie all the fucking time, to yourself mostly. But you're a good man.'

'I'm not sure I am. No matter what I do, I end up hurting people.'

'You hurt yourself most of all. The rest of us are just collateral damage.'

'What's done is done, isn't it? I can't change anything.'

'But the future's still ahead of you, Gav. Don't keep making the same mistakes.'

'It's not that easy, Steve.'

'It never is with you.'

'That's not fair.'

Steve smiled at him, only a hint of sadness behind his eyes.

'If we were teenagers nowadays,' Steve said. 'You'd be called pansexual. Or would you be bisexual, still? I don't know, there's a lot of labels, nowadays.'

'I don't know why we have to have labels at all,' Gavin sighed.

'Says the man who's been living as a straight man his entire life. You're happy enough with that label.'

'What am I supposed to do? I'm married with a kid, Steve. You're a gay man, you live as a gay man. At least your box fits. What box do I fit in?'

'Well, you're not straight, Gavin.'

'I'm not gay either. I live as a straight man because I'm married and I have a son. The only person I sleep with is a woman, so straight is as good a label as any.'

'Sexuality is about more than who you sleep with, Gavin, don't you get that? I worry you've... I don't know. Buried yourself.'

'I haven't buried anyone, Steve. You know how I feel about you but there's nothing to be done with that. I'm married and despite our problems, I do love Imogen. I'm not living a lie.'

'You're not living a truth, either.'

'Jesus, Steve! Things aren't simple for me, why can't you understand that?'

'You think things are simple for me? You think when you're gay you only come out once? Every new person I meet, every new situation, I have to come out. It's constant. But what's the alternative? Live a lie? Let people treat me like I'm straight when I'm not? I choose not to pass. You choose the opposite.'

'For fuck's sake, who I am isn't political. It isn't a statement. I've got a wife, Steve. What do you think I should do? Tell everyone I'm still in love with my teenage boyfriend?'

'Why not? It's the truth!'

Silence. The word love lingering in the air around them.

Weighty, not featherlike, not delicately brushing their skin.

'You're still in love with me,' Steve said quietly.

'I've always loved you, you know that.'

'You've never said it before.'

'I've never said a lot of things.'

'But you love Imogen, too?'

'Yes, she drives me mad and it's tough bringing up a kid, but I still love her. Underneath it all she's still the woman I met.'

'I'm glad,' Steve said. 'I'm glad it's real.'

Gavin nodded, swallowing and taking a deep breath.

'It's different to you and me but...' he trailed off for a moment. 'What even is it? You and me? We're like this fucking itch we can't scratch.'

'Do you want to scratch it?'

'I'd never be unfaithful to Imogen,' Gavin said. 'I'm not that guy.'

'That wasn't what I asked,' Steve said. 'I asked if you wanted to.'

Gavin shrugged his shoulders.

'Does it matter?'

'I think so,' Steve said quietly. 'I think it matters very much.'

They both lay back on the grass, this time side by side, fingers lightly brushing against each other as they stared at the sky.

'I'm glad you came today, Gavin,' Steve repeated at some point.

'Me too,' Gavin said, squeezing Steve's hand for a second before letting it go.

'You still live in Brighton?' Steve asked.

'Yeah.'

The sky was clear now, cloudless.

'The gay capital of England,' Steve finished. 'Funny that you ended up there.'

'Oh stop, will you!' Gavin laughed, shoving Steve playfully.

'I'm not pansexual. I don't think I'm even bisexual. Besides, Manchester is the gay capital, isn't it? Or is it London?'

'Brighton's pretty gay, though, right?' Steve ribbed.

'It's creative. Arty. And white. Brighton is so fucking white you wouldn't believe, it's the only thing I don't like about it. I work in London and it's normal there, you know? You see every colour under the sun, then you get the train back to Brighton and it's just... white.'

'I thought Brighton was diverse?'

'In loads of ways but not when it comes to race for some reason.'

'Are you happy there?'

'Yeah, can't imagine living anywhere else. After Uni, we stayed for the lifestyle. The clubs, the sea, the bars, the downs... that was all fine for a while but now I don't get to see any of it. I spend five days a week commuting, locked inside a crowded train, sweating my arse off and pretending I use the time to read. By the time the weekend comes around, I'm so tired, all I want to do is sleep, except I haven't seen Tim all week, so I have to try and make up for lost time with him.'

Gavin closed his eyes, visions of his real-life filtering in, remembering an argument he and Imogen had a few days before:

'Right,' he'd said, plonking a massive box of Lego down on the living room floor and grinning at Tim. 'What are we going to build? Space station? Fire station? You tell me, we've got the bits from a million different sets.'

Tim had been glued to *Teen Titans Go!* on Netflix so had barely even acknowledged him.

'Come on, mate? Turn the TV off and build something with me,' Gavin had pleaded as Imogen stood in the living room doorway, not trying to disguise her disdain for his efforts.

'He hates Lego, Gavin,' she'd said snippily. 'You'd know that if you were here more.'

Gavin had taken a deep breath, deliberately ignoring her and speaking directly to Tim.

'Come on, Tim,' he'd said more firmly. 'TV off. I've got all the instruction leaflets here – help me out?'

Tim had glanced at him sideways for a second.

'Let me watch the end of this.'

'Okay.' Gavin had smiled, grabbing his son for a cuddle. Tim had struggled to get out of the embrace, shouting 'get off me' but smiling at the same time, clearly enjoying the attention, the physical contact.

'Oh, for god's sake, Gavin,' Imogen had snapped. 'Just let him watch the television. He needs his down time too, you know.'

'You're having quite the pity party, aren't you?' Steve said.

Gavin opened his eyes to find Steve leaning up on one elbow staring down at him, face close to his.

'I'm serious,' Gavin said. 'Imogen controls everything to do with Tim, I don't get a bloody look in. On his last birthday party, I insisted she let me help with the party games... she always tries to do everything, you know, never lets me in. Anyway, she let me create a 'pass the parcel' in the end, said it was the only thing I wouldn't mess up. I didn't give much thought to the magazines and papers I used until Tim's friend Matthew ripped off a layer of newspaper to reveal Closer magazine's *My Sex Doll Hell* underneath. It was a disaster.'

'You didn't,' Steve burst out laughing, covering his eyes up in mock horror.

'I did... Imogen was mortified, of course, but I think underneath it all she liked it, you know? It gave her the high ground and confirmed my place as a useless father.'

'I'm sure you're not useless.'

'Feels that way. I never see him, I'm always at work.'

'Can't you change jobs?'

'I never wanted the job in the first place,' Gavin started, his eyes lighting up with another memory. 'I had a photography studio for a while.'

'Are you serious?' Steve's eyes lit up in return, mirroring Gavin's own enthusiasm. 'You did it? You actually did it?'

'Yeah, I mean, just family headshots, weddings and stuff to start with, to make ends meet, you know. But I loved it.'

'I'm so proud of you!'

'Don't be, I got rid of it. Didn't earn enough money with a kid on the way.'

'I'm sorry,' Steve said. 'I really am.' He paused, clearly mulling something over. 'You have choices, Gavin. You don't have to do what you think other people expect of you all the time.'

'I've got a son. Besides, Imogen can be very persuasive.'

'You could leave your job if you wanted to. Give the photography another go?'

'I've got bills to pay. A son in private school. It's not an option for me, my life's complicated.'

'You use that word all the time as if it makes you special. Everyone's life's complicated, Gav, doesn't mean you shouldn't find a way to *do* something about it.'

Time passed. Clouds rolled by in the sky.

'I didn't mean to go on about myself,' Gavin said. 'Today of all days.'

'It's okay,' Steve replied quietly. 'Life's hard for all of us, isn't it? I mean, I knew that as a kid but I thought it would get easier when I grew up. Nobody tells you that it doesn't. It's just becomes a different kind of difficult.'

'Life shouldn't be hard for kids, though, should it. Your life shouldn't have been so hard.'

'It was okay. I found you, didn't I? Could have been worse.'

'And we've found each other again.'

'Have we, though?' Steve said, sitting up and brushing the grass from the back of his arms. 'Because where does this go, Gav?'

'We can be friends, can't we?'

'You're married with a son.' Steve said, a distance appearing, as if the graveyard was warping and stretching out between them, pushing them further and further away from each other.

'And Imogen? Would you tell her we were friends again?'

'Steve,' Gavin said desperately.

'Would you?'

Gavin's shamed silence answered for him.

'I can't be that guy,' Steve said softly. 'I won't be your secret.'

'We're allowed to be friends, I'm sure she'd...'

'Just because we aren't fucking doesn't mean we're platonic. You know that. I know that. Imogen definitely knows that. Stop lying to yourself, Gavin.'

Gavin clenched his teeth shut, overwhelmed with a surge of anger he didn't want to let out.

Everyone lies, he wanted to shout. *We aren't doing anything wrong.*

Instead, he said quietly: 'Lies can be a good thing. They can protect people.'

'Not all lies, Gavin,' Steve said, leaning over and kissing him lightly on the lips. Not a sexual kiss but a goodbye kiss filled with years of sadness.

'Steve,' Gavin started.

'I should get to the wake,' Steve said, standing up and smoothing down his suit.

'Don't go,' Gavin pleaded. 'Not yet.'

'You deserve more than you allow yourself, Gavin. I wish you'd see that.'

Gavin couldn't breathe, his body rigid with... what? Fear? No, not fear, something else, something deeper, even more primal.

'Thanks for coming,' Steve said again. 'It mattered, it really did.'

'This can't be it?' Gavin said desperately, pushing himself to his feet so that he stood toe to toe with Steve. 'You can't just leave me?'

'Yes, Gavin, I can.' Steve replied, walking away, leaving Gavin shivering and alone in the graveyard.

~ Chapter 10 ~

When Gavin got home the next day, life continued as normal. Imogen asked how the funeral had been without really listening to Gavin's answers, which was handy because everything he told her was a lie anyway. Life was the same, yet nothing felt the same. Gavin had opened the lid to one of his internal boxes, where he kept the things that were too painful to look at or contemplate anymore. Try as he might, he couldn't fit the lid back on, its contents kept spilling out over every edge, running into the darkness, seeping into his system, infecting everything. Gavin had worried that seeing Steve again would open old wounds for Steve but it hadn't occurred to him they'd reopen his own wounds. He hadn't even realised he had any.

Steve had acted like he didn't want any contact with him but Gavin knew that wasn't true. They were connected, he felt that more keenly now than ever. One day, he waited for Imogen to take Tim out and flung himself on the sofa, grabbing his phone and opening his Facebook app.

Steven Killingbeck, he typed, pausing and adding in the word *Yorkshire* before hitting enter to search, jiggling his leg up and down nervously as he did so.

There he was. First search result.

Don't, he thought to himself. *Just have a shower and get ready. Steve clearly doesn't want you to contact him, you need to respect that, you need—*

Send friend request.

Shit.

No going back.

Ping.

Hi, Steve typed into messenger. *Ping me your number so we can move over to WhatsApp – I hate Facebook.*

Gavin's heart nearly exploded in his chest. No arguments, no recriminations, just friendship. That's all this was. Friendship.

Facebook owns WhatsApp, you know that, right? Gavin typed, adding a smiley face emoji for good measure.

At least they pretend WhatsApp is encrypted, though, Steve replied. *If I mention sweetcorn on here, I'll see ads for sweetcorn within five minutes.*

Are you likely to mention sweetcorn?

I just did.

Gavin sat up on the sofa, holding the phone tightly in his hands as he hunched over it, heart racing. Another mistake, he was making a mistake. What was wrong with him? They weren't just friends, they'd never be just friends.

Look, I've got to go, he typed. *We're going to a friend's for dinner.*

Okay, Steve replied. *I'll send you my number for WhatsApp. Speak later?*

Gavin threw the phone onto the sofa next to him, chest pumping, feeling jittery and disconnected.

Ping.

Was that him sending his number through already? Why did Gavin already feel like he was cheating on Imogen? He hadn't done anything. He grabbed his phone, only to see a WhatsApp message from Imogen, not Steve.

Back in five minutes, it said. *I've dropped Tim at Matthew's; we have to go shopping before we go to Louise's tonight.*

Okay, he typed. Then, in a panicked display of affection, he typed: *Love you x.*

You too, Imogen replied. *Grab the shopping bags from under the stairs.*

Half an hour later they pulled up in the supermarket car park together.

'You friended Steve on Facebook,' Imogen said as she shut the car door behind her, pressing the button on the key fob to lock it.

'I haven't got the shopping bags out of the boot yet,' Gavin replied, deliberately ignoring her, concrete slowly pumping through his veins, immobilising him. Silently, Imogen pressed the button to release the boot and Gavin got the bags out.

'You Facebook stalking me?' Gavin said eventually as they began walking towards the supermarket.

'You promised me,' Imogen replied stonily.

'Jesus, I'm allowed friends!' Gavin snapped, heart thumping. Imogen grabbed a trolley from the trolley park outside the shop and they walked in together in silence.

'He wasn't a friend, Gavin,' she said quietly, picking an apple up and cupping it in her hand, studying it as if it was of interest to her, as if she was inspecting it for bruises.

'Yes, he was,' Gavin started.

'No!' Imogen spat, cutting him off. 'I won't feel like the bad guy here. You promised.'

'When we were teenagers!' Gavin said, raising his voice slightly, enough that a young couple glanced over at them curiously. 'People change, they move on.'

'Or not,' Imogen said dryly, dropping the apple back into its crate. 'It doesn't seem like you've moved on at all.'

'Do we have to do this here?' Gavin said, glancing nervously around the Supermarket.

'Why not? Tim's at Matthew's, we rarely get any time alone together.'

'We're hardly alone... we're in public, do we have to argue?'

'I don't know, do we?'

Gavin shivered, the cool of the sandwich and snack fridge behind him creeping under his skin, penetrating his flesh and making its way through to his bones.

'It's nothing, all right? I just... when I was at the funeral, we bumped into each other, that's all. It was nice to see him.'

'You *saw* him? Oh, this gets better,' Imogen said sardonically, grabbing their empty trolley and pushing it down the aisle with purpose.

'I bumped into him, that's all. It's a small place. His mum's dead.'

Gavin wished he hadn't lied in the first place, wished he'd simply told her he was going to Steve's mum's funeral. He'd already dug a hole for himself, made it seem like he was doing something wrong which of course he wasn't.

'I'm allowed friends, Imogen. In case you hadn't noticed, I don't have any.'

'Absolute rubbish,' Imogen stopped dead, slamming the trolley into the side and spinning around on Gavin. 'You have your work friends, you go for drinks with them every week while I sit at home with Tim!'

'I fucking hate them,' Gavin shouted. 'I hate the job – the job you *made* me take – and I hate all the wankers who work there, including your uncle.'

'I didn't make you take the job, Gavin,' Imogen shouted in return. 'You had to grow up, we had a son on the way. I know men don't like to grow up, you all expect you can stay a child forever, doing exactly what you like, but life isn't like that. Not for the rest of us, at least.'

'Oh fuck off, Imogen. I worked, I made money, so did you! We didn't have to make the choices we did, we didn't have to be so bloody unhappy.'

There. He'd said it, the thing they never acknowledged, the thing they never admitted to one another despite the fact it was so obvious.

'Yet here we are,' she said quietly, turning back to the trolley and holding it, head bowed, not moving. 'Really bloody unhappy.'

'It doesn't mean anything,' Gavin said more softly, approaching Imogen from behind and touching her shoulder gently. 'Steve, I mean.'

'It means everything,' Imogen replied, glancing back over

her shoulder at him. 'I don't understand how you can't see that.'

'I'm lonely, Imogen. You have Louise, Alice, the mums from school. You have friends, connections. I don't know how it happened but I have nobody.'

'You have me?' she said, more a question than a statement.

It's not enough, he thought. *It hasn't been enough for such a long time.*

'I know I do,' he lied instead.

'Besides,' Imogen said, straightening herself up and standing more upright. 'You have other friends, what about Adam?'

'Adam?' Gavin frowned. 'He's a nice guy, but he's your friend's husband. That's not the same as being my friend.'

'He could become your friend. You have to make an effort to make friends, Gavin, it doesn't just happen. What do you think other people do? Must I do everything for you?'

'What do you mean?'

'I'll talk to Louise,' Imogen said decisively, picking up a packet of four free-range chicken breasts from the fridge next to them and putting them in the trolley. 'See if we can arrange something for you and Adam.'

'There you go again,' Gavin said, arms flapping angrily down against his thighs. 'Controlling everything.'

'I'm not controlling things, Gavin, I'm sorting them. Someone has to.'

'I didn't ask you to.'

'You never do,' Imogen snapped. 'Doesn't mean they don't need doing.'

'Fuck's sake,' Gavin whispered under his breath as she continued down the supermarket aisle.

'And Gavin,' she called back firmly. 'You need to unfriend Steve.'

They did the rest of the shop in silence, barely speaking as they picked Tim up from his playdate. As Imogen began getting ready to go out, Gavin took a shower.

'Come on, Gavin?' Imogen said. 'I've arranged a babysitter. Alice is coming tonight with her new boyfriend. Louise said he's a nightmare. Besides, I'm running out of excuses for you not coming now.'

Louise and Alice were friends from Imogen's ante-natal class. They all met at one of their houses for a dinner party once a month, alternating whose home their went to. Gavin often missed them, not because he didn't like Louise and her husband, Adam, but because it gave him a night to himself, some space without Imogen.

'I don't want to go,' Gavin said firmly.

'For God's sake, stop sulking.'

'I don't fancy it,' he replied to Imogen.

'You're always cancelling, they'll start to think you don't like them.'

'Heaven forbid,' he said absently.

Five hours later, Imogen staggered through the front door, slamming it behind her.

'I wish you'd come,' she called, slurring slightly, clearly drunk.

'Quiet, Tim's asleep.' Gavin walked out of the living room with a bottle of beer in his hand, pausing the film he was watching on the TV and throwing the controller onto the sofa as he did so.

'I've had an awful night, Gavin. Just awful,' Imogen said, eyes black from crying. She stood unsteadily in the hallway, every ounce of her begging to be comforted or cuddled.

'What happened?' Gavin asked wearily, not moving towards her, not wanting the drama.

'I just...' she started, before descending into tears again.

'What happened?' He asked again, glancing over his shoulder into the living room, realising the TV hadn't paused.

He scrabbled on the sofa for the remote and pressed pause again, before walking back into the hall.

'Sorry,' he said. 'What happened?'

'Louise invited that new friend to the party, you know, the guy who owns the garage opposite her café?' Imogen stood up straighter, wiping her eyes, standing awkwardly in the hallway.

'That guy I've seen Adam running with?'

'I think so,' Imogen replied, wiping her eyes.

Gavin had seen Adam and his new friend running on the downs. He'd been having a coffee at the top of Devil's Dyke and they'd run past, chatting and laughing, not even noticing he was there. There was nothing explicit, nothing said or done that Gavin could have pointed a finger at, but they'd seemed happy. Relaxed in each other's company in a way Adam never seemed to be when he was with Louise. At the time, seeing them had reminded Gavin of Steve, of their friendship, of how he never felt as relaxed in Imogen's company as he did with Steve. Stupid comparison, obviously. Adam and this guy were just running buddies, not—

'He's not the point,' Imogen continued dramatically. 'Alice was there with her new boyfriend, John.'

She paused, as if somehow Gavin was supposed to understand the importance of John's presence. Gavin didn't answer, didn't move. Imogen stared, wide eyed, waiting for some kind of reaction.

'So? I don't see...'

'I wish you'd have come,' she said plaintively. 'I need support sometimes, too. You never come and...'

'Oh, Imogen, for fuck's sake what happened?' Gavin snapped, exasperated.

'Be nice to me,' Imogen slurred.

'Come on, love,' Gavin said, trying to manufacture a softness in his voice that he didn't feel. 'You've had too much to drink.'

'No, it's not me, it was him,' she said, bending down and pulling her high heels off. 'Alice's new boyfriend. He called me a cunt. Right there at the dinner table, in front of everyone.'

She trailed off, sitting down on the stairs and putting her head into her hands.

'Christ,' Gavin replied, leaning against the doorframe of the living room door, mind racing.

'And nobody supported me, not Adam, not Louise,' she took a deep breath, staring at Gavin, clearly shaken up by it. 'But it's not okay, Gavin. To speak to me like that.' She shook her head. 'It's not okay.'

'What did you do?' Gavin asked, taking a swig of beer.

'What did *I* do?' Imogen stared at him in shock, betrayal eating its way through the flesh under her eyes. 'You're saying it's *my* fault?'

'I didn't say that. I just... you know what you're like sometimes.'

She stood up, wounded and alone and Gavin immediately realised he'd gone too far. He wanted to reach out and hug her but the moment had passed. Perhaps it had passed years ago.

'Doesn't matter,' she said quietly, turning to walk up the stairs.

'Imogen,' he called after her. 'Come on, I didn't mean it. Come down and talk to me.'

Days or weeks or months drifted by. For a while after the dinner party things were frosty between Imogen and Louise but at some point they'd clearly made up because one day, Imogen said:

'Louise has asked if you'll play squash with Adam.'

'Why?' Gavin replied absently, reading the paper on his phone and sipping coffee.

'You said you had no friends, remember?'

'For fuck's sake, Imogen, I'm not a child.'

'Then don't act like one.'

'I don't even play squash!'

'Then organise your own friends.'

'Nobody asked you to organise anything!'

'It's not just you. Louise is worried about Adam, says she thinks he needs to get out and make more friends.'

'Great, so we're both being bullied into it,' he said, dropping his phone down onto the kitchen table. 'I don't even play squash.'

'Exactly,' she said. 'I told Louise you could do with the exercise.'

A week later, he and Adam played squash. Unsurprisingly, Adam thrashed him, although he was a patient teacher.

'I used to play with Tom all the time,' Adam said, a far-away look in his eyes.

'Your brother?' Gavin asked as they walked into the changing rooms.

'Yeah, Tom.' Adam replied.

'Do you miss him?' Gavin asked stupidly, pulling his T-shirt off over his head. They'd been twins, of course Adam missed him. 'Sorry, I mean, of course you do, stupid thing to say.'

'It's okay,' Adam said, staring directly at him. 'You learn to live with it.'

'Do you?' Gavin replied before he could stop himself.

'Not really,' Adam replied eventually, pulling his shorts and underwear off and grabbing a towel before turning his back on Gavin and walking to the showers.

After they'd showered and changed, they went for a pint. Adam was pensive, distracted.

'We fell for each other *before* Tom died, did you know that?' Adam was clearly lost in his memories, pausing only to sip his lager as he spoke. 'Forbidden love, it's always the sweetest, right? My own twin brother's girlfriend. I mean, I used to fantasize about her all the time, but that's not unusual, right?' He flicked Gavin a glance, clearly checking to see if he still had his audience. 'Anyway, point is, it was just a private fantasy, nothing serious, I didn't think anything would come of it, didn't want it to, she was my brother's girlfriend. But Tom threw this Halloween party and I was standing there in the corner of the room...' His voice had dropped down to a whisper and Gavin had to lean in to hear him properly. 'I could feel these eyes on me, you know? When I glanced up, there she was, just staring at me. She didn't flinch, didn't avert her eyes, she just carried on looking and I knew she felt the same.'

'Christ.' Gavin exhaled, sipping his own beer and nodding his head for Adam to continue. 'So did you... you know, start an affair?'

'No, God no, I'd never have done that to Tom, never. But it was awkward, we both felt it after that, both knew what was coming. So I did the only thing I could, I ran away from Brighton and moved back to my parents' house in London. Anything to be as far away from her as possible.'

Adam downed the last of his pint and indicated Gavin's glass.

'Another?'

'No, I'm driving, aren't I, but you have one.'

Adam got himself a new pint and sat back down opposite Gavin.

'So you and Louise got together after Tom died?' Gavin asked gently.

'Tom wanted us to, how fucked up is that?' Adam traced curves on his glass with his index finger. 'He wrote both of us messages before he died, to be delivered after his funeral, telling us he wanted us to be together.'

'Fuck,' Gavin said, unsure how else he was supposed to respond.

'Yeah, fuck,' Adam made eye contact with Gavin and there was such a profound sadness there that for a moment it engulfed him, overtaking his own emotions. Gavin blinked, dropping his head, not sure how to respond.

'I keep thinking if he hadn't left that note, if he hadn't pushed us together...' Adam drifted off, shaking his head. 'I don't know. I just... I'm not sure we were actually meant to be, me and Louise. We were bound together by guilt or grief or... something. She loved Tom, see? She loved him so much and... well, thing is, I might look like him but I'm not him. He was always the best of me, smarter, more charming, more accomplished. She always loved him more, I think. I could never measure up.'

'I'm sure that's not true,' Gavin started.

'Don't,' Adam said, downing another load of his pint and shaking his head. 'I'm just saying. Forbidden fruit. Sometimes it's poison.'

They drifted into silence and Adam finished his pint, glancing at Gavin's nearly full pint before getting up and ordering another one for himself.

~ Chapter 11 ~

Gavin and Adam began playing squash once a week. At first, Gavin felt uncomfortable in the changing rooms, more a flashback to his school days than anything to do with Adam per se. Having to change and shower with Adam made him feel naked and exposed. Sometimes, though, Gavin would find himself staring at Adam, watching him undress, wondering if he was deliberately staying naked a little bit longer than he needed to so Gavin could snatch a glance or two before pulling on his underwear. No, of course he wasn't. He was married. Mind you, so was Gavin, so that didn't mean anything. And he was sure he'd seen Adam's gaze lingering a little longer than it should have. Or was he imagining it? No, he was being ridiculous. Besides, why was he sexualising a friendship? Why couldn't it be exactly what it was?

'You still running?' Gavin asked one day, towelling himself dry. 'I used to see you and that guy running.'

'He moved away,' Adam said simply.

'Oh right,' Gavin said, detecting a deep sadness in Adam's voice. 'You still running?'

'Nah,' Adam said. 'Probably should be, I guess. They say it's good for mental health, don't they?'

'Mental health?' Gavin replied, frowning. Adam didn't respond as they finished dressing and headed to the bar.

'Is it possible to have a breakdown without knowing you're having one?' Adam asked eventually, downing a third of his pint in one.

'What do you mean?' Gavin asked, stroking his own pint glass and studying Adam intently.

'I think I'm fucking losing it,' Adam said eventually. 'Even simple things seem difficult nowadays. I can't think straight anymore.'

'Has something happened?' Gavin said slowly, seeing the pain in Adam's face but not knowing how to respond to it.

'No. Look, it doesn't matter,' Adam said instantly, swigging back the end of his pint. 'Another?'

'No, ta, I've still got this one,' Gavin said.

'Okay,' Adam said, standing up, nearly tripping on the squash bag at his feet as he did so.

'Look, Adam,' Gavin said, standing up and putting his hand on Adam's shoulder. 'I don't know what to say, except... I don't know, I'm here if you want to talk. For what it's worth?'

'It's nothing, ignore me,' Adam said uncomfortably.

'Is it your brother, do you think? Did you ever get counselling after Tom died?'

'What's the point? They can't bring him back, can they? Talking won't do any good.'

Gavin stared at him for a moment, sad eyes, dark circles beneath. Red lips, moist, kissable. Without thinking, he leaned in and kissed Adam on the mouth. For the smallest moment, Adam seemed like he was allowing the kiss, before he recoiled and pushed him away.

'Shit, sorry,' Gavin said, flustered. 'I didn't mean... Shit.'

'It's okay, I just... it's not...' Adam replied, flustered.

'I thought, I mean...'

'Honestly, it's okay. Let's just forget about it.'

'I'm sorry,' Gavin said, heart smashing its way out of his chest. 'Fuck, I didn't...'

'Look, it's fine,' Adam said again, holding his hands up palms outwards.

Gavin leaned down and grabbed his squash bag from the floor and stood up quickly.

'Better get off,' he said quickly, awkwardly.

'Honestly,' Adam repeated. 'Calm down, it's okay. We'll pretend nothing happened, all right?'

When he got home that night, Gavin got into bed and kissed Imogen, holding her tightly and stroking the back of her hair.

'What's got into you?' she said sleepily.

'I love you,' he said because he needed to. He wanted to feel some truth in the phrase, some comfort.

The squash sessions with Adam dried up after that. At first Adam cancelled, then Gavin. Then something came up. And another thing. Gavin avoided the next monthly dinner party, much to Imogen's irritation. It was months before Gavin bumped into Adam again, on the street outside their local pub. Gavin stopped dead as Adam walked out. They stood awkwardly opposite one another for a few moments before Adam finally spoke.

'You didn't get it wrong,' Adam said.

'I don't...' Gavin paused, not sure how to respond.

'You didn't imagine it,' Adam persevered. 'The vibe, I mean.'

'No?' Gavin swallowed.

Adam held his gaze for a moment before nodding.

'But it's not... I don't know, I'm a mess, Gav, it's not what I need.'

'I know,' Gavin said, pursing his lips together. 'I shouldn't have done it, I'm sorry.'

'Okay,' Adam said, nodding with finality.

Gavin nodded in return.

'Right, I'd better go,' he said eventually.

'Yeah.'

'Maybe a game of squash again soon?' Gavin asked.

'Yeah,' Adam replied unconvincingly. 'Give us a shout.'

They didn't play squash again, of course. Time moved on and Gavin realised that was it, their friendship was over before it had begun.

'Adam's going off the rails,' Imogen said one day, spooning some cookies and cream Häagen-Dazs into her mouth. 'He's drinking every night as soon as the kids are in bed. Every night. Louise said he won't open up to her. She doesn't know what to do about it but worse than that, she's not sure she even cares.'

'That's a real shame,' Gavin said, his back to Imogen in the kitchen, not wanting to turn around or get involved in the conversation. 'They're a lovely couple.'

'What would you know?' Imogen said. 'You barely see them anymore. I thought you and Adam were friends, what happened? Louise said he needs someone.'

'Like you said,' Gavin said slowly, heart racing. 'He's always pissed. I don't think he ever got over losing his brother, to be honest. They were so close and...' he trailed off. 'I don't know, he's hard to be around. I can't help him, can I? I can't replace Tom.'

'Don't be callous, Gavin. You don't have to be his brother, you can be his friend, someone for him to talk to.'

'Men don't do that, Imogen,' Gavin said irritably. 'They don't talk.'

'Oh don't be ridiculous,' she said. 'You're more emotional than you like to admit, Gavin. Why don't you give him a call?'

'I don't want to, okay?' he snapped, gripping the side of the kitchen tightly.

'Maybe I'll try talking to him,' Imogen said.

'Jesus, no!' Gavin said in spite of himself. 'You'll just make things worse. The last thing they need is you turning up on their doorstep with homemade scones and sympathy.'

'Are you okay?' Imogen said, her tone softening. She walked over and stood behind him, touching the back of his arm. 'You seem tense.'

'Tough week, that's all,' he replied, turning around and putting his arms around Imogen's waist. 'Look, I'd like to think I could help Adam but honestly, I think we're better off staying out of it. I'm not a therapist, I don't know what's going on with him. Louise will help him sort himself out, she's his wife after all.'

'That's the point though, I think she's past caring.'

Imogen put her head onto his chest for a moment and he continued to hold her.

'She said they never have sex,' she said pointedly, lifting her head to make eye contact with him. He took a deep breath but didn't answer.

'Do you think we might have sex again sometime soon?' she said quietly, eyes searching his.

'Things are really stressful at work at the minute.'

'Yeah,' Imogen said, a coldness seeping into her voice as she pushed back to release herself from his embrace. 'You're under a lot of pressure.'

'Come on, Imogen,' he implored. 'You know what it's like for me at the minute.'

'No, it's fine,' she walked away, head low. 'I know how hard you work. It's just...' she stopped, looking back over her shoulder at him as she reached the kitchen door. 'When I see Louise and Adam, how their marriage is crumbling around them... I don't want that to be us.'

'We're nothing like them,' Gavin said. 'Adam lost his brother, he's got problems that are nothing to do with his marriage.'

'And us?' Imogen asked quietly.

'There's nothing wrong with us,' Gavin replied. The lie hung in the air between them, an invisible barrier obscuring their view of each other, making them opaque, out of focus, like wavelengths on different planes, blinking in and out of existence and never meeting.

Weeks later, Adam threw himself from Beachy Head. Imogen hung up the phone after Louise's call and cried into Gavin's chest, staining his shirt with mascara.

'Nobody could have seen it coming!' she sobbed.

Yes, they could, Gavin thought but didn't say. *We all saw it. We just refused to look.* In that moment, Gavin's clarity brought no comfort. He *had* seen the real Adam; trapped, isolated, no real friends to talk to. Gavin breathed deeply and held his wife close, stroking her hair and picturing Adam's anguished face the night he tried to kiss him. They were mirrors of each other, he and Adam. They'd never talked about it, of course. Why hadn't they talked about it? Why had Gavin run so far away? Could he have done something? Could he have changed Adam's path?

'We need to go over and see Louise,' Imogen said, lifting her head and releasing herself from his embrace.

'Of course,' he replied. 'Can we take Tim? Or would that be inappropriate? I don't know what you do in these situations?'

'He can keep Matthew and Maria company. They all need their friends around them at times like this.'

Gavin nodded, already haunted by the reflected light of his almost-friend's death. He was devastated for Louise and the children, of course. He was devastated for the man who could have been his friend. He was devastated by the idea that life had offered Adam no other options. There should have been other options. Someone should have been listening to him harder. Gavin should have listened harder.

Gavin would never forget the image of Louise as she stood with her back to them in her living room, staring at an enormous canvas print on the wall. It was a photo of her, Adam and the kids up on the downs somewhere, windswept, smiling and content. Adam was staring at Louise rather than the camera and there was real love in his eyes. Matthew and Maria were beside their mum and dad, arms around each other in a rare moment of sibling contentment. Gavin could see why they'd chosen that picture to blow up and hang, it was filled with love and emotion, an ordinary family on an ordinary day. Happy, beautiful, devastating.

'I called him,' Louise said quietly. 'I wanted to say I was sorry for the things I'd said. I wanted to tell him I loved him.'

Her shoulders begin to quiver and for a moment neither Gavin nor Imogen moved, then Imogen rushed forward, grabbing Louise and cuddling her, holding her close as she sobbed.

'I wanted to make things better.' Louise's voice was strangled, frog-like. 'I did this, I drove him to it.'

'No,' Imogen said firmly. 'You can't blame yourself, Louise.'

'You don't understand, I treated him so badly, it's my fault it's...'

'It's not,' Imogen repeated, a strength and resolve in her voice Gavin had never heard before. She hugged Louise closer, stroking her hair, tears streaming down her own face. 'This isn't on you, do you understand?'

Gavin stood dumbly in the doorway of the living room, listening to Tim playing cards with Matthew and Maria quietly in the kitchen.

'What are the kids going to do without him?' Louise said, as if it had only just occurred to her, lifting her head slightly to make eye contact with Imogen.

'You'll help them through it,' Imogen said, not releasing Louise from her embrace. 'You're a brilliant mother.'

'I'm not, I'm no good, I never have been. I can't do it alone.'

'You're not alone, you've got me. You've always got me.'

'I was so young when I lost my dad... now history is repeating itself for Matthew and Maria,' she trailed off, hand moving up to cover her mouth and squeeze her nose as more sobs rippled through her body. She stood up straight, breathing deeply and lowering her hand, fixing Imogen with a sad stare.

'*Better eyes, little one,* my dad used to say, *the world's always shimmering if you know where to look.*' Louise turned away again, staring once more at the canvas on her wall, lost in her own thoughts. 'But the truth is, I've never seen the shimmer. My world has always been tarnished. *Shimmers* have never been part of my life.'

'Louise, I don't know what to say,' Gavin said, but Imogen flicked him a dark look, telling him to shut up.

'I let him down,' Louise continued. 'Cheated on him, ignored his grief.'

'It's not your fault, Louise. It's not.'

'Then whose fault is it?' she screamed, clutching at her hair. 'I was his fucking wife, Imogen. I should have known where this was headed.'

Gavin stood back silently, remembering his almost kiss with Adam, unconsciously touching his lips.

'Imogen's right, Louise,' he said. 'It's not your fault. Adam had his own demons after Tom died.'

Louise turned around to face him, flanked by Imogen on her right.

'He never got over losing him, did he?' Gavin continued.

'No,' Louise said quietly. 'His other half. I think he felt guilty, like he should never have survived without him.'

'What do you need?' Imogen said, linking arms with Louise and squeezing her close. 'We can help out with the kids, Tim would love to have them to stay anyway. Or the funeral? Do you need help with the arrangements?'

'Thanks,' Louise said. 'I'll sort the funeral. Adam's mum's already trying to take over, so I'm already in the middle of that battle. But I could really do with some help with the kids.'

'Of course,' Gavin said from across the room. 'Anything you need.'

* * *

'Wait, you kissed Adam?' Jackie says through chalky lungs, heart fist-fighting in her chest. Late afternoon has brought a cooler breeze in the pond enclosure and she shivers a little, shocked by Gavin's latest revelations.

'I'm not sure you'd call it a kiss, not really,' Gavin says. 'I was such an idiot; my head was all over the place.'

'He never told his wife about it, though? It never got back to Imogen?'

'He was a good guy. Besides, he had other things on his mind, didn't he? Other demons. I wish I'd been a better friend to him. I think about it a lot, even now. Wondering what I could have done differently.'

Now or never, Jackie.
Be quiet.
Tell him you knew Adam.
I can't, he wouldn't understand.
Give him the benefit of the doubt, he might surprise you.
You've changed your tune.
I like him, I think you can trust him.

'We've been sitting here all morning,' Gavin says before she can open her mouth. 'All this talking is drying me out, I'm dying for a coffee. Shall we go to the café and get one?'

'No, I'd rather stay here,' Jackie replies, shifting uncomfortably, aware she's losing her moment. Now is the perfect time to come clean, to let him know of her connection to him except... where to start? How could she begin to explain who she is without frightening him off?

'I'll grab us both one and come back? If you still want to chat?'

'I'd love to,' Jackie said thoughtfully. 'White, no sugar.'

'Great,' he said, jumping to his feet. 'Be right back.'

Tell him.
I can't.
He seems nice, Jackie. You shouldn't lie to him.

I'm not lying.
You're withholding information, that's the same thing.
He's a stranger, so what?
He's not a stranger, though, is he?

'Here,' Gavin says, startling her from her thoughts.

'That was quick,' Jackie replies, taking the coffee from his outstretched hand and smiling in gratitude. 'What do I owe you?'

'Don't be silly,' he replies, placing his own coffee cup down on the bench and fishing inside his jacket pockets, producing two sandwiches. 'Realised it's lunchtime,' he continues. 'So I got us both a sandwich. Wasn't sure if you were a vegan or not, everyone is nowadays, you noticed? Anyway, I got one roasted red pepper and humous and one chicken mayo, both on granary. If you're not vegan, we can split them in half if you like.'

'I'm not a vegan,' Jackie replies, smiling contentedly at him and taking one half of the chicken sandwich as he holds it out to her, then half of the pepper and humous one. He hands her a bunch of serviettes and she places them down on her lap, taking the chicken one first and biting into it.

'You're very kind,' she continues, swallowing. 'And very unexpected.'

'Unexpected?' Gavin says quizzically.

'Yes, I don't know… not what you first seemed at all. You're quite different in fact.'

'In a good way?' he asks, frowning a little.

'Oh yes,' Jackie smiles. 'In a very good way.'

They fall into silence again as they eat their sandwiches, happily watching the birds and the breeze ruffling through the bamboo forest next to the pond. Jackie knows she should walk away and that talking to him is a bad idea. Yet she knows she can't let him leave, not now, not with so many unanswered questions.

'Thanks for listening,' he says, wiping his mouth with a tissue and throwing it into the bin next to him. 'I've been going on for hours, haven't I?'

'I asked you to,' Jackie says. 'I'm dying for you to finish your story.'

'You're a great listener,' he says, reaching out a hand towards her and touching her arm lightly. 'But you must be sick of the sound of my voice by now.'

'Not at all,' she says honestly. 'I could listen to you all day.'

'I feel selfish doing all the talking, though.' Gavin says. 'Why not tell me a little about yourself?'

'Not much to tell,' she lies.

'Still,' he replies. 'If we're going to be friends, I'd like to hear about you?'

'Friends?' she mirrors, the word alien on her tongue.

'Yeah,' he smiles. 'Friends.'

She shrugs, feeling her cheeks flush again, awkwardness overtaking her limbs, making her feel like a teenager, unsure of her own body.

'Come on,' he perseveres. 'It's a two-way street. I promise I'll finish my story if you share even a little bit of yours with me.'

'Honestly,' she replies, head bowed. 'There's nothing to tell.'

'Oh, everybody has a story, Jackie,' he cajoles.

'Not like mine,' she says, turning her back on him. 'If I open up, you'll run a mile.'

'I won't,' Gavin says seriously. 'I promise I won't.'

'Don't make promises you can't keep, Gavin,' Jackie says sadly, taking a deep breath and bracing herself.

'We've all made mistakes,' Gavin replies, touching her shoulder lightly. 'Done things we can't undo or forgive ourselves for.'

'Have *you*, Gavin?' Jackie says, frowning and looking back at him, her chin brushing his hand as it rests on her shoulder as she does so.

'God yeah,' he says darkly, squeezing his jaw shut. 'You haven't heard the other half of my story yet. I'll promise not to judge if you don't judge me. Deal?'

Jackie takes a deep breath and turns back to face the pond before her, glittering and unaware of the darkness swirling around it.

'Okay, Gavin,' she says, swallowing hard and nodding. 'Deal. Remember, you asked for it. When I've told you, there's no going back.'

'Honestly, Jackie, I don't think anything you've done could be worse than what I've done.'

'Let's see, shall we?' Jackie says quietly, glancing back at Gavin again. 'I knew Adam, you see. He's the reason I moved to Brighton.'

'What?' Gavin replies, wide-eyed. 'How? I mean...'

'I followed him here,' Jackie continued, memories crawling out from under their rocks and shady hidey holes. 'He was this... light, I suppose. I wasn't chasing him or anything, it wasn't like that. Maybe it was the idea of him, of people like him. The needy and the lost, you know?'

'Jackie, you're not making any sense. How could you have known Adam?'

'I moved here to start again, to forget my past. Isn't that why everyone comes to Brighton? But you have to believe me, I only wanted to help people, I didn't mean to do any damage.'

Part 2

Psychic Shirley

~ Chapter 12 ~

On her first day in Brighton, Jackie scanned the seafront promenade as the late summer breeze ruffled her long rain mac. About a metre away, a young guy with a massive, beautiful afro sat with one leg crossed under him on a bench, talking into his mobile phone and gesticulating wildly.

'Mum, leave it will you?'

She stared at the seafront. Peeling, rusting turquoise railings framed her view of the pebbled beach and sea. Mum.

'You should have stayed in London, in the house!' her mother's shrill voice whistled, deep inside her mind. 'You were safe there.'

'I was your prisoner!'

'So melodramatic!' her mother continued. 'Isn't Brighton a new prison? That tiny flat when you can afford so much more. It's no kind of life!'

'At least it's *my* life.'

'Poppycock,' her mother's voice continued, triggering a memory so sharp she found herself standing in her old living room in London many years ago, school uniform skew whiff, toes pointing inwards.

'You mustn't take your gifts for granted,' her mother said breezily, smoothing down her school cardigan and removing imaginary bits of fluff.

'I don't have any gifts, Mum,' she replied, staring at the family photos on the wall behind her mother, none of them including her.

'Of course you do, darling. You get them from your father.'

'Mum, I'm not psychic,' she said again, knowing it was pointless. It was *always* pointless. 'Neither was Dad.'

'I've bought you some books,' her mother said, still young

and healthy. Still alive. *Your psychic experience*, she slammed a book down on the table in front of them. *Cold reading for beginners*, slam. *The other window, perceptions in the nether realm*, slam. Her mother looked pleased with herself and, like any good daughter, she wanted to make her mum happy, aware it would make life easier for both of them. She wanted more than anything to be a normal 12-year-old girl but her mother had other ideas.

'I've booked you some appointments next week,' her mother said, fixing her hair with a clip and smoothing down her blouse. 'So you'd better get practising.'

'Appointments?' she said, heart assaulting her chest.

'For psychic readings, dear.'

'You want me to see a psychic?'

'Don't be silly.'

Her mum smiled, stroking her daughter's palm but the relief running through her young body was short-lived as her mother continued. 'You are the Psychic, Shirley. People are coming to see you!'

'No, Mum, I don't want to,' she cried, the tears immediate.

'You can't waste your gifts,' her mother repeated, not moving to comfort her, not relenting even slightly. 'Besides, they're paying £15 for a half-hour reading and we need the money.'

Years later, on Brighton seafront, Jackie squeezed her eyes shut and clutched the rusty Victorian railings in front of her. Shirley. The girl she used to be. The girl she'd never be again.

The guy with the afro was still arguing with his mum on the bench next to her, families were still enjoying the late summer sun, life was still being lived. She didn't want those memories, didn't want to go back there. She had a new life, a new purpose. She didn't need to think about anything that came before.

Nonetheless a photograph floated into her mind, old and yellowed, well studied. The only surviving photo of her mother that she kept after her death. Her father took it the day before his heart attack. In it, her mum sat on an armless brown, beige and cream sofa, all smiles and possibility, cradling a swaddled baby Shirley in her lap. The television screen didn't show in the photo, so Jackie had no idea what her mother was watching but the glow from the screen cast ominous shadows towards them, a portent of things to come.

Weeks later – so the social worker's story went – the neighbours alerted the authorities because of her mother's constant singing and the stench, the relentless, gut-churning stench seeping through the walls. The authorities bust open the front door to find her father dead, holding his screaming baby girl in a tight embrace. Her mother had placed her there while she went to the kitchen to make a bottle of milk, singing loudly at the top of her lungs as she did so.

'It wasn't your fault,' her foster parents and social workers used to say. 'The shock of losing your dad broke her.'

Unfortunately, her mother didn't stay broken forever and Shirley was placed back in her care at the age of seven. The photograph of her mother cradling her while watching TV had always fascinated Shirley because it was one of the last things her father did before he died, before her mother's mind snapped. The mum in the picture was complete and smiling. It was as if this captured moment, locked in time, filled with life and love, could have led to a brighter, alternate future.

Even without the picture in front of her, she knows every detail. Her mother, filled with excitement, staring at the camera, eyes glinting.

'Hey, beautiful girl.' She likes to imagine her young mum whispering to the baby in her arms, excited and breathless. 'We're going to have such a life together. Such a life.'

In the photo, the wooden table beside her mother was empty. There was no coffee cup and no camera but she knows from the social worker's notes that when they found her, the camera was sitting on the small square table, film still inside, intact, untouched in the weeks since her father had placed it there. A cold cup of coffee sat next to it, white mould growing on the inside walls of the mug. When her mother realised her husband had died, she'd simply refused to acknowledge it. She'd made him breakfast, lunch and dinner each day, scolding him for his lack of appetite. She'd given him his daughter for cuddles while she bathed and dressed. She'd chatted and sang as if nothing had happened – he'd loved to hear her sing, apparently.

She didn't want those memories, she'd come to Brighton to forget about them, not relive them. She stood up straight, breeze tussling her hair as she tied her rain mac tighter around her waist before adjusting her sunglasses. Enough melancholy, she told herself. Focus on the job in hand.

'Mum, I'm a teenager, not a child!' beautiful afro said loudly into his phone, standing up from the bench to gesticulate, as if his mother was in front of him and not on the other end of the phone.

Jackie looked away from him as another memory arrived unannounced.

'I don't want to, Mum, it feels wrong,' her teenage self said, terror rising. Jackie closed her eyes again, giving in to the memory.

'What have feelings got to do with it?' her mother snapped, her mood at odds with her impeccable, graceful 1960s wardrobe. 'The only feelings you need are psychic feelings, do you understand?'

'I don't have any psychic feelings,' she said for the millionth time.

'Then don't have any feelings at all. You're doing this, we need the money. Now go and sit at the kitchen table and I'll show them in.'

She gave the reading. It was a young single mum, no more than ten years older than Shirley, wanting to know if she was going to be okay, if her son was going to be okay. She saw great things for their future. America! She saw an American husband, more children, a new life, far away. The woman left happy, beaming and content.

'You see,' her mother said. 'It's a good thing you're doing.'

Shirley ran from the kitchen to her bedroom, flinging herself on her bed and crying. It never got easier, even as the appointments her mother made gained in pace and frequency. Back then, her mum even put cards in phone boxes, like her daughter was a sex worker. It was hard to fit in her schoolwork around the readings, but Psychic Shirley had quickly become their main source of income because of her mother's deteriorating ill health. Shirley dreamt of finishing school and moving away to university but fate, dressed in her mother's 1960s wardrobe, had other ideas. By the time Shirley was twenty her mother was mainly housebound and Shirley knew escape was never going to be an option. A life of her own was outside of her reach, a dream for another girl with another mother.

I didn't love you mother, she thought, allowing the thought in for the first time, setting it free, which is more than her mother had ever done for her. Twenty long years caring for her, cleaning her, feeding her, doing everything she asked. For what? Not gratitude, that's for sure. Even in her final moments, she hadn't told her daughter she loved her.

After her mother's death, Shirley rattled around their North London home, boxing up her mother's things, cleaning and, when the silence got too much for her, singing to herself like her mother would have done. Was she turning into her, she wondered? Would she become a bitter, lonely old woman whose only pleasure came from traumatising her own daughter?

No. Of course not, because she didn't have any children.

She'd never even had a relationship of note, her mother had made sure of that. The only time she'd come close was with the man who worked in the library who used to ask her to remove her knickers so he could masturbate into them and she was pretty sure that didn't count. Besides, she was nothing like her mother. She liked to think she was kind, that she wanted the best for people.

About a week after her mother's funeral, she finally ventured into her bedroom, the place where they'd spent so much time together in her final days. It still smelled of her, of sickness and unkindness and bitterness and anger. In the background, the home phone was ringing which could only mean one thing: a booking for Psychic Shirley. Later on, she'd rip that phone from the wall and smash it into tiny pieces. She was done with that life. Conning innocent people out of their hard-earned cash and for what?

'How do you think we'll afford to eat?' her mother used to say.

'You get a pension, you still get Dad's pension,' she would start. 'And I could get a job, I could...'

'And who would look after me then? Some stranger? Is that what you want to do to your own mother? To offload me?'

Yes! Her mind would scream, but of course she wouldn't say that. She'd swallow it down. Her mother was ill, in a lot of pain. She had a right to be angry and it was her job as a daughter to take that.

She sat down on the corner of her mother's bed, gently stroking the bedspread and taking a deep breath. She couldn't understand her own emotions. She was devastated, of course, but also relieved; she was free at last. Did that make her a terrible person? It couldn't be normal to feel relieved. Decent people wouldn't feel relieved when their mother died, they'd feel grief and anguish and longing. She did feel those things, but they were fleeting, like when she missed her mother's singing or when she wanted to tell her she'd seen something interesting on the television.

Forty years old and nothing to show for it other than caring for a mother who didn't love her and earning a living as a fake psychic. She was done with Psychic Shirley, done with greedy families who wanted to commune with their deceased Uncle Roderick to find out where he'd left his last will and testament or young women who wanted to know if Jason Knowles at the office fancied them or not.

She glanced up at her mother's wardrobe, which she knew was filled with glamourous, original 1960s outfits, all impeccably dry cleaned and covered in plastic. Her mother had always believed women should be glamourous at all times in public. She didn't understand modern culture, how women could leave the house without makeup.

'Now there was a woman with class,' her mother used to say, propped up in her bed as Shirley fed her soup, fingering a magazine photo of Jackie Bouvier Kennedy Onassis. 'Not like you young people nowadays.'

'I'm 40, Mum,' Shirley would say gently. 'I'm not so young anymore. The years fly by, don't they.'

'Take all my dresses to the dry cleaners, will you?' she responded, ignoring her daughter's comments. 'I know I can't get up and about to wear them nowadays, but I hate to think of them in there, gathering moth balls.'

She made sure her mother looked as glamourous as possible for her coffin, putting her in her favourite blouse and skirt combo and sending photos of Jackie Onassis to the funeral director for reference. The funeral itself had been a small affair, with only a distant aunt and a couple of their neighbours attending. They'd led a solitary life and after the funeral came and went, she began to realise just how solitary. Her relief, already tinged with guilt, gave way to another emotion entirely. Loneliness. Briefly, she contemplated becoming Psychic Shirley again, if only for the visitors, the company. She knew that wasn't the route forward, though. She didn't want to trick people anymore.

Spying her mother's enormous black sunglasses lying on her bedside table, she leaned forward and picked them up. The light had hurt her eyes, her mother said, even indoors. Shirley twirled them in her fingers and started to weep, surprising herself with the intensity of her emotion as she curled up and sobbed. She wasn't sure how long she lay there but when she finally sat back up, putting the sunglasses on her own eyes to cover their puffy redness, she glanced out of the bedroom window to see it was raining. She braced herself and walked over to the wardrobe, opening it slowly and taking out a black, slimline dress and a long, tight blue rain mac from the rail.

She didn't know where she was going or how long she planned to walk but the rain mirrored her mood perfectly. The rain mac fit tightly around her slim frame, the sunglasses hid her eyes and face. She felt anonymous, invisible. Perhaps that's how she'd always felt but somehow that day, she began to own the feeling. She didn't know who she was, she needed to find herself, a version she was happy with, not the one her mother had moulded. At some point, she came across a group of people at a bus stop. Despite the fact there was a lot of room under the bus shelter, they were all queuing for the bus so half of them weren't under the shelter and they were getting drenched. Shirley stood for ages watching everyone following protocol, too polite to stay dry despite the room under the shelter. Eventually, she joined the queue behind a young guy in a soaked woollen jacket, comfortable to be alone yet alongside people at the same time. They were all individuals, strangers, but they also had a common goal. The bus to Victoria. She didn't want to go to Victoria but she did want to be around people so it was as good a place to be as any.

'Waterloo,' she began to sing quietly. She wanted to fling her arms in the air and run into the street, like a character in a musical where all the other people at the bus stop would suddenly join in with her, knowing all the dance moves and lyrics. 'Couldn't escape if I wanted to,' she continued, attracting the attention of the young guy in the soaked woollen jacket in front of her who was clearly unsettled by her song. She was thrilled to realise she didn't care. She grinned manically at him and he frowned, squeezing his shoulders up against his neck, but as she held his gaze, his frown turned into the smallest of smiles, just for a moment. Then he turned back around, pretending she wasn't there. That moment, as the man smiled at her, changed something in her, she felt a fluttering in her stomach, a tingle all over her body.

She stood behind the man, humming Abba to herself and shoving her hands deeply into her mother's rain mac. When the bus arrived, she got on it, following him up on to the top deck and sitting next to him, despite the fact there were loads of empty seats. She didn't know what she was doing or why, all she knew was that she needed contact, she had to speak to someone and he had a nice smile. She knew she was probably unbalanced, that this wasn't normal behaviour but what was normal? Had anything about her life been normal? She was free of her mother, free to be who she wanted, behave how she wanted. If she wanted to sing in the street, she'd do it. If she wanted to talk to strangers on the bus, she'd do it. So what?

She could sense the man's discomfort as she sat down next to him, staring.

'Can I help you?' he said edgily.

'I doubt it,' she replied honestly. He stared at her and she was once again pleased that she had her mother's Jackie Onassis sunglasses on. They hid her face, her emotions, her fear. They made her nothing more than a mirror.

'Why are you wearing those?' he asked. 'It's raining.'

'Why do you care?' she replied, settling into her seat a little more comfortably. Her heart was still racing but it was slowing, little by little.

'I don't,' he said. 'I don't even know you.'

He looked straight ahead, a darkness drifting over his face, the smile disappearing so completely that she couldn't be sure it had ever been there. Something was wrong with him, she realised, deeply wrong and despite the fact he was a complete stranger, she was overcome with an urgent need to help him. To care for him in a way nobody had ever cared for her.

'What's wrong?' she asked quietly under her breath, as much to herself as to him.

'My brother died,' he replied, flicking her an awkward glance. She touched his hand lightly but as she did so, she could see there was something else on his mind, something else he wanted to tell her.

'But that's not all of it,' she said, taking her glasses off. It felt the right thing to do. By exposing herself, she could convince him to expose himself too. He looked at her again and she made contact with his sad, endless eyes.

'No,' he muttered. 'I'm in love with his girlfriend.'

That day changed her path forever. If that man had been someone else with a mundane life and no problems, things would have been different. She'd probably have gone home and pulled herself together. Got a job in an office somewhere, maybe? Shirley would have carved out a different life. But she didn't meet someone else, she met him. Grieving brother and guilty lover. The messy tapestry of his life had presented itself to her, unpicked and dangling, and she'd had the needle skills to fix it.

'Maybe I've always loved her,' the man said. 'But she loves Tom.'

'Your brother?' she said quietly as the bus jolted them along. 'He died and left this... hole. She misses him, I miss him.'

She didn't reply, she wasn't sure how to. They sat in silence next to each other for a while, their legs bashing into each other as the bus travelled over bumps in the road.

'I'm Adam,' he said, glancing at her from the corner of his eye but not looking at her directly. She knew he was expecting her to reciprocate, to tell him her name but as she opened her mouth, something stopped her. She no longer wanted to be her mother's daughter. She no longer wanted to be Shirley. In that moment, her name – her real name – summed up everything she was trying to escape, everything she was trying to change. She couldn't be her anymore. Daughter, carer, fake psychic. That wasn't who she was, wasn't who she wanted to be. She fumbled her Jackie Onassis sunglasses back onto her face and glanced down at her mother's long, dark rain mac.

'Call me Jackie,' she whispered, feeling the weight of a thousand lonely evenings lift from her shoulders. No more would she be the woman helping her mother go to the toilet or wiping her face or administering her medication.

'Call me Jackie,' she said again, more confidently, a pleasant shiver running down her body.

'I don't know why I'm telling you all this, Jackie,' he said.

'Everyone needs someone to talk to,' she replied. 'Maybe a stranger is easier than someone you know and love?'

That was the moment. Wasn't that what all those people had been looking for when they visited Psychic Shirley, after all? A connection? Someone on the outside to tell them things were going to be okay. She stayed on the bus chatting to Adam for another few stops, listening, helping him through his guilt, allowing him to open himself up to the possibility that it was okay to love his dead brother's girlfriend. Who was she to judge? Who was anyone?

When she got back to her mother's house, she knew she couldn't stay there, couldn't carry on living the life she'd led for a moment longer. She couldn't – wouldn't – be Psychic Shirley anymore, but what if she could become something else? That man had been going to Brighton. On the coast. It was as good a place to restart as any. The next day, she called the estate agent to put her mother's house – her house now – on the market. She sold everything except her mother's clothes, arriving in Brighton with nothing more than two suitcases.

So here she was, day in, day out on Brighton seafront or in Brighton's parks and gardens. Jackie. The strange lady in a rain mac and dark sunglasses in the corner of people's eyes. Barely real, an apparition with one aim: to help people.

She glanced at beautiful afro as he sat back down on the battered green wooden bench. Just beyond him on Brighton's street-level promenade was the majestic West Pier, iconic in its stunning dereliction.

'It's not fair,' he snapped into his phone. 'I told you, I won't finish with her!' he growled, jabbing his phone to disconnect it and slinging it on the bench beside him.

'And I think to myself,' she sang quietly, looking directly at him. 'What a wonderful world.'

Beautiful afro glanced up at her, a nervous half-smile on his face.

'Hi,' she said, walking over to sit down next to him on the bench.

'Hi,' he replied cautiously, frowning a little.

'I couldn't help overhearing your phone call. Is everything okay?' she beamed her best smile, extending her hand. 'You can call me Jackie.'

~ Chapter 13 ~

As the years passed, Jackie lost count of the amount of people she'd helped. Some, she could barely remember, others – like Adam – were tattooed onto her memory, their stories defining her more than she defined herself.

At night, she'd lay back on her bed and put the television on, throwing the remote control down next to half a glass of water on her bedside table. Each evening, she'd put off sleep for as long as possible to avoid the dreams but eventually, her eyelids would begin to close, carrying too much weight to stay open. Snugging down into her sheets, she'd curl up into a foetal position, giving in, knowing the dream would follow, the one with the familiar woman watching her drown. She couldn't remember when the dreams started, but the dark dream woman had quickly become a regular visitor, prickling the flesh on her back, like insects burrowing under her skin, laying eggs that would hatch later and feed on her.

'I told you this would happen,' the voice said sadly. Jackie couldn't answer. She was floating face down in the pond, not thrashing, not struggling, resigned to her fate. The woman with her wasn't moving forward to help, she was simply watching from the shadows as memories, tiny glints of light, flashed around Jackie's head, fireflies of the past or present, it was hard to tell the difference. Is that what she wanted, this familiar? Jackie's memories?

'Help me,' Jackie tried to scream as her lungs filled with water.

'Your story's finished, Jackie,' the dream figure replied quietly, leaning in closer, elbows resting on the railings around the pond, close enough that if she wanted to, she could have reached Jackie and saved her life. She could have grabbed her sodden shoulder and hauled her out of the pond, given her mouth to mouth. She could have compressed her chest again, again, again until she'd spluttered, until she'd coughed and choked water onto the stone slabs of the park enclosure as the sirens from the ambulance drew nearer and nearer and nearer.

'I'm sorry,' the familiar continued quietly, not moving a muscle. 'There isn't another way.'

'Why won't you help me?' Jackie wanted to scream.

'You don't know who I am yet, do you?' the shadow figure continued, leaning over the pond railings and staring down at Jackie flailing and thrashing in the water.

'Mum?' Jackie whimpered. 'Mum, is that you?'

The pond should have been cold but Jackie couldn't feel it. Her body was heavy, an armoured sleeve around her, weighing her down, pulling her under.

'Oh Jackie,' the voice replied sadly. 'Do you really think she'd care enough to come back from the dead for you?'

'Who are you?' Jackie shouted, inhaling a lungful of water as she did so.

Silence. Not even the sound of her own limbs thrashing around in the water. No birds singing, no people, no light. The darkness closed in around Jackie. The voice got fainter until she could barely hear it, until Jackie wondered which of them was the dream, which was the illusion. She stopped struggling and began to sink into the dark waters, ready to become nothing. Then she woke, wet through with sweat. She sat up, pushing her hair out of her face and scrabbling for the glass of water on her bedside table, gulping it down, still unsure for a moment what was dream and what was reality. Then her flat coalesced around her. Damp sheets, menopausal frame wrapped in them, wasted life dripping away.

At some point, she stripped the bed and put the sheets in the washing machine. She leaned against the side of her kitchenette, cupping a mug of coffee and scanning her small studio flat, in particular the open wardrobe to the left of her bed. She needed to get dressed, to get out and find someone, anyone.

One morning, after lengthy consideration, she chose a headscarf with white and red dashes of colour, paired with an open burgundy blouse and loose white trousers. Once dressed, she slipped on her long, open rain mac, less designed for the rain than for espionage. It was too warm for it and she knew she'd sweat a little but she didn't feel herself if she didn't wear it. It was a uniform, a comfort blanket, as much part of her as her own skin. To finish off, she fixed her mother's dark sunglasses on top of her headscarf and stared at herself in her full-length mirror, nodding in approval.

She wasn't sure where she was going, so she wandered aimlessly into town, finding herself near the train station when a woman, one half of a bickering couple with two young children, knocked into her by accident.

'Sorry,' the woman said gruffly. Jackie nodded, glancing up as she accepted the woman's apology. She was about to walk on when the woman continued speaking.

'Come on, Adam,' she snapped. 'We're going to miss the train.'

'Don't tell me,' a man replied, his voice light and familiar. 'Tell these two little monsters.'

Jackie stared as the man bent down and tickled first a little girl then a small boy in turn, a huge grin on his face.

Adam. Jackie's heart stopped. There he was. Older, of course, but undeniably the same man from the bus in London all those years ago. Slim, handsome face, sadness and loss in his eyes. Was this woman the dead brother's girlfriend? Were these *his* children?

'Are you okay?' Adam asked, looking directly at Jackie with concern. She was locked onto his face and a smile burst from her without warning. Would he recognise her? Would he reach forward and grab her in an embrace, thanking her for her advice that day so many years ago?

'Adam, come on. I should be at the café today, you know I should. If you want a family day out, don't ruin it by making us miss the train.'

'Louise, for god's sake calm down,' he said, looking away from Jackie and grabbing a child's hand in each of his own.

'You sure you're okay?' he repeated, glancing back at Jackie. 'Oh, yes, fine, sorry,' she stuttered, realising he hadn't recognised her at all. She was just a woman in the street that his wife had banged into. He nodded, following quickly after his wife, leaving Jackie dumbstruck and motionless in the street.

Jackie didn't know what to do but she knew instantly she couldn't let him go and lose him again. Could she get on the same train as him? No, he'd think she was stalking him. People bustled past her, knocking her out of the way, glowering at her as her mind whirred, trying to find a solution.

The café! The woman had mentioned a café. *Louise.* Surely not? Jackie lived in a small flat in Brighton's Hanover area but she walked all over the city and had often passed a café called *Louise* in the Seven Dials area of Brighton. What if *Louise* was Adam's wife's café? The thought gave her butterflies and as she watched Adam and his family walk away towards the train station, she already knew she would seek the café out to find out for sure.

She didn't know what she expected to find in the café, but what she found wasn't it. Plastic chairs, basic décor. A builder's breakfast café, not Brighton, not trendy. In the years following Adam's death, Louise would renovate it, cover the walls with bookshelves, making it softly lit and atmospheric but on this day when Jackie first found it, it was dated and crumbling.

Jackie sat silently sipping a cup of tea, listening to Bella, the woman serving behind the counter as she chatted to her husband on the telephone. She was telling him she'd be home late as she was on her own today and had to close up. Jackie glanced around the café, glad to note there weren't any men listening to Bella's conversation. As she cupped her mug, warming her palms, she thought hard about what she was going to do. Without knowing it, Adam had changed her life. Would he think she was insane if she tried to tell him that?

'Louise is back in tomorrow,' the woman, Bella, said into the phone as she lounged behind the counter. 'She's gone on a day out with Adam and the kids. They're past the point of no return if you ask me but looks like they're still trying...'

Point of no return? Jackie's heart strings tightened. They were Romeo and Juliet; Jackie had pushed Adam towards Louise, certain they were meant to be. Every marriage had difficulties, of course, bumps in the road. Jackie drank her tea as a new sense of purpose gripped her. Fate had sent her a message she couldn't ignore. Adam needed her help again, needed someone to make him see that he and Louise were meant to be and always had been. She'd offer her thanks to him by finding a way to straighten out his love life. Their chance encounter had once again given her a new purpose.

She took her time, not wanting to rush things and make a mistake. This wasn't a one-off encounter like she was used to, it was a longer-term project. It mattered. She took to drinking tea in the café a few times a week. Sometimes Louise and Adam smiled at her, once he even nodded. But she was simply a café patron, a new regular, nothing more.

When she wasn't in the café, she'd walk around Seven Dials, watching as one or other of them visited the post office or grabbed some shopping at the local Co-op. Often, she'd see them arguing in the street and quickly became convinced that Bella had been right. Something was very wrong with their marriage. It seemed to Jackie that Adam did all the childcare because Louise was almost never with the children. It looked like Adam didn't work, though, so maybe he was the stay-at-home parent? Either way, Louise spent a lot of time in the café rather than at home with her family.

After weeks of watching, Jackie decided to move away from Hanover across town to Seven Dials. Things would be easier if she was a little nearer. There was a small bedsit on Addison Road, equidistant from the café and Adam and Louise's house, so it was perfect for Jackie. As the weeks turned into months, Jackie built a picture of their lives from afar. She became a shadow in the café and on the streets of the local area, obsessed with helping them to repair their marriage. The longer it went on, the less able she felt to speak to them. What if Adam remembered her and thought she was stalking him? How could she convince him she only had his best interests at heart? Perhaps Louise was the better bet, then? She'd never spoken to her apart from to order coffee and being a café customer could work as a conversation starter anyway?

Each day was the same, Adam dropped the children at school and nursery. Louise worked all hours at the café. When they were together, they argued, even in public. Increasingly, it looked like Adam was drunk. Things were spiralling and eventually Jackie knew she couldn't watch from the side-lines any longer, she had to intervene before it was too late.

Choosing her day, she spent hours getting ready, picking the right outfit from her mother's old wardrobe. Which version of Jackie should she be for this most important of interventions? She opted for rain mac Jackie because that's who she'd been when she first met Adam and it seemed perfect, full circle.

At first, she went to the café, deciding it was by far the best place to begin a conversation. Louise chatted to customers all the time, it was easy, natural. Jackie probably wouldn't even have to do anything to draw attention to herself, she could simply start a chat. Her heart raced as she opened the café door, only to see Bella behind the counter with no sign of Louise.

'Is Louise around?' she asked Bella nonchalantly.

'Day off, she's back in tomorrow. Can I leave a message for her?' Bella replied.

'No, it's fine, I'll pop back in the morning,' Jackie said, leaving the café hurriedly. What if Bella told Louise she'd come looking for her? There was nothing chance about that, was there? She'd made a mistake, she had to think, had to adjust her plan. She walked quickly to Adam and Louise's road. She couldn't just knock on their door, could she? Maybe she could? Maybe she could just say 'Adam, I met you on a bus years ago and I followed you to Brighton. Actually, I've been following you both for months and I think I can help.'

That sounded weird, they'd run a mile. She had to try though. She should walk over there and knock—

The front door slammed hard as Louise stormed out, makeup smeared all over her face, crying. As she disappeared up the street, Jackie realised fate was intervening again. This was her chance. She followed Louise as she threaded her way through the streets, left and right from seafront to shops, laines to North Lane, no rhythm, no reason. Somewhere near Ship Street, Louise stopped abruptly and turned around, seemingly staring straight at her. Jackie stopped dead in her tracks, not sure what to do. Had she been caught out? Unsure what else to do, Jackie opened her lungs and began to sing as loudly and tunefully as she could. As Louise came close, Jackie stopped singing and beamed at her but Louise scuttled past, head down, heading towards a café further down the street.

For a few moments, Jackie stood still, losing her nerve.

Now or never, she told herself, turning and walking towards the café.

Jackie scanned the room, seeing Louise sitting down at a small table near the window, coffee in hand. After ordering a drink from two men who were clearly high on drugs, Jackie braced herself and walked over to the empty seat beside Louise and said: 'You okay?' in the most blasé way she could muster. She'd never felt more excited, more alive.

Jackie spilled her Earl Grey on the table as she sat down, forcing Louise to look up. There was mascara and makeup smudged across her face, although Louise had done all she could to clean it off with a tiny wet wipe from her purse, which was now screwed up on the table in front of her.

'You okay?' Jackie repeated.

'I'm fine, thanks,' Louise said tersely.

'My mistake. You don't look all right, that's all.'

'Excuse me?' Louise replied, clearly irritated, offended even. This wasn't going according to plan. Jackie painted on her freshest smile as Louise stared at her, hoping to soften her with kindness but it seemed to have the opposite effect because she burst into a new round of tears, as if the emotion inside her couldn't remain contained.

'It's okay,' Jackie said, reaching out and touching her lightly, desperately trying for a balance between being comforting yet not intrusive. 'It's probably not too late to fix things, you know,' she continued gently. 'Not yet.'

'God, I'm so sorry,' Louise said, scrambling in her purse to find a tissue to wipe her face again. 'Honestly, I don't normally cry in public.'

'Don't apologise, it's fine,' Jackie said. 'Here.' She handed Louise a clean napkin from her table and remained silent as she dabbed her eyes with it.

'It might help to talk?' Jackie said, heart furious. Louise was pretty, she could see what Adam saw in her. There was nothing overstated about her, nothing trying too hard.

'I've fucked everything up,' Louise said.

'Everything can be fixed, if you want it to be.'

'Not my marriage.'

'Everything,' Jackie stressed kindly.

'That's just it, I don't think I want to fix it,' Louise said sadly. 'Not anymore.'

'All marriages go through ups and downs,' Jackie started. 'Do you mind me asking what the problem is?'

Louise looked at her, frowning lightly.

'Oh God, no, it's fine. I'm so sorry, I didn't mean to break down on you like that.'

'I told you, don't apologise,' Jackie said. Then, extending her hand: 'Call me Jackie, by the way.'

'Louise,' she replied, taking Jackie's hand and shaking it. She paused before speaking again, as if she was weighing things up in her mind. 'I've cheated on my husband. More than once, actually, loads of times.' She stopped talking, shaking her head. 'I just feel so fucking empty all time, like there's this void I can't fill and I treat him like shit, you know? He doesn't deserve it. I grind him down and I hate myself for it.' Louise looked at Jackie nervously and while Jackie smiled in return, she knew she wasn't conveying any warmth because she wanted to slap Louise in the face and grab her and shake her.

Don't judge, Jackie thought to herself. One of her most important rules, the only important rule. Don't judge, everyone had their own baggage, their own reasons for behaving the way they did. *Don't judge* she repeated internally, again, again, again. *Don't judge.*

'I met this guy, a local mechanic. He used to come into my café. I really fell for him, you know? Got obsessed, lost sight of everything and then...' she broke off, a sob escaping from her, a look of pure fear crossing her face. 'Anyway, it wasn't like that for him, he was...' she stopped, swallowing hard and shaking her head. 'It doesn't matter, what matters is that it was the beginning of the end for me and Adam. We never recovered from it. *I* never recovered from it.'

'Adam found out about you and the mechanic?'

'Jarvis.' Louise said. 'No, God no. They were friends, used to run together.'

'So Adam never knew how you felt about this man?' Jackie continued.

'No,' Louise said nervously. 'Look, sorry, I shouldn't have said anything, you must think I'm such a cow.'

You've no idea, Jackie thought. Instead, she said through gritted teeth:

'There were others? Affairs?'

'Not affairs, just sex.'

'Do you still love Adam?' Jackie asked sternly.

Louise sighed heavily. 'I think it's too late, I've pushed him too far, let it all get out of control.'

Jackie was struggling to keep her composure, to maintain a kind and supportive façade.

'I've made such a mess of things,' Louise repeated, sipping her Americano and glancing at Jackie sheepishly. Jackie tried to manage her anger. This wasn't the woman she'd imagined. She'd known they had problems of course, but she'd imagined it all to be the pressure of a young family, a business. Perhaps Adam resenting Louise being the breadwinner? Something else, anything but this. Jackie had pushed Adam into the arms of a tart who couldn't keep her knickers on.

Don't judge.

'Things are rarely one-sided, Louise,' Jackie managed to say, hatred making her lip tremble lightly.

Don't judge.

'Talk to Adam,' Jackie continued. 'He might surprise you.'

'I don't know if I want anything from him anymore, even if I did talk to him. Things have gone too far.'

'Have they?' Jackie pushed. 'If that's true, why are we having this conversation?'

She didn't know how Adam would feel about Louise being

unfaithful but if they were to repair their marriage, Louise could at least be honest with him. She owed him that, didn't she?

'I've no idea,' Louise said, wiping her nose on a napkin. 'I don't even know you.'

'Shall I tell you something? Maybe the most important thing you'll ever hear?' Jackie said, a spike of irritation making her snappy. 'It's about time you gave Adam the benefit of the doubt before it's too late. The others are only interesting because they're a fantasy, an illusion of a life more exciting. But it sounds like Adam has always been there, he's always been real – maybe that's why you don't value him?'

'I don't think that's fair...'

'What's fair got to do with anything?' Jackie was angry and she couldn't hide it. Louise had destroyed all of her illusions, all of her dreams. This was no dream marriage; it was a nightmare. This woman was selfish and unkind, not good enough for Adam in any way.

Louise stared at Jackie with something like fear in her eyes. Jackie was no longer the sympathetic ear of a stranger, she was an antagonist, a judge and jury.

'Look, I'm sorry, I'd better go,' Louise said, standing up abruptly.

'It's not too late,' Jackie said, trying to regulate her voice, to sound calmer. 'You've got time to change, Louise.'

'You've been kind,' Louise said, but there was panic in her voice. 'I'd better go, try and beat the rain,' Louise continued, looking at the grey skies outside of the window and grabbing her bag.

'Don't try to beat the rain,' Jackie snapped, grabbing her arm 'just accept that sometimes you're going to get wet.'

With that, Louise ran out of the café into the rain, leaving Jackie desperate, confused and alone.

~ Chapter 14 ~

Jackie didn't leave her little bedsit for days after her encounter with Louise. It had turned everything she believed on its head. Instead, she sat nervously pacing, picking her nails, mindlessly watching daytime television, mind whirring, constantly whirring.

You were judgmental.
I know.
You scared her off.
I was angry.
Their marriage is not your business.
I pushed them together, I encouraged him to go to her...
He was on his way to her anyway, it had nothing to do with you.
I'm pointless? Is that what you're saying?
Nobody said that.
She's a cheating bitch! He deserves better.
You don't know her. For Christ's sake, you don't even know him.
Of course I do, we have a connection!
No. You don't. He doesn't even remember you.

'Get out of my head!' Jackie screamed, grabbing her head with both hands and squeezing the sides of her skull, falling to her knees, feeling the waxy, threadbare carpet against her skin, imprinting, denting, marking her.

The voice normally only spoke to her in her dreams, not when she was awake. She hadn't been sleeping properly, it was probably that. Nothing to worry about. She just needed to get out of the flat. Get back to normality. She showered and made herself coffee, staring out of the window onto the street as she drank it. Despite it being morning, it seemed dark, overcast. Maybe she should wait to go out until tomorrow? Except... she should find Adam and talk to him. She couldn't tell him Louise had been cheating but she could still help him, surely? She and he were connected, she was sure of it. He'd remember her if she just spoke to him again and stopped hiding. She'd remind him of the bus ride, of their conversation. She should have done it months ago.

Slamming her coffee down, she ran over to her wardrobe and got dressed hurriedly, filled with a renewed sense of purpose.

She tried the café first as she knew his routine by heart. He often dropped the kids off, then went to grab a coffee at Louise's café before returning home. As she entered, tinkling the bell, she could hear Louise's assistant, Bella, talking loudly to another customer through tears.

'To take his own life like that, it's unimaginable,' Bella said.

'Poor Louise. Those children, those poor, poor children,' the customer, a portly elderly woman replied, reaching over and grabbing Bella's hand.

'He did all of the looking after, you know,' Bella continued. 'I don't know what they'll do without him. Don't get me wrong, I love Louise but she's not mother of the year, if you get my meaning. Oh, I shouldn't speak like this, it's not fair, not with everything she's dealing with. You never think anything like this will happen to someone you know, do you?'

'No, Bella, it's awful. You're quite right to worry about those children, though. I never saw them with her, only with him. I never could understand how she could go to work and leave her babies at home like that. Men aren't natural caregivers, are they? It's not right. Are they going to the funeral? Of course they are, it's their dad, they have to pay their respects, don't they? But it's not a place for a child, is it? A funeral, I mean.'

'It's this morning,' Bella said, glancing at her watch. 'In about half an hour. Of course, I wanted to go, but Louise didn't want to shut the café, so I said I'd cover for her here. The least I could do under the circumstances.'

Jackie turned and ran out of the café, up the street, cold air
burning her lungs, acidic and unkind.

I was too late.

It's not your fault.

I could have stopped him. I could have done something.

It's not your fault.

If I hadn't been so judgmental, if I'd talked Louise into calling
him, he'd still be alive.

It's not your fault.

I waited too long and he needed someone. He needed me.

You weren't part of his life, Jackie. It's nothing to do with you.

I could have knocked on his door any day, I could have
intervened.

He didn't even know you.

Half an hour later, Jackie stood mutely on the corner of Adam
and Louise's road as his funeral procession drove past. She
couldn't breathe, couldn't fathom what she was seeing. Like
a statue, a ghost, she watched the procession pass. It felt like
she'd never be able to move again.

Time passed. Days turned into months and Jackie became
nothing more than a figure staring down from the first-floor
window of her bedsit, palm pressed against her window, a
single tear rolling down her cheek.

She hadn't saved Adam. Perhaps she'd never saved anyone.
As the darkness grew within Jackie, so did the power of the
interior voice, the one that no longer committed itself to her
dreams but intervened in her daily life.

You can't stay locked up in here like this.

Answer me.

Jackie, you need help, let me help you.

Why should I trust you? You want me dead.

It's for the best. One day you'll accept that.

Leave me alone.

Aren't you even curious?

About what?

About Louise? About Adam's children and how they're coping?

You said they were nothing to do with me?

I want you to know they're all right, Jackie. You need to move on.

The voice was persuasive. At some point, Jackie managed to leave her flat and found herself outside of Louise's café, staring through the window to see Louise smiling and laughing with the workmen who were clearly renovating her café, turning it from an ugly plastic space into a trendy spot for the local businesspeople and families to grab coffee and lunch. Jackie's curiosity began to give way to anger.

Look at her. Happy, moving on. She's free to prey on any man she wants now, isn't she? With Adam's life insurance money. She's probably over the moon that Adam killed himself.

That's unkind. She lost her husband.

She treated him like dirt.

You don't know that. You don't know anything.

Look at her. Carrying on as if nothing's happened.

What's she supposed to do? Lock herself in a bedsit and blame herself for eternity like you? .

That's not fair.

She's moving on, you need to do the same.

I don't think I can, I failed him.

He didn't even know you.

What do you know?

More than you think, Jackie.

147

Over the coming months, Jackie checked in on Louise from afar, being careful not to go into the café, not to become part of her life again.

You were never part of her life, don't you see that?

On the surface of it, Adam and Louise's children seemed okay and Louise was certainly spending more time with them than she had when Adam was alive, although Jackie supposed she didn't really have another option.

Still judging, Jackie?

Jackie began to get a feel for Louise's support network. First there was her best friend, Imogen. Jackie had seen her in the café a lot before Adam died, she'd listened in on her conversations with Louise many times. She couldn't say she liked Imogen much so she was surprised by how supportive she seemed to be. She visited Louise at the café a lot, sometimes with her husband, Gavin, but mostly without him. By the looks of it, their friendship was stronger than Jackie had given it credit for because she was the person Jackie saw Louise with most.

After a few months, a new woman with dark hair also began visiting Louise at the café. Whereas Louise had seen Imogen and Gavin at the café many times while Adam was alive, this woman was a new acquaintance. Jackie wished she could go into the café and listen in to find out her name and her story but she couldn't risk it. What if Louise remembered her from their chat before Adam's death? They hadn't parted on the best of terms, she'd overstepped, made Louise nervous and edgy.

I told you to move on, not start stalking her.
I'm not stalking her.
What would you call it?

148

I'm making sure she's okay, like you asked me to.

That was months ago, Jackie, this isn't normal, you know it isn't.

What Jackie couldn't do for herself, Covid-19 did for her. Louise's café closed and the world began hiding behind their front doors. Jackie's world grew smaller, Louise and her friends were cut off from her, removed with no warning, no time to prepare for the loss.

It wasn't only Louise she'd lost. Finding people on benches became more difficult as well. Jackie spent more and more time alone in her bedsit, with only the voice for company.

It's for the best, Jackie. You weren't well, you see that, don't you?

Night after night, day after day, Jackie stared down from her window at the parked cars and lampposts below, at old men with shopping bags as they struggled past, at middle-aged women with curly hair and small, white dogs. The only person to keep Jackie company was the voice from her dreams, ever more present, ever more insistent.

As life outside Jackie's window began to return to normal, her thoughts returned to Louise, to Adam's children. Were they okay? Had they made it through the pandemic?

This has to stop.

What?

You can't use Louise as some kind of umbilical to the real world.

I want to know how she and the kids are, that's not unreasonable.

Yes, it is, Jackie. You don't know them.

I do, I...

Jackie, stop.

Okay, I don't *know* her, but...

Jackie, stay away from her and her friends, promise me.

If anyone had been watching from the street, they would have seen a lone woman crying and nodding maniacally as she stared from her window, cuddling herself tightly for comfort.

Each night, as she fell asleep, the voice took more murderous physical form.

'You know I'm not your mother, don't you?'

'Yes.'

'Do you know who I am?'

Shadowy face. Indistinct, featureless yet somehow familiar.

'Do you understand yet?'

'I think so. Let me see you.'

No matter how hard Jackie stared into the would-be murderer's face, she couldn't discern any features in the shadows.

'It's not up to me, Jackie. You'll see me when you're ready.'

'You don't have to kill me.'

'I can't see another way.'

Silence. Darkness swirling around them. Two dream figures standing opposite each other in the pond enclosure, two metres apart.

'Are you going to push me in again?'

'I always do.'

'Yet I never die.'

'You aren't ready, that's all. But you will be.'

'Why? Because I know who you are now?'

'You've known for a while, Jackie. This pandemic has been good for you. It's broken some bad habits.'

'Perhaps.'

'What do we do now?'

'You're asking me? That's a first. You kill me, I suppose, like you always do.'

'I never succeed, though, do I?'

'You will this time. We both know that. But before you do, I want you to know that I don't blame you.'

'I appreciate that, Jackie.'

'It hasn't been *all* bad, though. I've helped, haven't I?'

'Of course. For such a long time I thought I hated you, but these past months, just you and me... I understand you now.'

'You needed me. Just because you don't need me anymore doesn't mean I wasn't useful.'

'I want to hear you say it.'

'What?'

'My name.'

'You're the one I hurt most of all.'

'Say my name.'

'I can't, not yet. Let me go back out there. To the park. Let me help one last person.'

'Help them or help yourself?'

'Them! If I have to die, let me have one last day, you owe me that!'

'I do, Jackie, I owe you that and so much more.'

~ Chapter 15 ~

'Jesus Christ, Jackie,' Gavin breathes. He's leaning with his back to the railings by the pond, sunlight glistening on the water behind him.

'I told you you'd hate me,' she says, standing in front of Elsie and Christopher's bench, arms squeezed tightly to her sides.

'I don't hate you, of course I don't but...' Gavin trails off, clearly unsure what to say.

'I didn't mean for it to end up like it did,' Jackie started.

'You've been stalking us, Jackie,' Gavin continues. 'Well, Louise and Adam, at least.'

'It wasn't stalking,' Jackie starts, tears welling in her eyes. 'I just... I wanted to help them and I couldn't, I couldn't stop it, I couldn't stop him.'

'Did you know who I was when you met me this morning?'

Jackie nods, swallowing hard. 'I saw you in the café before Adam died. With him, with Imogen sometimes. But I wasn't following you or anything, you were just their friends, you know? I wanted Adam to be happy, you see that don't you?'

'You didn't even know him!' Gavin says, raising his voice slightly. 'You met him once on a bus in London. That was it, Jackie.'

'Don't shout at me,' Jackie cries, turning her back and walking towards the exit of the pond enclosure, wanting to be as far away from him as possible. She shouldn't have trusted him, he's unsettled, of course he's unsettled.

Why is he unsettled?
I don't know, I...
Why is he unsettled, Jackie?
Because...
Because it wasn't normal. Following Adam and Louise around like

that.

I didn't follow them around, I just…

Your followed them around, Jackie.

I wanted to help.

They weren't your friends.

They could have been if I'd…

No, Jackie!

Jackie stops short of the small gate and turns back to face Gavin, taking a deep breath as she does so.

'I'm sorry,' she says quietly. 'I know how strange it sounds. I know I sound unbalanced but I'm not…' she pauses, waving her hand about erratically alongside her head. 'I'm not crazy, I just…'

'Look,' Gavin says gently. 'I'm sorry, I didn't mean to shout. It's just… it's a lot to take in. You can see why I'm weirded out, right? This is…' he holds his hands out in front of him, as if he's holding and shaking an invisible boulder. 'It's a lot.'

'I shouldn't have said anything, I told you I shouldn't have said anything,' Jackie says, shoving her hands deep into her raincoat pockets.

'No,' Gavin says, shaking his head. 'It's good that you've told me, I think maybe you needed to tell someone. You need help, like you help other people.'

'I'm not sure I've ever helped anyone, not really,' Jackie says quietly.

'That's not true, Jackie. I've been sitting with you all morning and I can see that you're kind. You care, it's obvious you care. But you've got to start forming real relationships, Jackie, not fantasy ones. You see that, right? You can't keep stalking people, you'll get arrested.'

'I don't stalk people I just…' Jackie says, trailing off.

'You stalk them, Jackie,' Gavin says, nodding. 'Own it.'

'I…' Jackie says, motionless, reality burning through her

veins. 'I never saw it that way, I never wanted to hurt anyone.'

'I know,' Gavin says gently. 'I can see that. I believe you, Jackie.'

'If I could have saved Adam, I would have,' Jackie says desperately, tears streaming down her face. 'I should have spoken to him sooner; I should have convinced Louise to call him. I could have stopped it.'

'Oh, Jackie, come here,' Gavin says, stepping towards her with his arms outstretched. 'There was nothing you could do. Adam had demons, things he couldn't get past.'

Jackie stands still, not moving towards Gavin, not sure what to do. She can't work out why he's being so nice, why he isn't running a mile from her. She can see it all now, her behaviour, how unnatural it's all been. The voice has been trying to tell her for such a long time and she's refused to listen but now she's said it out loud, she sees everything for what it is.

'I'm not well, am I?' she says quietly.

'I don't think you are, Jackie,' Gavin says softly, arms still outstretched, inviting her into his embrace. 'But you can get well. We can all get well if we work at it.'

'Do you think so?' Jackie whispers, taking her hands out of her pockets and wiping her cheeks.

'I know so,' Gavin replies. 'Now are you going to come in for this cuddle or am I going to stand here like a wanker all day?'

Jackie laughs at that, her body gently vibrating as she steps closer to him and lets his arms wrap around her.

'You haven't done anything so bad,' he whispers in her ear. 'Nothing you can't come back from.'

'Thank you, Gavin,' Jackie replies, not quite able to relax into his embrace.

'Hey,' Gavin says, releasing her and putting his hands on her shoulders to make eye content. 'I'm glad you talked to me. I think you needed to. It kind of makes sense now.'

'What does?' she says, gently stepping away from him as he

drops his arms.

'That... I don't know... sadness in you.'

'Sadness?' she says, forcing a smile.

'Yeah,' he says. 'You wear it as tightly as you wear your mum's rain mac.'

'Do you find me creepy,' she asks, heart racing. 'I think I'd find me creepy.'

'Little bit,' he says, smiling and holding his hands up, palms outward. 'But that's okay. Like I said, I'm glad you talked to me. Everyone needs to be *seen* and you've got a good heart, Jackie. I can see that.'

'Thanks,' Jackie says uncomfortably.

'You really never had anyone else?' Gavin asks. 'After your mum, I mean? No relationships? Nobody to love you?'

For a moment, Jackie is a teenage girl again, putting her soiled knickers back on in the library toilets after the middle-aged librarian had masturbated into them.

'You're a dirty girl,' he used to say as he walked out of the gents, thrusting them moistly into her hands.

'You asked me to,' she'd reply confused, close to tears. 'It wasn't my idea.'

'Put them back on,' he'd say. 'I like to think of you sitting in them as you read.' Then he'd wink at her and get back to his work until the next week, when he'd find her in the Spirituality section, cornering her by a pile of books, panting, 'take them off, give them to me,' with slavering lips.

Had that Librarian contributed to the woman she'd become, she wonders? Had he made it easier for her to retreat into caring for her mother, doing her bidding, earning money as Psychic Shirley and hiding away from life and love and relationships? No boyfriends, no husbands, no children, no friends. An entire life, lived on the outside edges, like a shadow pressing into other people's problems and dramas.

'No relationships,' she says quietly. 'No husband, no

children, no family. Just me.'

'And friends?' Gavin perseveres, sadness infecting his tone, filling her with shame. 'Real friends, I mean, not Adam or Louise.'

'No,' she says, shaking her head and shoulders, like a dog ridding itself of an unwanted stroke.

'Oh, Jackie,' Gavin starts, pursing his lips together. 'At least tell me you've *danced* a little.'

'Danced? Is that a euphemism?'

'Ha,' Gavin says, laughing, his face lighting up in a smile for the first time since her story. 'No, I just meant... No nights out where you've let loose? You were sitting here singing away when I met you this morning, there's so much *life* in you, Jackie.'

'I haven't danced. I mean, I haven't done any of the other things, either, if I'm honest, but...'

'Such a waste,' Gavin says. 'Look at you! You're stunning, like some sort of star from a bygone era.'

'Don't be silly,' Jackie says, cheeks blushing. 'I'm a menopausal woman with issues. No wonder nobody's ever wanted to dance with me. They're certainly not going to want to now, are they?'

'I'm not having that,' Gavin says, fishing his mobile phone out of his pocket.

'What do you mean?' Jackie asks, heart beating a little faster.

'Hold on a second,' Gavin says, pressing buttons on his phone. 'Here we go...'

For a second, nothing, then the slow, jubilant yet mournful tone of Nina Simone begins pumping out from his phone. He holds his hand out, an affectionate smile tattooed onto his features.

'Jackie, may I have this dance?' he says, taking her hand and gently leading her up off the bench. He puts his arms around her and holds her in a soft embrace and begins moving his legs, dancing slowly back and forth. At first she resists, not through embarrassment but through awkwardness. She isn't used to physical contact, it's alien, uncomfortable, yet... she likes it. She stands rigid, not moving her legs, but after a few moments, she relents, forcing herself to move her feet slowly, to go with it. She allows herself to gently embrace him back and rests her head on his shoulder as they move back and forth.

'There you go,' he says. She can't see the smile on his face but she can hear it in his voice. 'I'm afraid I'm a shit dancer, but I'll have to do, I'm afraid...'

The song seems to last for hours, the two of them swaying in each other's arms. She's not sure anyone watching would call it dancing, more shuffling back and forth, but she doesn't care. It's a moment of closeness she can't remember ever sharing with anyone, the sunlight warm on her face and back, the pond enclosure shimmering around her. As the music finishes, Gavin slowly releases his embrace, making eye contact with her as he does so.

'Thank you for the dance, madam,' he says, making an elaborate bow.

'No, thank you,' she replies quietly, sitting down on the bench again and crossing one leg over the other. 'And thanks for being true to your word. You haven't judged and you haven't run a mile.'

'Think you'll be able to do the same for me?' Gavin says, his smile disappearing as a darkness flickers beneath the skin around his eyes. 'Because I hurt people, Jackie. I didn't mean to and sometimes I didn't even realise I had but...'

'Okay,' Jackie says, fumbling with her sunglasses, making sure they're still covering her eyes. 'Let's hear the end of your story.'

'Who said it's ended?' Gavin replies, walking over to join her on the bench and sitting next to her again, staring at her face intently.

'No judgements, remember,' Jackie says. 'I promise.'

'Don't make promises you can't keep, Jackie,' Gavin says, a sad smile still infecting his face.

'I promise,' Jackie reiterates, feeling her chest clamp shut, stealing the breath as she forms the words, not sure what to do with the emotions surfacing in her, one superseding the other before they can declare themselves.

'Okay,' Gavin says in barely more than a whisper. 'Where was I?'

'Adam had just died,' she says, reality flooding back in.

'Okay,' Gavin says quietly, a sombre cloud descending over him. 'It's not just you, Jackie. I feel guilty, too. Like I could have done something to stop him. But in some ways, his death was a wake-up call. Is that a terrible thing to say?'

'No,' she whispers. 'You're just being honest.'

'After he died, I could see myself going down the same path as him, spiralling down, you know? His suicide made me stop and think, I knew I had to do things differently. I had to start *choosing* a different path, you know?'

'And did you?' Jackie asks, pushing her hand up beneath her sunglasses to brush away her tears.

'Hey,' he says. 'Come on, you're going to be okay. I'll help you.'

Jackie covers her mouth and swallows, regulating her breathing for a moment before she can speak.

'Thank you,' she says. 'I'm fine, honestly. Carry on.'

'Okay,' Gavin nods, reaching over and squeezing her hand lightly. 'As you know, Adam's death left a legacy. It left scars behind, for *all* of us...'

Part 3

Changing Cages

~ Chapter 16 ~

Before. Such a powerful word. *After* was somewhere quite different, harder to navigate. Adam's death had somehow flung their lives up in the air. Now everything was waiting to drop and find a new place, a new position in the world, but gravity hadn't kicked in yet, so everything just floated, unsure of itself or its purpose.

Imogen pottered around the kitchen, wiping the already-clean surfaces with a cloth, nodding her head with palpable disinterest as Gavin spoke.

'Commuting is killing me,' Gavin said, taking a bite of cold lasagne. He'd promised to be home from work on time, a promise they'd both known he wouldn't be able to keep.

'What are you talking about?' Imogen replied, opening the fridge without looking around.

'Commuting to London every day,' he continued, taking another mouthful. 'I don't think I can keep doing it.'

Travelling by Southern Rail was all consuming. Every day was punctuated by squeezing into a tin can filled with soul-dead husks who, like him, used to believe life would offer them something more appealing.

'Oh, Gavin, you'll cope. When it comes down to it, we all cope.'

'Adam didn't,' Gavin snapped.

'Not this again.' Imogen stared at the contents of the fridge, clearly deciding whether she should have the cheesecake or a glass of wine. She'd choose both, she always did, but he knew she liked the dance of deception. She enjoyed pretending she'd only go for one sin or the other.

'You're nothing like Adam,' she said, somehow making it sound like an insult.

Aren't I? Gavin thought. Because he wasn't sure, he wasn't sure at all. Adam's death had left a long-lasting unease he couldn't put his finger on. As time passed, Gavin felt a mounting terror, a chest-squeezing anxiety he'd never experienced before, robbing him of sleep, of calm, of any other emotions. If anything, time was making it worse, not better.

'I never see you,' Gavin said, more to himself than to Imogen. 'I'm lucky if I see Tim at all in the week.'

Imogen took the cheesecake out of the fridge with one hand, the bottle of wine with the other, slamming the fridge shut expertly with her hip.

'What would we do for money?' she said irritably, pouring her wine and taking a spoon out of the drawer. 'We can't live on air, Gavin.'

She spat the word Gavin like it was a swear word, an insult of the highest order. Without waiting for a response, she wandered into the other room to watch TV.

Gavin finished his dinner in silence, then went upstairs to bed without saying goodnight to Imogen. On his way, he gave Tim a kiss and stared at his sleeping face. On weekdays, this was the only version of him Gavin got to see, pale and shadowy. A sleep-child, barely real.

The next day was Friday, which meant only one thing: his weekly night out with his workmates. Work mates. Work, not mates. Fridays after work always involved expensive social clubs, filling their nights with anything possible, spending the money they earned so they could pretend it didn't make them feel desolate. Champagne, shots, lager, tedious hours of listening to Greg, Essex boy 'done good', telling of his latest relationship woes.

'Mate, you know I went on that lads' holiday?' Greg said. Gavin suspected he called him 'mate' because he couldn't remember his actual name. Gavin nodded and feigned interest as he sipped a bottled beer. 'I was on the sauce all week,' Greg continued. 'Didn't know what I was doing most of the time.

Anyway, this bird ended up back at my apartment... shouldn't have occurred, obviously... but she was there, right, so I had to sort her out, didn't I? Anyway, I got found out. I wouldn't mind, but my girlfriend lives with me and I pay for everything... everything. She works, she's training to be a nurse, but she earns fuck all, so I don't mind paying the rent and bills and shit. But she was well angry with me and I'm like, really?... Like she gets to judge me when I pay for everything...'

By 11pm, James from floor six had started throwing up in the street and it was safe to leave to get the Brighton train home without being called pussy whipped. Because in Gavin's work circles, if you had respect for your wife or girlfriend, you were somehow seen as less of a man. In fact, anything remotely resembling emotion relegated you to 'gay', 'pussy-whipped' or 'ladyboy'.

Walking to Victoria Station, Gavin tucked his hands into his pockets against the cold and turned the corner, only to be punched hard in the face. He reeled backwards against the wall. The second, third and fourth blows mirrored the first, hitting the same target just below his cheekbone. The fourth headed south a little, crushing his lip against his teeth. All on the left side, not the right. He didn't know if his face was angled in that direction or if his assailant was right-handed and that's just where his fists naturally landed, always in the same spot, over and over again. In the background, he could hear traffic and as he fell, as his mugger rummaged in his pockets, he felt weirdly calm. Calmer than he'd felt in years, truth be told. The mugger didn't take his laptop bag, which struck him as weird, just his phone and wallet. After a while, he pulled himself to his feet, brushing himself down and continuing towards the train station. Patting his inside pocket he felt his train pass, deciding not to call the police to report it. What would be the point, apart from a crime number for the insurance?

He sat on the train with a swollen lip and throbbing head,

staring out of the dark window wondering, like he did every single day, how his life had become so lifeless. Being mugged had been almost welcome, exciting even. At least it had been something tangible, animal brutality in a sea of nothing. He rubbed his head, realising he had blood in his hair, just a little. Didn't matter, as long as it wasn't too obvious, as long as he didn't have to explain it to Imogen or Tim. Shit, would he be swollen or bruised? Leaving his laptop under the seat, he ran to the end of the carriage to try the toilet, which was, of course, out of order. Wandering back up the carriage, he ran his hand along the blue and yellow trim of the unlovable seats. Past the guy coaxing his bleach blonde girlfriend to go down on him 'it's all right, nobody will see, no one is looking', past the guy opposite them who was trying to film them surreptitiously on his mobile. Back into his seat, staring straight at his reflection in the dark window. Slight bruising. Swollen cheek. Explicable. Probably. Got pissed, lost his phone and wallet. Fell over. Silly. Drunk. Sorry Imogen, it won't happen again.

'You said that last time.'

'I mean it this time.'

Next to him on the rough, dirty train seats, sat an old paper.
Have we got addiction all wrong?

He picked up the paper, scanning the article. Scientists had taken a bunch of rats and made them drug addicts – heroin, cocaine, whatever. So far, so normal, scientists had been doing that for decades. But this study was different. Everything everyone had been told about addiction was wrong, the study suggested. Traditional experiments with rats had always been versions of the same thing: rats were placed in a cage, alone or in pairs, with two water bottles. One had only water, the other was laced with heroin or cocaine. Predictably, the rats developed an obsession with the drug-laced water, so much they eventually overdosed and died. So far so expected. The results of this type of experiment had become accepted dogma: drugs were highly addictive. If you took them, you wanted them more and they would enslave you. Except one scientist – Dr Bruce Alexander – wondered why the rats were always put in cages alone or in pairs. This didn't reflect rat society – or crucially – human society. Rats and humans are social mammals, the article argued, neither lives in solitary confinement. To address this, Dr Alexander designed some new cages. They were massive, with balls to play with, things to climb on and many other rats to interact with.

Like the previous experiments, the rats were given access to two water bottles – one with only water, the other with drug-laced water. The results were quite different. The rats tried the drugs, of course. Some liked the drugs but none of them became heavily addicted. None of them overdosed and none of them died. Stimulation and social connection changed everything, it seemed. Addiction was more about the rats' 'cage' and its social connections than it was about the drugs themselves. In fact, many of the rats in the nice, social cages tried the drugged water once or twice then shunned it evermore for the normal water. Other studies followed, all flying in the face of accepted dogma. Drugs didn't inevitably cause addiction, the studies found: the 'cage' was crucial.

The crux of the argument was this: addiction was an adaptation to circumstance – increase the rat's (person's) positive social connections and you would have a much better chance of beating the addiction. Addiction was a symptom, not a cause. This research was decades old, the article said, so why hadn't attitudes to treatment changed?

As Gavin sat on the train with the taste of blood in his mouth, he knew there were fundamental truths in this article that could help him, if only he could work out how to apply them. Addictions. He'd never thought about them before, not really, but sitting on that train, he couldn't think about anything else.

He wasn't a drug addict or an alcoholic but he was definitely an addict. He was addicted to money, to his lifestyle, to the pretence of it all. His life had become a never-ending pursuit of 'more' and if he didn't keep accelerating, achieving, buying, spending... What? What would happen?

The blindingly obvious question reared its head: What if he simply stopped doing all the things that made him so empty and unhappy? What if he changed his 'cage'? Would he realise those things weren't so important, just like the rats realised the drugged water wasn't all it was cracked up to be?

What if he stopped serving up the smiling outside version of Gavin, the dependable breadwinner he'd so skilfully painted himself to be? What would happen? He shivered; eyes boring into the bloodshot eyes of his dark, train-window reflection.

'Stop,' he whispered to himself. 'Just stop.'

Adrenaline began to flood his system as one singular thought took hold: he had choices.

Didn't he?

He leaned back in his seat and closed his eyes, resolving to change things. He would not keep commuting to a city job he hated. He would not keep going out for drinks with colleagues he couldn't stand. He would not keep sitting on a bloody train, day after day, not seeing his wife and son. Brighton to London, London to Brighton, listening to the same shitty announcements, the same sorry excuses: We're sorry for the delay to this service. This train will not be running past Haywards Heath. Please get a bus service from Three Bridges. This train will now be stopping at all stations and won't arrive in Brighton until 3.30am and we are sorry for the delay. We are sorry about the guy who just pissed under the seat at the back of your carriage, but what was he supposed to do? All the toilets are overflowing or out of order. What's that you say? The alcohol-stench-urine is slowly running down under the seats from the back of the carriage and is now seeping into the fabric of your laptop bag, so when you pick it up and put it on your back, his piss will soak into your shirt? Oh well, never mind. Did we mention we must put up ticket prices again because... because we can... Captive market and all that.

As his train finally pulled into Brighton, he was jolted awake, already suffering a hangover, a repeated mantra running around his head: he had to change cages.

By the time he arrived home, trudging up the hill from the train station in the cold gloom, it was the early hours of the morning. Choosing the downstairs bathroom so as not to wake Tim or Imogen, Gavin first emptied his laptop bag and rinsed the piss from the train off it. Then he shed his clothes and showered, wincing as he massaged shampoo into his swollen scalp. He spent a long time standing under the falling water, enjoying the heat on his shoulders and neck. He always ran the water a little too hot. Imogen could never understand how he could stand under it, she always said it would burn her skin if she tried. It had been a long time since she'd joined him in the shower anyway – certainly long before Tim was born.

Drying himself off, he stared at his face in the mirror. He was surprised how little it hurt but maybe that was the alcohol in his system. He pulled at his skin, relieved to see that while his lip was swollen the bruising was mainly inside and not out and – while it hurt him to open his jaw fully and his cheek throbbed, there was only mild swelling and no bruising. No black eye. He could probably get away with the 'fell over drunk and lost my wallet' line in the morning. Imogen would be pissed off, but better that than an inquisition about the mugging or the endless needling for not reporting it to the police.

Staring silently at his face in the yellow orange light of the downstairs bathroom, Gavin nodded to himself. He would change his cage and the first step towards that would be leaving his job.

~ Chapter 17 ~

The next morning, Gavin woke to find Imogen already out of bed and downstairs, helping Tim with his breakfast before karate.

'Tim's got an open classroom next week,' Imogen said without looking around at him.

'What day? I'll take the day off and come along.'

'How does that make sense? You said you aren't hitting your targets, you can't take days off whenever you like.'

'I'd like to come.'

'I'll be there already, Gavin. He doesn't need both of us, what he needs is financial support.'

'There's more to fatherhood than that,' Gavin said quietly, leaning against the doorframe.

'How was your night?' Imogen asked, hovering over Tim's shoulder and pouring milk onto his Weetabix.

'He's not a baby, Imogen, he can pour his own milk,' Gavin said, being careful to angle his face away so the swollen side didn't show. 'You've got to stop babying him.'

'Oh, you're in one of *those* moods,' she said without even glancing his way. 'How wonderful for us all.'

'Don't start.' Gavin walked up behind Tim and kissed him on the head. 'Morning superstar, did you sleep well?'

'Yeah,' Tim replied through a mouthful of Weetabix. 'Can I watch TV after breakfast?'

'You've got karate, but maybe later on this afternoon, if you're good.' Gavin smiled, ruffling his son's hair.

'Oh, that's it. TV. Silly me for thinking you might like to do something with your son this afternoon. You haven't seen him all week,' Imogen said.

'The other day you were going on about TV being good for him to relax,' Gavin started, walking to the fridge and grabbing a can of Diet Coke. 'I can't win.'

'It's not a competition, Gavin,' Imogen said, secure in her victory. Gavin fell silent, his mind still turning over his decision from the night before.

'I'll take Tim to karate,' he said, ignoring his wife's barb. 'Then do you want to grab lunch somewhere after? I want to talk to you about something.'

'Sounds ominous,' Imogen said, leaning down to cuddle Tim and saying: 'Do you want Daddy to take you to karate? Or Mummy, like usual?'

'Mummy,' Tim said, jumping up from the breakfast table and running into the hall, shouting over his shoulder 'can you get my Karate things for me, Mum?'

'Get them yourself,' Gavin called after him, 'they're in your drawer where they always are.'

'Don't worry, I'll get them,' Imogen shouted after their son, pushing past Gavin to get out of the kitchen. Then, without turning back to look at him, she said: 'Meet you in the café at St Ann's Well Gardens at 12 after I pick Tim up? Louise will be there with Matthew and Maria, Tim's desperate to play with Matthew.'

'Can't we talk before that?' Gavin asked, breathing in, out, in, holding it. 'We can't talk if Louise is there.'

Later that day, he sat in the park waiting for Imogen to arrive with Tim after karate. He closed his eyes and thought of his marriage. Too many years, not sad years, not happy years, just years, piled one on top of the other, fallen dominoes behind him, stacked ones ahead, none of them leading anywhere good, anywhere different. All of them screaming that he had no choice, crushing everything else under their weight. Choices were for other people, the ones he sometimes watched as they scurried past his living room window, or past him in the park, carrying coffee, smiling and laughing and enjoying life and its rich tapestry of emotions where stress was only one ingredient, anxiety only one outcome.

The world wasn't going to give him space, he had to take it. If Adam had taught him anything it was that you had to slam on the brakes, you had to heed the warning signs before your train gathered too much pace, before there really were no other options. Life had other paths apart from the one he was on, he had to believe that.

He had money. He'd only recently had his yearly bonus and coupled with his final salary and savings, he could last a while before running into problems, even with Tim's school fees. He would hand his notice in on Monday. He was sure once he'd explained it to Imogen, she'd be okay with it, she'd understand.

Imogen and Tim walked towards him from the other side of the park, with Louise and her children, Matthew and Maria, beside them. Tim was still in his Karate whites, which was strange because normally Imogen made him change out of them before the park in case he got muddy.

'I'm quitting my job,' he said over and over inside his mind. Of course, when they arrived at the table, Imogen was deep in conversation with Louise, so instead of speaking, he paused. A fatal error.

'Hey,' Imogen said warmly. She was always a little nicer to him when her friends were around. 'I'm an idiot, I forgot to bring Tim's change of clothes.'

'You should have messaged me to bring some,' he said, smiling up at her. She leaned down to give him a kiss lightly on the lips, noticing the bruising on his face for the first time.

'Shit! What happened to your face?' she asked.

'Oh nothing,' he replied, 'fell over last night, nothing to worry about.'

'Gav, it looks bad,' Louise said, sitting down next to him and touching his knee lightly. 'Have you seen a doctor?'

'No, no, honestly, it's fine.' He painted on his biggest smile.

'Now, kids,' he said, raising his voice, 'what type of ice cream do you want?'

As the kids ran off over to the café to choose their ice creams and lollies, he smiled at Imogen and gently stroked her arm. She smiled back, apparently satisfied with his explanation.

'Hey,' Louse said breezily. 'Tim sounds excited about Tuesday. Are you going in?'

'What do you think?' Imogen answered before he could. 'He never makes Tim's open classrooms. Luckily one of us is able to be there to support him.'

Gavin sat silently on the dented silver café chairs, mouth squeezed shut.

'Anyway,' Imogen said, sitting down in one of the seats next to him. 'What was it you wanted to talk about?'

'Nothing,' he replied quietly. 'Doesn't matter now.' Then, changing the subject he smiled widely at Louise.

'How are things with you? I'm so impressed with how you're coping with Matthew and Maria on your own.'

'Oh, you know,' Louise replied, returning his smile with an extra touch of sadness. 'We're muddling through.'

'For God's sake, Gavin, do you have to be so insensitive all the time?' Imogen admonished, leaning over and squeezing Louise's hand tightly.

As Imogen chatted to Louise and the kids disappeared into the bushes to climb trees, Gavin stared numbly across the park. It felt like nothing around him was real, as if he was the only solid thing in the entire universe. He could hear the sound of children playing, dogs barking, conversations rising and falling, yet only he existed, only his thoughts, only his skin bristling as the breeze brushed him. He took deep breaths, trying to calm his heartbeat, his blood flow, his mind. The birds tweeted; the wind rustled. The bees, impossible, clumsy yet graceful, gently moving from flower to flower. Beautiful accidental pollinators.

The ants in the soil, scurrying, seemingly randomly, without form or cohesion until one ant found a chip – a massive, oily chip – and magically, they all began to form a line, carrying it with purpose on shoulders that shouldn't have supported its weight.

'Gavin?' Imogen's voice broke into his solitude and he blinked, seeing Louise walk away from the table towards the café. He and Imogen were alone, for a few moments at least.

'What's up, Gavin?' Imogen said. She sounded genuine, so he turned his gaze towards her, gripped with transient bravery.

'I'm not happy, Imogen,' he said.

'Well, that's not news,' she said bluntly. 'Neither of us are happy. It's been a long time since happy came to visit us,' she carried on sarcastically.

'Imogen, I'm serious. I'm going to quit my job. I know your uncle stuck his neck out for me but...'

Imogen's pause was monumental. Glaciers could have formed within it, entire civilisations could have risen and fallen, leaving no trace of themselves in the fossil record, like they'd never existed at all. Eventually:

'And what would we live on, Gavin? How would we pay for everything?'

'I'm not saying I wouldn't work... but I need some time to reprioritise, work out what I want.'

'Reprioritise? What does that even mean?'

'I just... we live this life that's all about earning more, having more and... and I don't think it makes us happy,' Gavin pleaded. 'It wasn't what we planned, was it? When we met, I mean. We were happier before.'

'Oh, Gavin, we've never been happy, not really!' Imogen said.

Silence.

'Don't you remember, at Uni? All of our plans, Imogen.'

Silence.

'We need to change our cage,' he pleaded, leaning forward and grabbing her by both hands.

'What are you talking about?'

'I'm serious.'

'I know you are, that's what worries me. What have cages got to do with anything? We *all* have to do things we don't want, Gavin. It's called being an adult.'

'That's not fair,' Gavin implored. 'I never wanted this job in the first place!'

'Do you want us to lose our home? Want Tim to have to move schools? Because that's what you're talking about, that's the result if you quit with no plan.'

'Would a reset be so bad? You know, start from scratch, try and remember what we wanted from life?'

'You're not thinking straight,' Imogen snapped. 'I don't know what's got into you.'

'Tim doesn't have to go to that school,' Gavin continued, but the fight was already leaving him. 'Or you could get a job again?'

'Oh, here we go again. You've no idea how much hard work bringing a child up is, Gavin, because you don't do it.'

'Because I spend my life at work or on a train commuting!' Gavin almost shouted. 'Just like you wanted me to do!'

Imogen couldn't reply because at that moment, Louise came back from the toilet, sitting down and smiling at them both, clearly sensing the tension.

'I know that woman,' Louise said, indicating a woman with long dark hair on the table behind them, absently eating a packet of wafers and staring into space. 'She came to my bereavement group once. Natalie, her name is. Lost her husband in a car accident. Terrible, she saw it happen right in front of her.'

'Go over and say hello,' Imogen said, all fake smile and pleasantry.

'No,' Louise said, glancing over at the woman again. 'Sometimes you want to be alone with your demons, you know?'

'Maybe she'd like someone to talk to?' Gavin said pointedly, hoping Louise would take the hint.

'I don't think so,' Louise said quietly. 'Not today.'

Gavin retreated back into isolation as Imogen and Louise began to chat again, leaning into his cold metal chair and staring at the trees where the children played. Maybe she was right? Maybe he could carry on as he was. He could tolerate his job – most people had to. His marriage could carry on in a stream of crossed words and misunderstandings, fumbled moments of anger or, worse, lack of any interest at all. Fatherhood could continue to be a snatched weekend pursuit, with both he and Tim skulking in the shadow of Imogen's disapproval.

No. He needed to start breathing again. He'd find a way, with or without Imogen's support. The breeze in the park picked up, bringing with it an invasive smell, like old piss and alcohol. Gavin opened his eyes and focused on a figure leaning against the low railings between the table tennis table and the old bowling green. The smell was overpowering and as the man, dishevelled, clearly homeless, began stumbling towards the tables, Gavin wasn't the only one to notice. Both Louise and Imogen were looking his way, as was Natalie, the woman Louise said she knew, whose table was much closer to the man than theirs.

'Time to go,' Imogen said, eyes rolling back in disgust. 'I'll round the kids up.' She walked off towards the trees where Matthew, Maria and Tim were climbing. Louise grabbed her bag and smiled at Gavin as he stood to his feet.

'You okay, Gavin?' she asked.

'Yeah, of course.' He smiled. 'I'm always okay.'

She leaned over and kissed him on the cheek.

'So was Adam,' she said softly, walking across the grass after

Imogen in search of her children. Gavin stood stock still, he could hear his heartbeat in his chest, feel the blood pumping through his brain. Running his hands through his hair, he walked after Louise, holding his breath against the smell of the homeless man as he did so, wondering for a brief moment if he should reach into his pocket and take a £10 note out to press into the man's hands. Would that be patronising or okay? He wasn't sure so he scurried past and did nothing instead. Nothing always seemed like the easiest option. As they left the park, Gavin could hear the man shouting: 'I'm here!' at the top of his lungs, unsettling Gavin more than it should have.

That was the moment he changed path. That was the exact moment he made the final decision to quit his job, toppling the first in a new line of dominoes, letting one softly knock into the next, then the next, each with perfect precision. Dominoes falling into the future. Event leading to event leading to event, unstoppable, gathering pace and force with a faint clickety clack, clickety clack, growing louder and louder as the days passed, leading ever forwards until finally the last domino, tombstone in size and significance, fell and shattered their marriage to pieces.

~ Chapter 18 ~

On Monday, Gavin got up as normal and got ready for work. He kissed Tim and Imogen goodbye and swung his laptop bag on his back before walking to the café around the corner from home, the opposite way to Tim's school so Imogen wouldn't see him. Then he had a black coffee. And another, but decaf to avoid the shakes and anxiety that came from too much caffeine.

Taking a deep breath, he picked up his mobile phone.

'Yeah, Greg, is Harry in yet? I need to talk to him.'

'What about?' Greg's bored voice responded.

'I'm quitting, mate.'

No going back. He knew he should have discussed it with Imogen first, knew he was storing up trouble. But it wasn't like he hadn't tried and if he'd told her before doing it, she'd have stopped him, talked him out of it, talked some *sense* into him.

'Legit?' Greg breathed down the mouthpiece.

No going back. He needed to be strong, to go through with it. Except he was sick of being strong, that's what had brought him here. Life had to be about more than that, surely? It had to involve more than holding it together, day after day, secretly wishing he could collapse in a corner and cry or scream to release the pressure, all the while knowing emotional release was denied to him. His only role, his only value lay in remaining *strong*. If he couldn't do that, what could he do? What kind of man was he?

Yet he knew if he carried on, didn't quit, he'd end up deeper in the rabbit hole, alone in the darkness with no way back. Right now, he was keeping all the plates spinning despite wanting to smash them all. If he didn't do something soon, he'd have a breakdown or worse.

What if he had a breakdown? Everything would stop,

temporarily at least. But no breakdown was in sight, no matter how much he fantasised about it. Was that weird? To spend his days wishing for a breakdown? He didn't want to be strong, he wanted to crumble, to falter. He wanted Imogen to notice how desperate he'd become. He wanted her to care. He had no experience of breakdowns. If he had one, he imagined it would be deeply unpleasant and he might regret wishing it upon himself, but he'd reached the point of needing change so desperately, so drastically, that anything other than reality would do. He needed the treadmill to stop. He needed a new cage with soft furnishings instead of the razor-sharp edges life had provided him with.

'Yes, Greg, I'm done,' he said more confidently.

There never seemed to be a 'right time' to tell Imogen what he'd done. He didn't work directly in her uncle's team and they weren't even based in the same offices, so he probably had a little time before he'd find out and tell the family. He decided to wait until he had something else concrete in the pipeline before letting Imogen know. Surely that was the best thing for her? He scoured the web for local jobs in Brighton and Sussex, things far removed from his last job, from the city and its related pressures. How did people survive on the wages on offer? Every job that looked like he might enjoy wouldn't cover Tim's school fees let alone their mortgage and credit card and loan repayments. His city job might have been soul destroying but it had been lucrative.

If he were to truly change his life, he had to bring Imogen on board with the ride, they'd have to sell up, move somewhere cheaper. Tim would need to go to a state school. So many changes, so many choices but at the other end of it, happiness, he was sure of it. Not the demi-existence he'd been living before. Day followed day and when his notice was up, he still hadn't told Imogen, despite the consequences for her and Tim. Each morning, he carried on leaving the house, pretending to catch the train. The longer it went on, the more difficult it became to tell his wife. How could he make her understand anything? Did he even want to? Her uncle would find out and call her to let the cat out of the bag any day now, he should tell her. Tomorrow. He'd tell her tomorrow. Always tomorrow.

He settled into a new routine. Each day, he got up, showered, put his old work clothes on and smiled. He kissed his wife and son goodbye. Then he walked. Nowhere to go, no plan, no idea what his future held. He hid in local cafes and parks, anywhere he felt sure Imogen wouldn't happen upon him doing whatever she did with her Brighton days while Tim was at school.

He had enough in savings and with his last bonus, he didn't have to worry financially for a while but that wouldn't last forever. Neither would her uncle's ignorance.

Twenty-four-seven, his temples throbbed, pulsating with the pressure, a faraday cage around his neural network, dampening the connections so information couldn't process properly. He couldn't think, couldn't focus.

Day by day, week by week, the world became something of a fantasy around him, not real at all. The lives other people lived, the clothes they wore, the food they bought, their carefree ability to *be*, it was all other-worldly, ephemeral. In his own dark world, Gavin was crippled with the knowledge he had jumped without looking and was now in freefall with nothing but broken glass beneath him. He had no plan. Why had he quit with no plan?

For a while, he found himself in the pub by late afternoon, nursing a pint, waiting until a time when it would be safe to go home. Stroking the misty glass, feeling the moisture on his fingertips, he'd remember Adam, always getting 'one more' drink, despite the fact he'd already had two more than anyone else at the table. Gavin knew he needed a different plan and, with no better ideas, he stole Adam's other coping mechanism:

running. It hadn't stopped Adam's descent but he and Gavin were different people.

Time moved on and Gavin's lie continued to grow in direct proportion to the dwindling of his funds and savings. Imogen, not unreasonably, carried on as if nothing had happened.

'Do we have to go?' Gavin asked one evening, staring imploringly at Imogen's unzipped back.

'What's with you?' Imogen replied, sitting at the dressing table and studying herself in the mirror as she put her diamond stud earrings in. 'You spend all of the time moaning you don't get to experience living in Brighton, then whenever we're doing something locally with our friends, you don't want to do that either.'

'They're your friends,' Gavin said, standing naked in the doorway of the en-suite bathroom, towelling his dark hair dry. 'Monthly dinners with them aren't what I meant about experiencing Brighton and you know it.'

'I'll cancel, shall I? We can go out with your friends,' she said pointedly, pouting at herself in the mirror.

Touché.

'I didn't mind when Adam was around... but now it's just a bunch of people. I don't like making small talk.'

'You barely came when Adam was alive,' Imogen muttered.

'Besides, who has a dinner party on a Sunday?' Gavin draped his towel around his neck and walked over to his underwear drawer.

'I told you, Louise's friend Natalie couldn't make it last night and she really wants us to meet her.'

'She was probably trying to get out of it as well.'

'Get dressed and shut up, will you?'

'But it's a Sunday. Nobody can get pissed or let their hair down properly on a Sunday, can they?'

'I'm sure you'll manage.'

'What's that supposed to mean?'

'Nothing, I'm just saying. Anyway, we should enjoy it while we can because the way you're going, we won't be able to afford to go out soon.'

'This again. I told you, the business has taken a downturn, nobody is getting their bonuses.'

Gavin had told this lie so many times over the past months, it tripped off his tongue with ease.

'Even Greg the wonder boy?' Imogen continued.

'What?' Gavin shivered, goosebumps covering his flesh as the lingering warmth from the shower gave way to the cool evening air of their bedroom.

'Greg. Your nemesis,' Imogen said, putting the finishing touches to her eyeliner.

'Even Greg,' Gavin replied.

Imogen glanced at him for a moment, letting her eyes wander down his naked body in a way she hadn't done for years.

'Are you sure everything is okay?'

There was a softness he'd forgotten she was capable of in her voice, if only for a moment. 'You've cut off my credit cards, told me I can't shop in Waitrose anymore. I'm worried, Gavin.'

'It must be terrible for you to have to use Sainsbury's now and then,' he said sardonically.

'Daddy,' Tim interrupted, appearing in the bedroom doorway. 'Why can't I come with you and have a sleepover with Matthew?' he used his best whiny tone, the one reserved for life's most unfair situations like not being allowed a packet of chocolate buttons or being told he couldn't stay up late playing Minecraft on a school night.

'We've been through this.' Gavin, still naked, walked over to Tim and crouched down to his level. 'We'll see if you can have a playdate soon, but you've got school tomorrow.'

'Put some clothes on will you, Gavin. Neither of us need to see your hairy appendages before dinner.'

'I'll wax it all off like you, shall I?'

Imogen rushed over to Tim, covering his ears.

'Not in front of Tim, Gavin. I don't know what's wrong with you sometimes.'

'Then maybe you should ask,' Gavin snapped, walking over to his underwear drawer and getting a pair of tight-fitting boxer shorts out.

'I just did. You ignored me. You can't have it both ways.' She took her hands away from Tim's ears. 'You can have a playdate with Matthew soon, sweetheart. But can you go and get your jim jams on for me now?'

'Look, big man,' Gavin interrupted. 'We'll arrange a playdate next week, okay?'

Tim nodded and turned away.

'Karen is babysitting tonight,' Imogen called after him.

'Not Karen,' Tim moaned, turning back and flapping his arms. Karen had been his keyworker at nursery and knew him back to front. Whereas other babysitters couldn't cope and ended up still trying to get him to bed at 11pm, Karen took no shit and had him in bed by 7.30. Gavin loved her for it.

'Why? What's wrong with Karen?' Imogen said, a slight panic in her voice, obviously imagining some previously unreported neglect or abuse from their favoured sitter.

'She makes me go to bed at, like, 5 o'clock,' Tim drawled, dragging his feet along the corridor to his bedroom to find his pyjamas.

Like clockwork, less than thirty seconds later:

'Muuuum, I can't find my pyjamas,' he shouted.

'Okay. love, I'll get them for you, hold on,' Imogen shouted back.

'He's 8 years old, Imogen. His pyjamas are in the drawer they're always in. Let him get them for himself.'

'What's your problem with me doing things for him, Gavin? It doesn't hurt.'

'He'll never feel any kind of self-worth if he's not allowed to

181

actually do something for himself.'

'Oh, shut up, Gavin. What kind of tree hugging self-help book did you get that from?'

'Jesus, Imogen, it's not tree-hugging it's just...'

'Someone's been filling your head with these ideas, haven't they? Who is it?'

'What?' Gavin turned his back on Imogen, heart punching his chest again, again, again, remembering lying with Steve behind the gravestones, guilt spiking him before he pushed it away, locking it down before it could take hold. He walked over to the wardrobe to get his shirt, controlling his breathing before he spoke to make sure there was no hidden cadence in his voice that might give him away.

'Don't be ridiculous,' he said, keeping his voice even.

'It's not like you, that's all,' Imogen said quietly.

'Come on, love, when would I have time for an affair with my job?'

'You had time to friend Steve on Facebook,' Imogen said coldly, slipping a diamond encrusted bracelet on her wrist and turning around to present her back to him. He zipped her up and they continued to dress in silence.

'Don't you think you're a little overdressed for Louise's house?' Gavin said eventually.

Imogen shot him a withering glance and pushed past him and walked out of their bedroom towards Tim's room.

'Let me help you find your pyjamas, sweetheart.'

~ Chapter 19 ~

Louise, Matthew and Maria still lived in the house they'd shared with Adam. Gavin always wondered how that felt for them. Did they feel closer to him, somehow? Or were they locked in a prison of daily reminders, knocking them back as they tried to move forward? He'd always wanted to ask her, to talk to her about Adam but he never knew what to say or how to bring it up. Besides, Imogen was Louise's friend, he was just the husband.

Their house was a ten-minute walk away but Imogen convinced Gavin to get a cab after the babysitter arrived. Anything to spend more money they didn't have. When they arrived on Louise's doorstep, they stood in silence.

'You okay?' Gavin asked, frowning. 'You didn't say a word in the cab.'

'Why wouldn't I be okay?' she replied, glancing at him with steely eyes. 'You haven't done anything that would make me not okay, have you?'

'Do you have to ruin the whole evening?' he started. 'Can't you just tell me what I've done wrong and I'll...'

At that moment, Louise flung open the front door, bottle of Prosecco in hand, ushering them all into the hall, kissing Imogen on the cheeks as she did so.

'I see you've upgraded from Cava to Prosecco,' Imogen said. Gavin had long ago lost any sense of perspective where his wife was concerned and couldn't work out whether she meant this as a playful and affectionate jibe, or if it was a barbed insult. From Imogen's mouth, it all sounded the same to him.

'Oh, fuck off,' Louise replied to her friend lightly, touching Gavin's arm gently in greeting. She'd clearly chosen to accept Imogen's comment as a joke, so he would too. Breathe deeply, ignore her. Talk to the other guests. Everything would be all right.

'You okay?' Louise said, glancing at him quizzically.

'Yeah,' he replied hastily, putting on his best smile. 'Looking forward to one of your roasts.'

'I'm not sure you've ever had one before,' she said. 'We might be calling for take out later if it all goes tits up.'

He couldn't help but notice how relaxed she was. So different to the woman she'd been when Adam was alive. He was sure she'd loved him but they hadn't been happy, that much was clear. It was awful to say but she seemed lighter without him, like she'd already shed some of the baggage he'd left her with. A part of Gavin, deep down in the hidden places he wouldn't acknowledge, felt envious of her. She'd found a freedom of sorts. Widowhood agreed with her.

'Natalie and Dan are in the living room,' Louise said, ushering them out of the hall and into the living room, holding the Prosecco bottle up. 'Go through and I'll get some drinks, Prosecco for you or a beer, Gavin?'

'Beer for now,' Gavin said.

'Gotcha,' Louise replied, wandering down the hall towards her kitchen. 'There are snacks out on the coffee table, help yourself.'

They walked into Louise's living room to find an attractive dark-haired woman and a tall ginger man already there.

'I'm Natalie,' the woman said, her northern accent dulled by years down south but still detectable. As she introduced herself to Imogen, Gavin studied her face, feeling a faint pang of recognition.

'Natalie,' Imogen said, smiling. 'We've met, in Louise's café? Lovely to see you again.'

'Yes, hi, it's Imogen, isn't it?' Natalie said, leaning in to give her a single kiss on the cheek, despite Imogen offering the other cheek as well. Natalie smiled at Gavin, the warmness of her gaze settling on him for a moment before freezing and turning to discomfort.

'Gavin,' he said, smiling. 'I recognise that accent, you're from near me, right? When did you move down south?'

'Years ago,' Natalie replied, nodding and looking quickly away.

'You look familiar, have we met?' he persevered.

'No,' she replied quickly.

'Right,' Gavin nodded. 'What town are you from because I could swear...'

'I'm Dan,' the tall, ginger man by her side interrupted and reached his hand out.

'Dan,' Gavin repeated, grasping the man's hand firmly. He was softly spoken but Gavin couldn't tell if this was because he was gentle or because he lacked confidence. Perhaps it was a little bit of both. He was friendly looking but there was something nervy about him that put Gavin on edge.

'Are you still doing that little bookkeeping job?' Imogen said to Natalie.

'I'm a Finance Director,' Natalie replied, not quite masking her indignation.

'Of course,' Imogen said, as if talking to a school child. 'I knew it was something like that. You met Louise at her bereavement group, didn't you?' she continued seamlessly. 'You lost your husband? You're so lucky to have found someone new so quickly.'

She scanned across from Natalie to look at Dan, dagger teeth smile.

'I...' Natalie started, clearly stuck for words.

'I suppose it's a lot easier nowadays, with all that swiping left. Or is it right?' she reached out and touched Gavin lightly on the arm, as if this was supposed to be pleasant or reassuring for him: a silent affirmation that she'd never use Tinder and didn't even understand its mechanisms.

'Fuck sake, Imogen,' Gavin muttered under his breath.

Natalie stared defiantly at Imogen but didn't respond as Imogen extended her hand out for Dan to take, the gesture of a woman who expected him to gently take her soft, manicured hand and kiss it. Dan didn't move, he simply clasped his own hands together nervously and started picking his fingernails, looking at the floor. A moment's more silence and Imogen turned on her heels and wafted from the living room to join Louise in the kitchen, shouting back over her shoulder: 'I'll help Louise with the drinks.'

Stilted silence followed, punctuated by the sound of Dan picking his fingernails.

'I'm sorry about her,' Gavin said awkwardly. 'She's not usually like this, I don't know what's got into her.'

Dan pursed his lips into an ineffective smile and Natalie flicked Gavin another uncomfortable glance. Gavin squeezed his lips together in apology and went after his wife, grabbing her by the arm in the hallway just as she reached the kitchen doorway.

'What's with you?' he hissed.

'What's with me? Oh, here we go. Terrible Imogen, everything's always my fault.'

'I don't see anyone else behaving like a dick, Imogen.'

'Don't you, Gavin?' she said, fixing him with a hard stare. He shifted uncomfortably under her gaze, breaking eye contact and looking at the floor.

'Go and mingle, Gavin,' she said, pulling her arm away and strutting into the kitchen. 'You could probably do with the company.'

'What's that supposed to mean?'

'I don't know, Gavin, what *is* it supposed to mean?'

'Fuck sake, will you just…' Gavin started.

'What's up?' Louise interrupted, catching Gavin's eye over Imogen's shoulder as she stood in the kitchen.

'What could possibly be up?' Imogen said, looking back at Gavin pointedly as she walked over to Louise.

'Have I missed something?' Gavin asked, leaning against the doorframe of the kitchen and trying to sound more relaxed than he was for Louise's benefit.

'Please, you two, not tonight. Can't we just have a nice dinner party, like the old days. I just... I could really do with a bit of normal.'

'Sorry,' he said instinctively. 'There's nothing that can't wait.'

Imogen stared at him stony-faced.

'Is there, Imogen?' he said, less certain by the second.

Later.

'Here,' Gavin handed over a bottle of beer to Dan and chinked it with his own. 'Louise said the starters won't be long.'

Louise hadn't said anything of the sort, but Gavin had no idea what else to say because Dan's awkwardness was off-putting. After a few moments of excruciating silence, Gavin continued with:

'I'm Gavin.'

'You said, yes,' Dan replied. Then, looking down at his bottle as if he'd remembered something vital, he said 'Oh, thanks. For the drink, I mean.'

'You okay, mate?' Gavin asked as tactfully as he could. 'I know Imogen was... well. She'll calm down.'

'It's not you,' Dan took a massive swig of beer and trailed off. It took another 10 or 20 seconds for Gavin to realise he wasn't actually going to finish the sentence.

'Right, okay. As long as it's just you, then,' Gavin joked. To his relief, Dan smiled and his shoulders dropped a little.

'I don't normally do parties. Even five people is pushing it for me...'

'Well, there's only four tonight, excluding you,' Gavin said.

Dan shifted uncomfortably from one foot to the next, looking back at the floor.

'You look familiar,' Dan said eventually, still not making eye contact but seemingly finding Louise's wooden floors fascinating.

'Really? I could swear I've seen Natalie before as well. Where do you live?'

'Seven Dials,' Dan said, 'near St Anne's Well.'

'Near us then.' Gavin glanced around the room, hoping someone else would join their stilted conversation and rescue him.

'I should get back to Natalie,' Dan said, looking over towards his girlfriend as she sat across the room, quietly sipping a Prosecco. 'She's on her own.'

'Okay.' Gavin downed the rest of his bottled beer in one. 'I'll see how Imogen and Louise are getting on with those starters.'

'No need.' Louise poked her head through the living room doorway breezily. 'I'm just serving now so if you all want to come next door into the dining room?'

As they ate, even Imogen seemed to relax a little and conversation began to flow more freely and Louise began topping Imogen's glass up with Prosecco instead of Champagne, giving Gavin a knowing wink as she did so.

Dan worked at a local agency down the road and Natalie was the finance director for a large tech company based near the train station. So far, so small talk. Gavin swigged back his beer, a little bored, wishing he'd stayed at home to watch Netflix instead of coming. Then:

'You're the only commuter here, Gavin,' Imogen said pointedly, popping the last of her starter into her mouth and staring at him. His heart swelled to twice its normal size and stopped beating, pushing further and further out of his chest until he was sure it would be visible to everyone at the table.

'Yeah, I guess I am,' he said, making every effort to sound nonchalant, trying desperately to think of a way to steer the conversation away from his job and commuting.

'Do you commute?' Dan said. 'I thought you worked locally.'

'I'd love to work locally.'

'Oh right. It's just, I've been trying to place you. You look just like this guy I saw running in the park the other day.'

Oh fuck.

'No, mate, not me,' Gavin said quickly.

'Looked just like you. Might have been on your day off or something.'

'Gavin doesn't have days off, do you, darling?' Imogen said pointedly.

Stony silence. Gavin stared down at the table and put his cutlery down. When he looked back up, everyone was staring at him, including Imogen, who had her teeth clenched shut.

'I'm always on that fucking train, aren't I,' he said, smiling his best fake smile. 'When would I have to time to run in the park?'

'My mistake,' Dan said. 'Everyone's got a doppelgänger, right? So they say. An alter ego.'

'Dan,' Natalie said, her tone one of concern. Gavin had almost forgotten she was there she'd been so quiet. 'That's enough, eh?'

The table descended into an uncomfortable silence and Louise pushed herself to her feet.

'Let me clear these plates and I'll serve the main course,' she said. 'It's lamb.'

'Here,' Gavin said, standing up and grabbing Dan and Natalie's plates and stacking them on top of his own, heart pummelling his chest. 'Let me help you.'

'Is everyone okay for drinks?' Louise said, fake breezily, as Gavin grabbed plates and cutlery clumsily, desperate to be out of the room, away from the conversation. 'There's red and white still on the table so help yourselves and shout if you want any more beer.'

'Oh, I doubt Gavin will want more to drink,' Imogen said, staring at him coldly. 'He has work in the morning. Don't you, darling?'

~ Chapter 20 ~

'What's up with her?' Louise asked, putting her pile of plates and cutlery down by the sink.

'Fuck knows,' Gavin sighed. 'Does she need a reason?'

'Something's on her mind, she's not normally this bad.'

Gavin shrugged, putting the plates down and leaning back against the fridge opposite Louise.

'Was that you Dan saw? In the park, I mean?'

Gavin's heart missed a beat.

'It's all a bit of a mess,' he said slowly.

'Want to talk about it?' She turned her back and started scraping plates into the bin, stacking them in the dishwasher after.

'Not really.' He clenched his jaw tightly. 'Talking doesn't help, does it.'

'The old me would have agreed but after Adam...' she drifted off, pausing mid plate-scrape. 'I don't know, I think talking might be the only thing that does help.'

'Even if it was,' Gavin said, touching her back lightly, 'you're Imogen's best friend. I can't talk to you, can I? You fraternise with the enemy.'

He walked over to the hob and stirred a pan of congealing gravy sitting on top.

'You want this warming up?' he asked. Louise nodded, but was clearly not ready to let go of the conversation that easily.

'Is that what she is?' Louise continued, shutting the dishwasher door and rinsing her hands under the tap. 'The enemy?'

'No, I'm being unfair. I've got myself into a situation that I don't know how to get out of, that's all.'

'Trust me, I'm not one to judge. We all make mistakes, Gavin, me more than most.'

'Thanks,' he said evasively.

'If you won't talk to me, talk to Imogen,' Louise said. She laid some warm plates out on the side as she spoke, beginning to serve vegetables and roast potatoes from the oven onto them. Gavin laughed, stirring the gravy as it warmed and loosened up, glancing back over his shoulder at her.

'You've met Imogen, right? Listening and empathising aren't really her thing. Not nowadays, anyway.'

'She might surprise you; she's been a life-saver for me after Adam, you know that.'

Louise pulled him away from the gravy and handed him a large knife and a massive two-pronged fork. He took them, standing mutely, not responding or moving.

'I'm serious,' Louise continued. 'Your wife gives good advice sometimes. Don't be so hard on her.'

'Really? Like when?'

Gavin put the overlarge knife and fork back down on the side.

'I couldn't have got through the past year without her.'

'She's different with you.'

'Why not give her a chance to be like it with you, then?'

'I've tried to talk to her so many times but it's like... I don't know. I think she hates me.'

'Don't be ridiculous.'

'I'm serious, there's no affection there anymore.'

'And from your side?'

'We've got a son together,' he countered.

'That's not enough, you know it isn't. How do *you* feel about her?'

He wanted to say *I don't love her anymore* but something in him overrode the emotion, told him it was the wrong thing. Louise was loyal to Imogen. All this chat, this support, meant nothing. He didn't doubt she meant well but when push came to shove, her best friend was just that. The two of them would close ranks. Honesty with Louise was not the best policy, no matter how genuine she seemed.

'Forget about it,' he said.

'A guy wanted to pay to sleep with me once,' Louise said out of the blue, her tone matter of fact, like she was telling him where she'd bought the lamb and roast potatoes.

'What?' Gavin half laughed, studying her face to see if she meant it or not. 'Are you serious?'

'Yeah,' she said, drifting off again, like she was replaying the event inside her mind. 'And I thought about it, you know? You only live once.'

'Jesus,' Gavin said, not moving, uncomfortable. 'What did you do?'

'He was a customer in the café, used to come in all the time. We'd shagged a couple of times but it wasn't that long after Adam so I didn't want a relationship.'

'So? What happened?'

'I told him I didn't want to see with him again, tried to remain friendly. But he got really angsty, couldn't take no for an answer. So many guys are like that. Take it so personally. They can't believe a woman could have the audacity to *not want them*. Anyway, he used to come in the café all the time. Got really jealous if I talked to any other guys, even customers. He'd make a scene, start ranting. Then one day, out of the blue, he offered to pay to have sex with me. I think he meant it as an insult, as a way of calling me a slag, you know?'

'He sounds like an arsehole.'

'He was. Is. But the next week, he came in and he was calmer, more normal. And he was all like "No, I'm serious, how about it? I miss you, I'll pay you". And... I thought about it. Is that terrible?' she stared at Gavin as if she was gauging his reaction, trying to see if he was judging her or not. 'It seemed a bit dangerous, you know, and even though I wasn't interested in him, that made it sexy, somehow.'

'Christ,' Gavin said. 'Did you do it?'

Louise laughed, leaning her head on his shoulder for a moment before continuing.

'Your wife talked me out of it. "Look at all the grief he caused you," she said. "You'll never meet someone nice if you do something like that."' Louise smiled again, walking over to the sink to wash her hands. 'My point is, maybe you should trust her more? She cares more than you think.'

'Fucking hell, Louise.' Gavin replied, not sure what he was supposed to say.

'Anyway,' Louise said thoughtfully. 'Turns out he wanted to piss on my face while his mate watched... once I knew that, it didn't seem so sexy anymore. It was hardly *Indecent Proposal*, was it?'

'Fucking hell, Louise,' Gavin repeated, laughing uncomfortably. As the sound came out of his mouth, it morphed into a weird concerned whimper. 'Seriously? Are you okay?'

'You get used to it,' she said. 'Men being wankers, I mean.'

'I bet you do,' Gavin said quietly, pursing his lips together and squeezing his own guilt down tightly.

'Anyway, the point is,' Louise continued, mock breezily, 'you have to decide whether you want to salvage things with Imogen before it's too late.'

'How was that the point of your story?' Gavin laughed. 'How was some random wanting to pay you to piss on your face supposed to make me want to open up to my wife?'

'I don't know,' Louise replied, smiling. 'It felt relevant when I started.'

'I think you went a little off-piste.'

'Stop changing the subject.'

'Technically, I think you were the one who changed the subject...'

'Are you going to talk to Imogen or not?'

'I don't know if she's still in there. The woman I met, I mean.'

'Of course she is. You have to want to find her, that's all.'

'And what if I don't? What then?'

They stood in silence, a compassionate moment of understanding settling over them.

'Right,' Louise said eventually, picking up the carving knife and fork again and shoving them back into Gavin's hands. 'Do the manly thing and slice the lamb will you, before everyone dies of hunger in there.'

He silently sliced the meat and Louise served it onto the plates.

'Grab that gravy from the hob and pour it into this measuring jug, will you?' she said.

'Don't you have a gravy boat?' Gavin asked, rinsing his hands and picking the measuring jug up, immediately dropping it onto the hob where it smashed, showering glass everywhere. 'Fuck! Shit, I'm so sorry.'

'Did glass go into the gravy?'

'I don't know… hold on.' Gavin opened Louise's cupboards until he found a sieve while Louise picked up the larger bits of glass and wiped down the sides before grabbing the dustpan and brush from under the sink. Gavin took the gravy saucepan from the hob and, holding the sieve over the sink, he poured the gravy into it. Louise came to join him, standing by his side with dustpan and brush in hand, staring as the gravy drained away down the plughole.

'You're a fucking imbecile, aren't you,' she said.

'What?' he said, staring down at the sieve in his hands, full of broken bits of glass.

'You've drained the gravy and kept the glass,' Louise clarified.

'Oh,' Gavin said quietly.

'What are we supposed to do?' she said, a smile breaking out across her face. 'Sprinkle glass over the lamb?'

'Not everyone's.' Gavin smiled. 'Maybe Imogen's?'

'Don't.'

Louise slid down the side of the kitchen cabinet to sit on the floor, the dustpan and brush still in her hands. 'Why do I do these dinner parties? They're always a disaster.'

'Memorable, though.'

Gavin dropped the sieve in the sink and slid down to sit next to her.

'What would you know? You miss half of them. Even before Adam died you didn't come,' she said, staring at the glass shards in the dustpan, clearly losing herself in thoughts of her dead husband.

She was right, he had missed a lot of their dinner parties. Sometimes because he and Imogen had been arguing, latterly because he'd felt uncomfortable around Adam.

'Were you and Adam happy?' he asked. Louise didn't reply but instead moved imperceptibly to the left so her shoulder was no longer leaning against his.

'Sometimes,' she said. 'No couples are happy all the time, are they?'

'No, I guess not,' Gavin replied quietly. 'Do you miss him?'

He wasn't sure whether he was supposed to or not but now he had, he felt like he had a million questions.

'Yes,' she said simply, clutching the dustpan full of broken glass a little more tightly.

'You're doing really well,' Gavin started, trying to think of something else to say, something better. The look in her eyes told him to stop. She was clearly only doing really well at making it seem like she was doing really well and that wasn't the same thing at all.

'I tried to kill myself once,' she said simply. Gavin swallowed hard, not sure what to say or how to say it. 'Before Adam succeeded, I tried and failed. He stopped me.'

'Jesus...' he started, then clamped his mouth shut.

'It's okay.' She glanced at him, clearly aware she'd made him uncomfortable. 'I... well. I didn't stop *him*, did I? He saved *me* but when he needed me to save him, I let him down.'

'You can't blame yourself.'

'I took a bottle of pills,' she continued, staring ahead, glazed over. 'Adam found me, took me to hospital, got my stomach pumped. As soon as I came around I knew I'd made a mistake, knew I didn't really want to die. But he never got the chance to find that out, did he? Because I didn't get to him in time to stop him.'

Her voice was quiet, almost like she was talking to herself and not to him.

'If I'd been better, kinder, less wrapped up in myself...'

'I don't think it works that way,' Gavin said gently, feeling completely out of his depth. 'He was struggling with losing his brother, his twin. We both know he never got over Tom, not really. You don't do something like he did if you're in a healthy state of mind.'

'I know that up here,' she said, tapping her temple. 'But I don't feel that in here,' she continued, tapping her chest.

Gavin started at her silently, not sure what to say or how to make her feel better.

'Sorry,' she said. 'Didn't mean to get melancholy. Sometimes it just comes over me. I think I'm fine and then *wham*, I'm drowning in it again.'

'I know that feeling,' Gavin said. 'Not the grief. The drowning, I mean.'

He paused, searching her troubled face and regretting his words.

'I'm sorry, I shouldn't have brought Adam up, I just...'

'No,' she said, pushing herself back up and emptying the last of the glass into the bin and surveying the gravy-less plates on the side. 'To be honest, I like it when people mention him. Too many people think the best thing to do is pretend he never existed.'

'Does Imogen help? I mean, do you talk to her?'

'She distracts me and she'd do anything for me. It's all a front with her, the bitching and moaning. You know that.'

'I used to,' Gavin said. 'I'm not so sure anymore. I think she might be dead inside.'

'Christ, you're so dramatic,' Louise said, rinsing her hands. 'You know she loves you.'

'Maybe I made her like she is? You didn't know her before. When we met, she was so different.'

'Was she? Really?'

'I think so.'

'I'm not so sure we change that much, not really.'

'I think we do,' Gavin said, picking up two of the plates from the side. 'At least, I think we can. I have to believe that.'

'Look, I've got no idea what's going on with you, but talking to Imogen has got to be better than holding it all in, hasn't it?'

'I'll guess I'll find out, won't I?' he said, grabbing a couple of plates from the side. She nodded at him and they held each other with a look for a moment before Louise said:

'Right. Let's serve this main course before it's freezing cold, shall we? I've got some mint sauce somewhere, that'll do instead of gravy, won't it?'

Gavin and Louise served the gravy-less main course and dinner drifted into dessert, all accompanied by mildly pleasant but dull conversation that Gavin neither engaged with nor ignored. He spoke when it felt relevant, fell silent when he could get away with it.

At some point after pudding, Gavin found himself standing in the garden with Dan, their gender drawing them together in the same way their wife and girlfriend had drawn together with Louise in the living room. Gavin couldn't help feeling he'd have had more interesting conversations with the women but it was an unspoken rule that this wasn't entirely appropriate.

'I should find Natalie,' Dan said anxiously, fingering the label of his beer bottle. 'We ought to get off soon, work in the morning.'

They descended into uneasy silence.

'So, how did you and Natalie meet?'

'I was homeless,' Dan replied, making Gavin choke on his drink.

'Are you serious?' Gavin exclaimed, unable to contain his joy that Dan had broken dinner party small talk protocol.

'When I met Natalie, I mean,' Dan continued, kicking his feet and staring at the ground, almost adolescently.

Dan made eye contact with Gavin for the first time and he realised something strange. Dan's eyes weren't the same colour. One was blue and one was brown.

'Wow!' Gavin said, flustered. 'I mean... I don't mean wow like that, I just mean... I don't know. Someone with an actual story that isn't, "My name's Brian and I work for an insurance company."'

'Do you know anyone called Brian?' Dan asked, deadpan.

'That's not what I meant.' Gavin squirmed, unsure if Dan was serious or not. 'I just meant you've got a real story.'

'Right,' Dan said, shifting awkwardly and stroking his glass manically with his finger, over and over again. 'It's not a story, though, Gavin. It's my life.'

'Look...' Gavin tried, unsure what to say and terrified of continuing to dig the already deep hole he was in.

'It's okay, I didn't mean to make things awkward,' Dan said, trailing off again. Another mind-chilling silence.

'How did you meet her?' Gavin said. 'If you don't mind me asking? If you were homeless? Did she work in a shelter or a soup kitchen or something?'

'A soup kitchen?'

'Well, I don't know, they have soup kitchens, don't they?

Aren't they a thing?'

'They have soup kitchens, yes,' Dan said, smiling. 'Sort of. But that's not where I met her. It's a long story, to be honest, probably not something for a Sunday night dinner.'

'Ah come on, mate, you can't stop there, I'm intrigued now.'

'Honestly, it's complicated. Another time, maybe.'

Gavin was about to probe him more fully when Imogen came sashaying through the open patio doors out into the twilight of the garden, champagne glass filled with Prosecco swinging between her fingers.

'So, this is where you're hiding,' she said. 'Man talk is it?'

'Not anymore it isn't,' Gavin replied, irritated.

'I was just telling Gavin how I met Natalie,' Dan said quietly as Imogen stared at him coldly.

'Were you?'

'Yeah, but I shouldn't have said anything,' Dan looked immediately uncomfortable. 'I'm not very good at... Chat. Never know what's appropriate.'

'Mate, don't be silly,' Gavin said. 'I'd like to hear about it.'

'Patronising much, Gavin?' Imogen slurred.

'For Christ's sake, Imogen!' Gavin snapped. She held his gaze, swaying slightly before swigging back another mouthful of her drink.

'I should find Natalie,' Dan said again.

'I'm sure we don't know the half of it, do we, Dan?' Imogen said, smiling with no warmth at all.

'I need the toilet.' Gavin said, turning his back on his wife and heading back inside to avoid the anger bubbling away inside of him.

After a long, alcohol-fuelled piss, Gavin washed his hands and stared at his reflection in Louise's bathroom mirror. Eyes slightly bloodshot, but otherwise no outward signs of inner turmoil. He knew he had to tell Imogen what had been going on since he quit his job but he couldn't be anywhere near her without an unexpected fury rising in his stomach. Also, she was in a mood tonight, it wasn't the right time. He was sure if he thought long enough, he could find a lot of other excuses. Tomorrow then. Or another day.

Opening the bathroom door, he walked back into the dimly lit hallway, bumping into Natalie as he did so.

'Shhh,' he said, smiling. 'Maria and Matthew are asleep.'

He nodded towards the children's bedrooms behind Natalie.

'Stay away from me,' she hissed, pushing him backwards.

'What?' he started, frowning.

'I mean it,' she said, rushing past him into the toilet and slamming and locking the door behind her.

~ Chapter 21 ~

'There he is,' Imogen crowed as Gavin walked back into the living room, still perturbed by Natalie's performance upstairs.

'Oh shut up, will you,' he said, pursing his lips in apology and looking at Dan and Louise in turn. Silence enveloped the room as they all stood awkwardly sipping their drinks. When Natalie came back down, she deliberately avoided eye contact with Gavin and walked over to Dan, taking him by the hand.

'I think we should go,' she said.

'Okay,' he replied, the relief visibly escaping his body, taking it from rigid statue to rag doll.

'So, husband,' Imogen said darkly. 'Tell me about work. Busy at the moment?'

'What's wrong with you tonight?' Gavin said quietly, taking Imogen's arm and trying to draw her to one side.

'What's wrong with me?' she said, shaking his arm off, clearly intent on performing to the room. 'You don't need me to tell you, I'm sure everyone in this room has an opinion on what's wrong with me.'

'You're drunk,' he said. 'We should go.'

'Do you think I don't know what people say about me?' she said, still twirling, glass held high in the air. 'That I've got this perfect life. Money, adoring husband and son.'

'Trust me, that's not what they say about you...' he started.

'Well, my life isn't perfect. *You're* not perfect.'

She jabbed Gavin hard in the chest, spitting the word 'perfect' out and wobbling, unsteady on her feet. The room around them hushed, all eyes on them.

'This isn't the place,' Gavin said, trying to keep his voice calm.

'Then where is, Gavin?' she said, her voice trailing off into a whisper as she made eye contact with him.

'There are things we need to discuss,' he replied softly. 'But not here, eh?'

'He doesn't love me,' she said loudly, making everyone visibly uncomfortable, so much so they seemed to step back into the shadows a little, distancing themselves for what should have been a private moment. 'Actually, he's never loved me.'

'And you think she loves me?' Gavin spat, ashamed that he'd been drawn into her game, that he too was addressing the room and not his wife directly.

'I've always loved you,' Imogen said quietly, almost like she meant it.

'No, you haven't,' Gavin said, reaching out and placing a hand on each of Imogen's shoulders, which she instantly shook off. 'You love the idea of me, that's not the same thing.'

Imogen snorted, not with humour, with distaste. 'I didn't make you go into denial, Gavin, you did that all by yourself.'

'Oh, here we go,' he shouted, feeling the full weight of the room's eyes, eating into his back, burrowing deep into his flesh.

'I was a rebound, you see,' Imogen said, looking from Natalie to Louise and nodding. 'Nothing more. A woman to hide behind.'

'That's bullshit and you know it.'

'Well, you're still Facebook friends with him,' she sneered. 'Couldn't quite manage to click *unfriend*, could you?'

'Oh for fuck's sake, Imogen, I haven't even spoken to him.'

'You like every picture he puts up though, don't you?'

'I had a relationship before you, so what? You were hardly an angel before you met me, quite the opposite in fact...'

'You were still in love with him when we met.'

'But I married you!'

'You never loved me!'

'Not because I loved Steve,' Gavin shouted, 'because you're not that lovable!'

Gavin could feel the room holding its breath around him, all of them learning something private, something that wasn't their business to learn. For some reason, mention of Steve was like pressing hard on a fresh bruise, even after all those years. Steve was *his* past, *his* story, it wasn't her secret to tell and he was furious.

'Oh, don't worry,' she said, barely whispering. 'Whether you're gay or not is the least of my worries right now.'

'What are you talking about?'

'I know, Gavin,' she said pointedly, her voice pitchy, uneven.

'What?' Gavin mouthed, dry lips sticking to his gums.

'Who else knows?' Imogen screeched, her voice octaves higher than normal.

'Knows what?' Gavin was light-headed, unbalanced. His anger from moments before replaced with fear and panic, a wash of emotions, each fighting for supremacy, none individually identifiable.

'You know what!' Imogen spat. 'Does everybody else know what a fool you've been making of me?'

'I haven't been making a fool of you, I don't know what you mean...'

'My uncle called me, Gavin!' Imogen shouted. 'Do they all know? Do they?'

Imogen swept her arm around the living room as everyone stood sheepishly, eyes averted but still listening, obviously still listening because it was impossible not to.

'Let's face it, you certainly don't talk to me anymore! You spent hours in the kitchen with Louise earlier, chatting away. When was the last time you talked to me?'

'When was the last time you listened?' Gavin shouted back.

Without warning, Imogen launched herself at him, nails bared, gouging at his face, leaving him stinging, wet with blood. He frantically grabbed her wrists to stop her attack. Somewhere in the background he could hear Louise telling Imogen to calm down, to listen to his explanation.

'Stay out of it, Louise,' Imogen screamed. 'I don't need relationship advice from the black widow. How many have you buried now? Two? Three? I can never keep up...'

'That's out of order,' Gavin said, letting go of Imogen's arms as she collapsed back against the wall, wiping the snot from her nose. 'Louise hasn't done anything.'

'Out of order?' Imogen looked around the room for support, her face smeared not only with snot but with Gavin's blood. 'There always has to be a drama at your parties, Louise, doesn't there? Remember when you invited that gay mechanic around? You'd have *loved* him Gavin, shame you missed that one.'

'That's enough, Imogen,' Louise said coldly.

'I haven't even got started,' Imogen continued, barely drawing breath. 'He quit his job, did you know that? Not today, oh no. Not last week. Not last month, even.'

She started laughing emptily, humourlessly, until it gradually turned into sobs.

'Six months ago.'

Her arms dropped down to her sides and she leaned back against the living room wall again, smudged black tracks from her eyes meeting the blood and snot on her cheeks as she stared at Gavin accusingly.

'What?' Louise said, looking at Gavin quizzically. 'You can't have, you didn't say...'

'And he didn't tell you?' Natalie piped up from across the room. 'Standard Gavin, I guess.'

'What the fuck would you know?' Gavin frowned, shooting Natalie a cold frown, irritated with her interjection.

'I wanted to tell you,' he continued desperately, looking back at Imogen.

'The credit cards, the belt tightening, it all makes sense now. You could have just told me!'

'I wasn't making my bonuses, anyway, I wasn't selling

anything. Nobody was. Brexit uncertainty meant nobody was making any decisions, clients weren't signing, it was a nightmare. Got so I couldn't sleep at night.'

'So you quit?' she said, voice getting louder with every syllable. 'You gave up and lied to me? Pretended to go to work every day hoping I'd never find out?'

'It wasn't like that,' Gavin implored, struggling to find the words to explain.

'Then what was it like, Gavin?'

'I was suffocating. I either had to hold my breath and jump like Adam or...' he trailed off, shocked by his own words, looking guiltily sideways at Louise, who had raised her hand to cover her mouth.

'Louise, I'm sorry,' he fumbled. 'I shouldn't have said that, I...'

'It's okay,' she said quickly, nodding. 'Honestly, it's okay.'

'Okay? None of this is okay!' Imogen said, not quite talking, not quite shouting.

'I wanted to tell you,' Gavin repeated uselessly.

'You have to get it back,' she said coldly.

'What?'

'Your job.'

'No, that's not... I'm not. I've got a plan, an idea for a business, I...'

'I'm not putting up with...'

'Will you just listen to me?' Gavin reached out to grab her arm, frustration and shame and anger all fusing into one single, red-hot emotion.

'Get your job back. If you don't, you'll lose everything,' Imogen shirked him off, refusing to let him touch her.

'Don't be...'

'Don't tell me what to be, you've lost that right. Sort this Gavin or we're over.'

He fell into silence, his arm dropping back limply by his side.

'I didn't mean to lie to you, Imogen. I know I made a mistake but...'

'Bullshit,' she snarled. 'You don't accidentally lie for six fucking months, Gavin!'

'I wasn't okay, Imogen, don't you understand? I'm not okay.'

'Everyone finds life difficult, Gavin! Get your job back because I swear if you don't, I'll get custody of Tim, I'll get the house. You'll be lucky if you even see him every other weekend. Mind you, that wouldn't make a difference, would it?'

'Christ, Imogen,' Gavin squirmed. 'What happened to you?'

'You did, Gavin.'

She drew the words out, stretching and contorting them in disgust. The room around them wasn't breathing, it was held on pause, juddering, out of focus.

'It's about time you grew up.'

'Time *I* grew up? What about you? Sitting there refusing to get a job like a 1950s housewife while I'm drowning alongside you, doing the job you made me take when you knew I'd hate it. If you think you're blameless in all of this, think again.'

'Oh, cos your shitty photography was going to keep us in the lap of luxury, was it? You never had any talent, Gavin! Everyone was just too polite to tell you.'

'Oh, here she is,' Gavin sneered, sweeping his arms around, looking at everyone else in the room. 'Meet the real Imogen everyone, meet the woman I live with!'

'You had to get a proper job, Gavin,' Imogen continued hotly. 'We weren't kids anymore.'

'We got by. We were happy!'

'No, we weren't, at least I wasn't. I wanted more.'

'Then you should have got it! You got a better degree than I did, you've always been smarter than me, why did I have to go and work for your fucking uncle?'

'Because I was having a baby, Gavin!'

'There were other options, Adam used to look after the kids

while Louise went to work.'

'Well look what happened to him!' Imogen shouted, her hand covering her mouth almost instantly, as she shot a look at Louise. 'Christ, I'm sorry, I didn't mean that.'

Louise stood stock still, mouth clenched shut.

'Take your argument home, you two,' she said eventually.

'We could have worked through all of this together,' Gavin continued, trying to keep his voice more level instead of shouting. 'All I'm saying is, I never wanted your uncle's job. You made me take it anyway.'

'You're a grown man, Gavin, you could have said no,' Imogen replied quietly.

'You know that wasn't an option,' Gavin said.

'So, it's all my fault, is it?'

'I'm not saying that, but...'

'Fuck you, Gavin!' Imogen said, tears streaming down her face. She turned and ran out of the living room and up Louise's stairs, slamming one of the bedroom doors behind her.

'I'll go after her,' Louise said wearily. 'I think maybe it's a good idea if you all leave.'

~ Chapter 22 ~

Gavin sat in one of Louise's armchairs and held a piece of kitchen roll to his cheek, stemming the flow of blood where Imogen had scratched him. Dan stood awkwardly in the doorway as Natalie walked towards Gavin, a strange look on her face, not quite hatred but something not far off.

'You haven't changed at all, have you?' she said.

'What?'

'You and Steve, though?' Natalie continued. 'I'd never have guessed, not in a million years. Not after what you did to me.'

Gavin's heart stopped beating as his chest and stomach contracted, crushing his internal organs moment by moment as he made eye contact with her.

Nat.

'You're Nat,' he said eventually, letting his hand with the tissue drop from his face, allowing the blood to trickle down.

'I'm Natalie,' she replied coldly.

'Look, Nat,' Gavin started, his entire body running cold.

'Natalie,' she corrected again, furiously. 'Nobody calls me Nat anymore.'

'Look,' he repeated, trailing off.

'She's going to leave you,' Natalie continued, standing in front of the armchair he sat in, looming over him, making him feel small, powerless. 'I know it's hard for men like you to understand but she's clearly done with your bullshit.'

'Look,' Gavin repeated for a third time. 'My marriage isn't any of your business.'

'You just made it our business, didn't you?'

Gavin took the tissue away from his cheek to inspect the blood, then pressed it back against the wound silently.

'I mean, don't get me wrong, she seems like a nasty bitch,' Natalie continued, venom in her voice. 'But that doesn't mean she deserves you.'

'Natalie?' Dan questioned, clearly shocked, taking a step towards his girlfriend.

'Just a minute, Dan,' she said without turning to face him. Dutifully, he did so.

'Do you remember what you did?' she said slowly, deliberately.

'We were teenagers. I know I was a dick but...'

Gavin ran his hand through his hair. He wanted her and Dan to leave, he wanted Imogen and Louise to come back downstairs, he wanted to go home with his wife and explain everything to her, to make things right. Couldn't Natalie see this wasn't the time for this?

'Do you still see Steve?' Natalie asked, her accent softened by years in the south like his own, but still recognisable, still a lynchpin to a past they shared. 'You were always in each other's pockets but I never would have guessed you were fucking.'

'We weren't fucking,' Gavin started, shaking his head. 'Look, I'm sorry for treating you like I did,' he replied. 'But it was a long time ago and in case you hadn't noticed, I've got other shit going on.'

'Is that it?' she said coldly, holding his gaze.

'I called you frigid,' Gavin said, shame rising in him as the words came out. 'Shamed you in front of everyone. I shouldn't have done it but it was 20 fucking years ago, Nat.'

'Is that it?' she repeated, her face waxwork.

'I didn't want anyone to know about me and Steve and... Look, I'm not proud of it. You know it's not what I was like. We were teenagers, I made a mistake Steve was really pissed off with me, he...'

'Steve?' she interrupted, her face melting into anger again. 'You're sorry because *Steve* was pissed off with you?'

'It was nothing to do with you, I wanted to impress the lads, that's all.'

'So you assaulted me to impress the lads?' Her voice warbled slightly as the words came out, followed by tears which she furiously rubbed from her cheeks, as if their very presence had betrayed her.

Gavin dropped the tissue from his cheek and stared dumbly at Natalie, pushing back in his armchair, physically wanting to be further away from her, to distance himself from her and the accusation.

'That's not what happened. We kissed, we fumbled around a bit, you said you wanted to stop and we stopped.'

'I *made* you stop,' she said tersely. 'If I hadn't, I don't think you would have done.'

'That's not what happened,' he repeated, doubt already creeping in. 'It wasn't like that.'

'I'd barely kissed a boy before you,' she said. 'After the camping trip and how kind you were... when I saw you at the party, I was so excited. But it was like you were possessed, hands all over me. Kissing wasn't enough, we had to go into the toilet. You were groping me and...'

'We were teenagers!' Gavin interrupted. 'That's what *everyone* was doing! It's what we were *supposed* to be doing, wasn't it?'

'You put your finger inside me, Gavin,' she shouted, flicking a look over her shoulder at Dan guiltily.

'I thought you wanted me to! That's what we were there for, wasn't it?' Gavin's conviction was wavering as he stared at her horrified face. Whatever else was happening, this was her truth, he had no doubt.

'We were just kids, Nat, I...' he continued, voice quietening to a whisper before trailing off.

'You keep saying that like it means something,' she spat, face flushed with emotion, anger, hurt, fear. Christ, fear. Despite being a grown woman there was a part of her that was *scared* of him.

'I didn't know,' he whispered, realising how empty it

sounded but not knowing what else to say. He held his hands in the air, palms out towards her, as if to prove he wasn't a threat, that he wasn't going to do her any harm. 'I'd never hurt anyone.'

'But you did, Gavin.'

He squeezed his eyes shut, desperately trying to replay the events of that long-ago evening in his mind. He didn't remember it the way she did. He'd been drinking, he'd been focused on Steve, on the gang. She'd barely been important at all. How terrible was that? Here she was, still damaged all these years later and apart from his shame at humiliating her, he'd barely remembered it.

'I'm sorry,' he said eventually. 'I know that's empty, that it doesn't take anything back. I didn't know,' he fumbled uselessly. 'I didn't realise.'

'I had to shove you off of me!' she said.

'I didn't know how to behave with a girl, I thought I was supposed to... I don't know. Take charge.'

'Bullshit.'

'I'm not making excuses,' he said, swallowing hard against his heaving stomach. 'I didn't have a clue what I was doing, I was scared, you'd think I was...'

'I felt violated,' she said, her voice low, measured. 'I *was* violated.'

Gavin pressed his palms hard into his eye sockets, wanting the pain, needing it.

'I'm sorry,' he said again, unsure what else to say. Part of him was desperate for absolution, was selfishly desperate for her to tell him she understood he hadn't meant it. The other part knew it wasn't about him, that she needed to expunge her demons in his direction.

'I need to hear you say it,' she said, some of the fire extinguished from her voice.

'What?'

'That you understand what you did.'

Everything had slowed around him except his breathing which was fast and erratic. Red and black smudges of light surrounded the edges of his vision where he'd been pressing his palms into his eyes and he was dizzy, rooted in unreality. He knew he'd been trying to impress Jamie, Michael and the gang that night, knew he'd been an arsehole but never in his wildest imaginings could he have known he'd treated her so badly.

'I understand,' he said quietly, trying to focus on her.

'You treated me like I was nothing,' she said. Her face hadn't softened, the pain was still there but something was lifting. 'You were the first to treat me like that,' she continued, 'but believe me, you weren't the last. Turns out, most guys just take what they want.'

It wasn't like that, Gavin wanted to shout, but his deeper self knew he couldn't. It *had* been like that. All he'd been thinking about was himself, proving himself, trying to be *a man*. Gut churning guilt, self-hatred. He clamped his mouth shut to make sure his defensive self didn't take over, didn't start speaking for him because he couldn't allow that, wouldn't allow it. The only thing he had to offer by way of atonement was silence and acceptance.

'What can I do?' he said eventually.

'It's done, Gavin.'

'I thought it was just a pissed fumble...' he started.

'Don't you get it? That makes it worse,' she said, voice raising again, just a little. 'If you didn't even know you were doing it, what else have you done since?'

'Jesus, nothing! I'm not like that.'

Gavin let silence envelop the room again, thinking about Imogen, the only woman he'd ever slept with, his only true sexual partner, always taking the lead, always in charge.

'I'm sorry,' he repeated. 'You have to believe me.'

'I don't have to do anything.'

'I didn't mean...' he swallowed back a round of vomit as it

rose in his throat.

'Your face is still bleeding,' Natalie said, leaning down and picking up his discarded tissue and offering it back to him. He took it silently without making eye contact again, pressing it against his face.

Breathe in. Hold it.

Breathe out. Hold it.

His mouth was dry. He clutched the side of the armchair. His breathing was a little too fast and he couldn't stop trying to take in large gulps of air over and over and over.

'Natalie, we should leave,' Dan's voice muttered, a million miles away.

'Dan, I need to resolve this,' Natalie said quietly.

'I *am* sorry,' Gavin said, 'for what...' he paused, swallowing the words he was about to say: *for what happened.* 'For what I did to you.'

'I told a teacher, you know,' Natalie said slowly. 'After Ursula's party.'

'What?' Gavin said, frowning. 'Nobody said anything to me.'

'Of course they didn't. You were just doing what teenage boys did, apparently. She told me I shouldn't have been so naïve. I believed her, that's the worst part. For such a long time, I believed her. I'd kissed you; I'd gone into that bathroom with you. And it was just a finger, nothing major, right? No big deal, it was nothing.'

'It wasn't nothing.'

'I know it wasn't,' she snapped, raising her voice slightly. 'It took me a long time to know that, but *I do know.* That's not what I need from you.'

An impasse wrapped a cold silence around them.

'What *do* you need from me?' Gavin asked.

'The truth.'

'You could have been anyone,' Gavin said awkwardly. His mouth was completely dry, his tongue scratchy against his teeth as the words came out. Natalie stared at him coldly but he could see she needed his words, even if she didn't want them.

'I was desperate to prove something to the guys... to prove something to myself, really. And after our camping trip, I knew you liked me and...'

He trailed off, not sure what he was saying, the words falling out, one after the other.

'Any girl would have done, that's the truth of it. It was nothing to do with you.'

'Is that supposed to make me feel better?' she asked.

'You asked for the truth,' he said. 'I didn't realise what I'd done or how you felt but I'm not denying it.'

He paused.

'They bet me a fiver I couldn't finger you.'

She remained silent, a statue.

'A bet,' she said slowly, face flushing. He nodded, shame colouring his cheeks.

'I was going through the motions, doing the things I thought I was supposed to do and...' he stopped talking, aware he was dangerously close to trying to justify himself.

'You didn't even fancy me?'

'I did but that wasn't the point. I was trying to prove something. It was nothing to do with you. It's complicated.'

'It's not complicated at all,' Natalie said coldly, clenching her jaw tightly, skin white-purple. 'You didn't want anyone to think you were gay, so you fingered me and told everyone I was frigid. Do you know how long that stuck? It wasn't even the guys from home, I could have escaped that. Some of the boys from school went to the same Uni as me, they labelled me frigid there, I couldn't even start fresh.'

'I'm sorry,' he said again, not sure what words could make any of this better.

'Good,' she replied, nodding. 'You should be.'

'I didn't mean to hurt you like that,' Gavin continued. 'I was a dick.'

'I thought I'd hate you,' she said quietly. 'I thought if I ever saw you again, I'd... I don't know. I don't hate you... It would be easier if I could, to be honest.'

Gavin nodded quietly, swallowing hard.

'If you want to make a difference, try and raise that son of yours right,' she said, turning her back on him, grabbing Dan by the hand and walking out of the living room. 'Teach him a thing or two about consent.'

With that, she walked into the hallway, dragging Dan behind her, and she was gone, slamming the front door as she went.

~ Chapter 23 ~

'Do you hate me?' Gavin asks, staring at Jackie intently. Jackie doesn't speak for a moment, squeezing her eyes shut behind her sunglasses.

'What you did wasn't okay,' she begins slowly, taking deep breaths.

'I know,' Gavin says, holding his hands up. 'I'm not asking for absolution, I'm not.'

'There are levels, though, Gavin. That librarian I told you about, the one who used to... you know... with my knickers. He was a predator. It makes me sick to think that I normalised what he did to me and how he behaved. How many other girls did he do that to because I didn't speak up?'

'Jesus, Jackie, it wasn't your fault...'

'Thing is, Gavin, Natalie said she didn't think you were going to stop, but you did. You did stop,' Jackie says, breathing deeply, every fibre of her being working to offer him the same kindness he'd offered her: no judgement.

'Being young, being confused, none of it's an excuse,' Gavin says, shaking his head. 'I didn't give it a second thought, how I'd treated her. I just... forgot about it, like it was nothing. Natalie was right, we have to bring up our boys better than that.'

'What did you do? After Natalie left that night?' Jackie asks.

'Felt sorry for myself, mainly,' Gavin replies. 'Tried to convince myself I wasn't the arsehole she said I was.'

'Typical man,' Jackie says quietly.

'So... shall I carry on, or have you had enough now? I totally understand if you want me to go.'

'I'm not going anywhere,' Jackie says. 'We made a promise to each other, didn't we? No judgements. I'd be quite the hypocrite if I ran out on you, wouldn't I?'

'I wish I could say things get better after that but I'm not sure

217

they do.'

'Jesus, what did you do next? Push Imogen out of the first-floor window?'

Gavin laughs at that, the sadness not quite leaving his face, but glimmers of the man she's spent the day with returning nonetheless.

'No murders, Jackie. Just me fucking up again.'

'We all fuck up, Gavin. Maybe in the end, all we can do is learn to forgive ourselves and move on.'

'Easier said than done, Jackie,' Gavin says quietly.

* * *

After Natalie and Dan left, Gavin sat shellshocked in Louise's living room, paper towel pressed to his face where bloody scratch marks were now congealing. He stood up and made his way into the kitchen when Louise's daughter, Maria, appeared. She was already halfway down the stairs, clearly woken by the noise of the front door slamming.

'Where's Mummy?' she asked.

'Don't worry, sweetheart,' Gavin said, focusing his mind as much as possible so as not to appear distressed. 'She's in her bedroom talking to Imogen.'

'Why are they in her bedroom?' Maria asked sleepily, tugging at her unicorn onesie and brushing the hair out of her face.

'They're having a bit of a heart to heart,' Gavin said. 'Go back to bed, it's all fine. Besides, you've got school in the morning.'

He went upstairs and waited while she used the toilet, making sure she was safely back in her bed and poking his head around her brother Matthew's door at the same time. Matthew was like Tim, it seemed, once asleep, it would take a fire truck to wake him. He stood outside Louise's door for a moment, unable to make out what the women's hushed voices were saying inside. He stood poised to knock for a moment before deciding against it. Imogen would come down when she was ready.

He went back downstairs and, for want of anything better to do, he washed up and tidied the dining room before having another drink. He didn't know how long he sat drinking whisky alone but by the time Louise came down, he was drunk.

'What does she have to say for herself?' he slurred.

'You shouldn't still be here,' Louise said tetchily. 'I told you to leave.'

'I didn't mean for any of this,' he said, standing up and leaning into Louise, his face close to hers. 'It all got out of hand, that's all. Everything always gets out of hand.'

She pushed him back slightly.

'That's because you don't deal with anything, Gavin.'

'I do, it's jush...'

'You're drunk, for fuck's sake, Gavin, don't you care about your marriage at all?'

'Isn't she coming down? We need to talk.'

'She's not coming down,' Louise said quietly. 'She's not coming home with you at all.'

'What?'

'I said she can have our spare room for a few nights. When you've both sobered up, you can talk.'

'Wait? Is she... is she leaving me?'

'Look, Gav, it's nothing to do with me. When you've both sobered up, I'm sure you can work something out.'

'Fuck her,' he said, staggering unsteadily into the hallway and looking up the stairs.

'Gavin,' Louise said firmly, taking his arm. 'Go home. No good will come of doing this now. I'll call you a cab. Do you have enough cash?'

He nodded, slumping against the wall.

'For the babysitter as well?'

Gavin nodded.

'Okay,' Louise said, pushing his coat into his arms.

Gavin fumbled with the front door, managing to open it on his third attempt.

'Hold on,' she said, gently pushing it shut again. 'I haven't called a cab yet, just sit down for a minute.'

'Yeah, I need a cab, please, as soon as you can...' Louise said into her mobile.

'Don't bother,' Gavin said. 'I'll walk.'

'Don't be stupid, you're drunk,' Louise said, putting an arm on his shoulder. He shirked it off, opening the front door on his first attempt and staggering into the garden.

'Gavin,' Louise called after him as he walked out of the garden.

'Leave it,' he called back, flapping his arm behind him without looking back.

The night air was cold and his cheeks felt as if a million tiny needles were penetrating his skin. His fists ached, like the joints were seizing up. Pausing to lean against a lamppost, Gavin stood still, shivering, mind broken, splintered into thousands of tiny pieces, all floating away from each other, embers from a fire disappearing into the night sky. What did people do when they couldn't cope anymore but had no choice but to carry on coping? That was the most exhausting thing, the endless necessity to continue, stretching into infinity, choking him while being careful to allow enough air in to keep him alive. On TV, in soap operas, when people were having a tough time, there was an end to it. There was a climax to the storyline. The pressure built up and up and up until the character had a moment of madness, they smashed the kitchen up or hit someone with a frying pan before falling to the floor, sobbing uncontrollably. Their breakdown was the beginning of healing for them – they had their moment where all the stress and pressure and anxiety exploded out of them and their friends and family realised how much they'd been going through before stepping in to help turn things around. Life moved on and the flood subsided. Air flooded back into their lungs.

In real life – or Gavin's life at least – there was no end. The pressure kept building and moment by moment he was able to breathe a little less. He could have gone home and smashed his kitchen up, thrown glasses and plates, ripped cupboard doors off and screamed at the top of his lungs. He could have crumbled into the corner sobbing but now that Imogen had left him – because that's what she'd done, he was sure of it – who would have been there to help but Tim? He'd have had to explain to his son that on top of his mother leaving, his father had smashed their home up.

He gritted his teeth together, grinding them as tears, unexpected, unwelcome, exploded out of him, coming from every pore, every available outlet until his entire body was a quivering, silent scream. A lifetime of trying to keep his emotions locked down and now they'd escaped they ran rampant, intoxicated with freedom. The more they attacked him, the more he hated himself. He had no right to self-pity, no right to feel shame or guilt or embarrassment because Nat and Louise were right, he'd brought all of this on himself.

The next morning, Gavin woke fully dressed on his bed, not remembering how he got home or getting rid of the babysitter. He got up, took some Aspirin and drank two pints of water as Tim wandered into the kitchen sleepily.

'Daddy!'

Gavin rushed towards him and grabbed his son, squeezing him tightly and lifting him from his feet, hugging him close and burying his head in his shoulder, overwhelmed by his son's presence.

'Hey, sweet boy,' he said, releasing Tim from his cuddle and looking deep into his son's eyes.

'Can I have breakfast?' Tim asked, then, staring at his father more carefully: 'Are you okay, Daddy?'

'Fine, big man,' Gavin said, still holding his son in the air. 'Now let's get breakfast because you've got school today.'

'Where's Mummy?' Tim said as Gavin put him back down on the floor.

'She's staying at Louise's for a couple of days,' Gavin said slowly. Tim walked over to the tall cupboard where they kept the breakfast cereal and opened it, looking over his shoulder at Gavin as he did so, frowning.

'Why can't I stay with her?' he asked.

'It's complicated,' Gavin said quietly. 'But things are going to be okay.'

While Tim was at school, Gavin sat on the sofa and stared at the walls, terrified and empty and... relieved. The thing he'd been waiting to happen had happened. He'd been trying to break his life and he'd broken it. This was the beginning. So why did it feel so scary?

That evening, Gavin put Tim to bed, trying to keep things as normal as possible. He read him a couple of stories and tickled him and assured him Mummy would be home soon and there was nothing to worry about. As his son fell asleep, he lay next to him stroking his hair and holding him close. At some point, he kissed Tim's sleeping forehead and went downstairs, leaning against his kitchen wall and closing his eyes.

How was he going to be strong enough to support Tim through what was to come? What *was* to come?

He poured himself a glass of wine – hair of the dog – and sat down at the kitchen table as his mobile pinged in his pocket. Taking it out, he saw a notification.

Hey x

Steve. A kiss. What did that mean? Did gay guys put kisses at the end of everything like it was nothing? Straight guys didn't put kisses on the end of sentences like that. Why was he messaging now? Despite what Imogen thought, they hadn't been in contact, not really. Just a few comments on Facebook, no real interactions. Not quite what Imogen asked for but nothing to feel guilty about either.

Hey, he typed into WhatsApp. *What's up?*

Nothing, I was just thinking about you, so thought I'd say hi.

Right, Gavin typed, taking a large swig of wine.

You seen the news? Steve typed. *That virus in China is all over Europe, apparently. They've shut all the ski resorts, it's crazy. There's a guy in Brighton with it. Wanted to check you were okay?*

Imogen left me.

A long pause.

…

(Steve is typing)

…

A long pause. Gavin drank more wine. He stared at his mobile screen waiting for Steve's response. He could almost see him typing something, deleting it, typing something else, deleting it. Eventually:

You okay?

It took him that long to type two words?

Not really, Gavin responded.

…

…

(Steve is typing)

…

…

Can you come down? Gavin typed, not waiting for Steve's response.

…

(Steve is typing)

…

Sure.

The next morning, Gavin got up and got Tim ready for school, using his best 'it'll be fine' smile.

'When's Mummy back?' Tim asked as Gavin gave him a huge hug and ushered him through the school gates. 'She hasn't even rung.'

'I'm not sure,' Gavin said, ruffling his son's hair. 'But we'll have fun together, won't we?'

'Daaaddy,' Tim said, flattening his hair back down and giving his father the smallest of smiles.

'Love you, big man,' Gavin said. 'Don't worry about Mum, it'll all work out for the best, I promise.'

It was a promise he knew would be hard to keep. He went home and showered before making a coffee and toast, mind vacant. He assumed Imogen was still at Louise's but she couldn't stay there indefinitely. Should he call her? Wait for her to call him? Was she trying to prove a point, leaving him alone with Tim? She'd always said he couldn't cope, maybe she was trying to show him he couldn't?

He stared through the back windows into the garden. It was March and a lot of flowers had already emerged because the sun had arrived early this year, like it knew something Gavin didn't. He was about to go out and sit in the garden when there was a knock at the front door.

'You came.' Gavin held onto the door for support, staring at the face before him, choking slightly.

~ Chapter 24 ~

Steve hadn't changed, not really. Maybe that's how it was with some people, they stayed who they were to you, whatever their age.

'Of course I came,' Steve said, a smile lighting his face. The same smile that a sixteen-year-old boy had as he read Jane Eyre on a bench. Without thinking, Gavin grabbed him, hugging him tightly, every cell in his body electric, charged, primed to explode. For a moment, Steve did nothing, then he hugged him back with the same ferocity, the same emotion. When they finally let each other go, Gavin ushered Steve into the hall and closed the door behind him, putting his hand on Steve's chest, lost in his face, his kindness.

'How did I ever lose you?' Gavin said.

'Don't,' Steve said uncomfortably, placing his hand on top of Gavin's and holding it against his chest for the tiniest of moments before gripping it and removing it. 'I'm with someone, I'm not here to be your rebound, just to offer support.'

Gavin nodded, turning around so Steve didn't see the tears, the emotion he couldn't contain.

'Hey!' Steve grabbed him by the shoulder and turned him around. 'It's okay.'

Gavin shirked him off and walked towards the kitchen.

'I'll always come if you need me, Gavin.'

There was genuine warmth in his voice, a compassion Gavin had all but forgotten.

'Yeah,' Gavin said quietly, leaning back against the kitchen counter, heart drumming loudly in his chest.

'Do your parents know?' Steve asked awkwardly, loitering in the kitchen doorway. 'About Imogen leaving you, I mean.'

'No,' Gavin replied absently, plucking up the courage to look directly at Steve again.

225

'Okay,' Steve said. 'We can deal with that later. First, put the kettle on and tell me what's been going on.'

As they sat and drank tea, Gavin told Steve everything, about feeling suffocated at work, about quitting, about his flirtation with Adam.

'And he killed himself?' Steve said, reaching over and squeezing Gavin's hand.

'Yeah, but not cos of that... I think it was about his brother. Christ, what if it wasn't? What if there was more going on? I should have been a better friend.'

'It wasn't your fault,' Steve started.

'I know,' Gavin interrupted. 'I do. But it made me think. I ran away from him like I run away from everyone, didn't I? I don't let anyone close.'

'You let Imogen close. You let me close.'

'Are you kidding?' Gavin snorted, a snot bubble coming out of his nose. 'Look how I've treated you both.'

'You're too hard on yourself.'

'I've fucked everything up, I've no idea what to do.'

'You'll work it out,' Steve said gently, hand still on top of Gavin's. 'You're more resourceful than you think. Look at how successful you've been. This house is amazing.'

'Paid for with a career I despise and a job given to me by Imogen's uncle. This house is a weight around my neck, proof that I lack a backbone.'

Gavin searched Steve's face, eyes flitting back and forth, his entire body exhaling in relief just to be near him. Steve stood up and walked over to Gavin's side of the table, taking Gavin's hands away from his face and crouching in front of him.

'I'm here,' he said. 'You're going to be okay.'

Steve put his arms around him, hugging his head to his chest, stroking him gently as Gavin released tears that shook his entire body, a rhythmic flow of breaths and sobs that Steve contained in his arms, not speaking, not offering any comfort other than his presence. It was enough.

At some point, when the emotion started to dissipate, Gavin became aware of the wet patch on Steve's shirt where his head has been resting and shame started to creep in.

'Sorry.'

He lifted his head and wiped the patch with his hand.

'I've got snot all over you.'

'Stop apologising.' Steve released his embrace and wiped one of Gavin's cheeks dry, holding his hand there and staring directly into Gavin's eyes. 'You do a lot of that.'

'I don't think I do enough of it, actually,' Gavin said, attempting a laugh but not managing it. He felt exhausted, as if the emotions that had flooded out of him over the past 24 hours had taken all of his energy with them.

* * *

'Steve came back!' Jackie exclaims excitedly, grabbing Gavin by the hands and squeezing him. 'What happened? Did you get back together?'

Gavin turns away from her and she hears him take a deep breath. He's clearly still lost in his own past as he lets go of her hands and wanders back over to the pond, staring distractedly at the water.

Conversely, Jackie feels a new warmth flood her entire body. She likes spending time with Gavin, he's entirely unexpected, nothing like she could have imagined from eavesdropping on Imogen and Louise. He's open, brave with the truth, even when it's difficult, like with Natalie. Most people would hide their mistakes and faults and flaws but he wears them openly. Is he at peace with things now? Perhaps he is? The man before her now isn't the same man he's telling her about, at least not completely.

Maybe his mistakes, his problems have helped him to grow?

You can do the same, Jackie. Evolve.
Not now.
I think you were right this morning. You needed this.
I didn't know I'd meet him.
Fate moves in mysterious ways.
I don't believe in any of that, you know I don't.
You were supposed to meet him, I think he can teach you something.
Like what?
Growth, Jackie. Things can change, no matter the mistakes you've made.

'As ever, things were complicated,' Gavin says quietly. 'He already had a boyfriend. My timing was terrible. Besides, I still wanted to save my marriage.'

'And did you?'

Gavin is about to respond, when instead he begins pointing madly at the pond.

'There *are* fish in the pond since the refurb, do you see?' he exclaims, looking back at her without any embarrassment, taking pure childish pleasure in them. 'They've put some fish back in at last.'

'No point in a pond if it's sterile,' she says quietly, hand moving unconsciously to her stomach. 'I knew they would eventually.'

'Did you?' he says, swivelling around to look at her. 'I didn't. I thought they might leave it to the weeds and lilies and be done with it.'

Jackie stands up and walks over to him, taking her sunglasses and headscarf off, taking a moment to tie her hair back from her face in a low ponytail with a hairband from her pocket.

'That makes you look different,' he says, leaning back on the railing and smiling at her.

'*Menopause* makes me look different,' she says sadly. 'It's turned my hair to straw. Nobody tells you that'll happen on top of everything else.'

'I think your hair looks great.'

'Thanks,' she says, ill at ease with the compliment, knowing it to be a lie. They stand quietly side by side for a while, Jackie's mind wandering to her past again, her mother, abusive librarians, years of solitude apart from conversations with strangers. Choices, all choices she's made.

'You're lucky, you know,' Jackie says, her hand moving unconsciously to her stomach again. 'To have Tim, to have a family. Don't underestimate how important that is.'

'I don't,' Gavin says, holding her gaze firmly. 'Do you regret not having a family, Jackie?'

'I regret a great many things, I think.'

'You think?'

'Just because you've been on a journey of self-discovery, doesn't mean we all have,' she says, smiling lightly. 'I think I've been hiding for a long time.'

'Are you ready to stop?'

'Hiding? I'd like to think so. Maybe I was meant to meet you, Gavin.'

'I don't know about that,' Gavin says, pausing, as if trying to find the right words.

'Do things work out okay for you, Gavin? You seem so more certain and secure than the Gavin in your story. Past you was a mess, if you don't mind me saying so, but you seem... I don't know. Different.'

'I'm not sure things ever work out okay or not... life's a continuum, right? It carries on, it doesn't stop, there isn't an end to the story.'

'No, but you can change. You're different, you're not the man you're telling me about.'

'Yes, I am, he's within me, part of me. The teenage dickhead, the scared adult letting his wife make all the decisions for him. They're all part of me. But I've grown some new parts as well, parts I prefer.'

'I don't think I understand.'

'You know people are always saying it's okay not to be okay? I get that, I do. Past me needed to hear that, he was always pretending to be fine, not talking to anyone, that's what caused his problems. He wouldn't acknowledge he wasn't okay until he'd all but destroyed his entire life, along with everyone around him. He couldn't let himself be happy.'

'I don't understand,' Jackie says, frowning.

'Even when I was sorting myself out, I self-sabotaged. As soon as I started to feel okay about anything, I'd find reasons not to. I'd find a way to feel shit about stuff, you know? Like I didn't deserve to be happy. I carried a lot of guilt and shame, so I made sure I punished myself. At some point, I had to tell myself it was okay to feel okay. That I was *allowed* to be happy. I didn't *have* to feel guilty all the time. I could make choices that made me happy even if other people didn't agree with them. I don't know, I'm probably talking shit but...'

'No, I think I get it,' Jackie says softly, swallowing into a dry throat. 'And it is.'

'It is what?' Gavin frowns, looking away from her towards the cloudy waters of the pond.

'Okay to be okay,' Jackie whispers, closing her eyes against the summer sun.

You understand, don't you?

Why I have to die?

Yes. Are you ready?

Nearly. Let me hear the rest of his story first, though. I need to know how things end for him.

Of course, there's no rush. Take all the time you need.

'So?' she asks Gavin without opening her eyes. 'You and Steve? Did you ever get together? What happened with you and Imogen?'

'Well,' Gavin said, a grin crossing his face. 'I told you my timing was terrible, didn't I? When Imogen left me, Covid was about to hit, wasn't it? If things weren't bad enough already, that arrived and turned all of our lives upside down.'

Part 4

Visible Lives

~ Chapter 25 ~

Within a few weeks of the first UK lockdown, the pre-Covid-19 world seemed like a dream to Gavin. In many ways, it had improved Gavin's life. It was a guilty feeling to acknowledge this, one tinged with the understanding that other people were dealing with unimaginable loss, but for Gavin, it had offered respite when he desperately needed it. Everything in his world had been hurtling towards a cliff edge; the disintegration of his marriage, the exposure of his lies and his impending financial meltdown. Perversely, coronavirus had provided him with payment holidays on credit cards and loans and mortgages that meant his dwindling savings could stretch a little further. Even Tim's school had a hardship fund for parents who were struggling with the fees which he'd taken up, despite Imogen's horror.

'Nobody will know,' he'd said softly over the phone. She hadn't replied, she'd simply hung up, her version of acquiescence.

In short, lockdown had given Gavin space. Valuable, previously unconscionable space and he was grateful for it.

Gavin stared at the screen in front of him, sipping a bottled beer while he waited for Imogen to connect to his Zoom call. Tim appeared in the kitchen behind him, coming up and leaning his chin on Gavin's shoulder.

'Hey, Daddy,' he said happily.

'Hey, sweet boy, what are you doing out of bed?'

'I wanted to say hi to Mummy,' he said, putting an arm around Gavin's neck as Gavin put one arm behind his back and hugged him tight.

'A quick hello, then back to bed, okay? You're going to hers for a few days tomorrow, anyway,' he said, smiling. 'Give

Daddy a break from home schooling.'

'Me and Matthew have created this world in Minecraft and I've made a trampoline on the top of one of the buildings,' Tim said, as if they'd been discussing Minecraft and not his absent mother. 'Do you know how I did it? I can show you. Also, did you know you can make dogs go upside down? I mean, actually upside down, like they walk around upside down and everything! If you name them...'

'Here's Mum,' Gavin interrupted, thankful for Imogen's presence as he accepted her into the Zoom meeting.

'No, she's not,' Tim said, staring at the black screen for a second. 'Why does it say Louise?'

'She's on Louise's computer, remember?' Gavin said. Then Imogen appeared, sitting at the small table in Louise's spare room, double bed and wardrobe lurking in the background, lit by a tall angle poise lamp on the floor.

'Tim!' she smiled. 'I didn't expect to see you tonight. Have you had a good day, darling?'

'Yes,' he said coyly, the screen robbing him of his words instantly.

'Are you looking forward to seeing Mummy tomorrow?' Imogen asked, not quite masking the ache in her voice. Gavin felt the same thing when Tim wasn't with him and he wasn't even used to spending as much time with Tim as Imogen, so he couldn't imagine how hard it was for her. They'd all get used to it, he supposed. They'd find a groove and make this work, for Tim's sake if not theirs.

'Mummy,' Tim said, 'can you tell Maria to leave me and Matthew alone while we're playing, she always comes in and ruins things.'

'That's not very fair,' Imogen said. 'Maria hasn't got anyone else to play with in lockdown, has she? Can't you find something that all of you can play rather than being on those tablets all the time?'

'I'm on my Switch, not a tablet,' Tim corrected. 'Anyway, it's not my fault she doesn't like Minecraft. She can talk to her friends on the computer, can't she?'

'All right,' Gavin said, squeezing Tim affectionately. 'Enough. You can work all this out tomorrow when I drop you off at Mummy's, can't you?'

'It's not Mummy's, it's Louise's,' Tim corrected.

'All right,' Gavin repeated, kissing Tim on the forehead. 'Now bed,' he said firmly. 'Say goodnight to Mummy.'

'Goodnight Mummy,' he said quietly, leaning into Gavin for one last cuddle before sauntering slowly out of the kitchen, not shutting the door behind him as he went. Gavin stood up and walked over to close the door, opening the cupboard to grab a packet of crisps out on his way back over to the table and Imogen.

'How is he?' she asked, more businesslike now Tim had left the room.

'He's holding up okay,' he replied as he sat back down and rubbed his stubble nervously. 'He's missing you.'

'It's not my fault I'm not in my own home,' Imogen said tersely.

'You left me, remember?'

'For a few days! The plan was that you'd move out and get a flat.'

'I didn't plan the coronavirus, Imogen. Estate agents aren't open. There are no flats or viewings, you know that.'

'Louise said you can stay in the flat above the café until you find somewhere.'

'We've been through this, what would I do with Tim in that little flat with no outside space? We're only allowed out for an hour a day; it wouldn't be fair on him.'

'This isn't fair on me!'

'Louise has a big house; Tim has his friends there. Besides, you're in lockdown there now, you aren't even allowed to move somewhere else!'

'You could swap with me?'

'And how would Louise feel about that? It's one thing having her best friend and son to stay, it's quite another to have me there for God knows how long.'

'She already said she wouldn't mind.'

'Look, Imogen, it would be too weird.'

'What would be weird about it? She's your friend, too.'

'It won't be forever,' Gavin said. 'Besides, Louise isn't really my friend, Adam was.'

'Barely,' Imogen said dryly.

'Come on, drop it, will you. I'm sure it won't be long before things get back to normal.'

'I want my house back, Gavin,' Imogen said, sipping her wine slowly.

'Do we have to keep having the same conversation?'

Imogen grunted, screwing her nose up a little, but Gavin could sense a little more warmth there than previously. The house was a stick to beat him with but they both knew if he said he'd swap places and move in with Louise, she'd never agree to it anyway. She wouldn't trust the two of them together for one moment.

'This bloody virus,' Imogen said. 'It's turned the entire world upside down.'

'At least we're all healthy,' Gavin said. 'Things could be worse, couldn't they. Your mum and dad are fine, so are mine. Although Mum can't stop going to the fucking supermarket every day like all the food is going to run out.'

'She probably has to top that toilet roll store up, doesn't she? Tim said she's already filled up the spare room with them. I'm sure she can find space for more in the boiler cupboard.'

Gavin smiled, taking another swig of beer.

'I think they'll have to ease things soon, don't you?' Imogen mused. 'Did you see the news?'

'Yeah, numbers aren't dropping yet.'

'It doesn't feel real, does it.'

They fell into comfortable silence, both drinking their drinks, staring at each other through their respective screens.

'What happened to us?' Gavin said eventually.

'You did,' Imogen replied but there was no malice there. Resignation, perhaps, but not malice.

'You left me, remember,' he pointed out again, leaning back in his chair and staring up at his kitchen ceiling instead of at Imogen on the screen before him. 'After scratching my face to shit.'

'Don't keep doing that,' she said firmly.

'Doing what?'

'Putting the onus on me, as if I caused this. I didn't.'

Gavin opened his mouth to speak, to defend himself, but stopped before the words came out.

'Besides, you didn't exactly fight for me to stay, did you?' Imogen continued.

'Why was that do you think?' Gavin asked.

'You don't love me,' Imogen said, matter of fact. 'Maybe you never did.'

'I *did* love you.'

'Maybe,' she said thoughtfully. 'But all the life went out of you. All the fun, the laughter. With it went the love, don't you think?'

'We stopped looking after each other, didn't we?' he leaned back into his chair and sighed. 'We shouldn't have. I wish we hadn't.'

Imogen nodded, pursing her lips.

'I keep thinking about where it went wrong, the start of it all. I mean, we were probably doomed from the start but… I don't know, I keep thinking about your bloody cages.'

'My cages?'

'Do you remember? That morning when you told me you

wanted to quit your job, that you needed to change your cage.'

Gavin nodded, remembering the rat article, remembering everything about that morning and his loneliness.

'But a cage is always a cage, Gavin,' Imogen continued. 'Even if you change it, furnish it nicely, make it look like something else. It's still a cage.'

'I don't know what you mean,' Gavin said.

'You didn't need to change your cage, you needed to escape from it. From me.'

'It wasn't like that,' Gavin started. 'I didn't mean...'

'No,' Imogen said, holding her hand up to the screen. 'It's okay. I think I was in a cage as well, really. We'd put each other in one, hadn't we? I couldn't see it then, but I do now.' She paused, leaving a silence for Gavin to fill, except he didn't know how to.

'I'm sorry I made you take that job with my uncle,' she said finally. 'I knew how unhappy it would make you but I insisted on it anyway.'

'We had a baby on the way, I get it,' Gavin said.

'Whatever the reasons,' Imogen continued, 'we somehow managed to turn each other into people we hated, didn't we?'

'Yeah.' Gavin smiled sadly. 'We really did.'

They fell quiet again and, not for the first time, Gavin felt a stirring of love for her. She was part of him and not just via Tim. The old Imogen, the lively university student full of life and ideas was still nestling in there somewhere. Perhaps navigating out of this marriage wasn't as easy as he'd imagined it would be. Perhaps he didn't even want to get out of it.

~ Chapter 26 ~

Shortly after his split with Imogen, before lockdown began.

'I know it's hard,' Gavin said, crouching down in front of Tim and smoothing his already smooth new school shirt and tie down. 'But we'll be okay, I promise.'

It was one thing having his son for a few hours at the weekend when Imogen was out shopping, but now he was a single father in sole charge for three days every week, Gavin realised just how much invisible work had gone into Imogen's parenting, and not only the practical elements.

'I want Mummy to come home,' Tim replied, his lower lip trembling.

'Daddy is looking for a new place nearby,' Gavin said. 'Then Mummy is going to move back here. We're going to get everything sorted, I promise.'

'Why can't things go back to how they were before? Mummy said things were fine before you left your job.'

'It's not that simple, Tim, I wish it was. Look, I know this is difficult, but we'll be okay, I promise.'

'You can't promise, you don't know!' Tim said, tears welling up in his eyes. Gavin grabbed him, kissing the tears from his cheeks and hugging him close.

'How about we go for an ice cream after school?' he said desperately. Tim pulled away from the hug and shrugged, walking in through the school gates and leaving Gavin feeling inadequate and alone.

When Gavin went to pick him up at the end of the day, Tim was silent, head hung low as he stood on the veranda next to his teacher, holding her hand.

'Mr Daley,' she said softly. 'There were some incidents today.'

'Incidents?' Gavin said, grabbing Tim and holding him close to his chest, then taking his face between his palms and searching his son's eyes. 'You okay, sweet boy? What happened?'

Tim didn't respond, his simply stood limply, a broken child held together by his own silence.

'One of the boys... well.'

His teacher was struggling to find the words as Gavin stood back up to full height, squeezing his son's hand as he faced her.

'There was some name calling.'

'Name calling?'

'About the separation,' she continued, squeezing her eyes and mouth tightly. 'One of the boys said Tim's mum didn't love him and that's why she'd left. He's been disciplined, but I thought you should know because Tim was quite upset.'

That night, Gavin lay with Tim as he cried himself to sleep, sobbing into his arms and wetting Gavin's T-shirt with snot and tears.

'We'll get through this, big man,' Gavin said, stroking his hair. 'I know how tough this is, but we'll find a way through it together. You and me, okay?'

'Why do you have to split up?' Tim asked, the endless question Gavin had no answer for.

'Sometimes grown-ups are complicated,' he said. 'Mummy and Daddy still love you as much as ever, whatever is going on with us.'

As his son continued to sob, his small, 8-year-old body convulsed. As each new round of emotion attacked the boy, Gavin held his son and cried silently alongside him, whispering in his ear as he did so.

'It's okay to feel hurt, it's okay to feel angry. But remember that Daddy loves you.'

'And Mummy?' Tim asked, lifting his head from Gavin's chest to look into his father's eyes. 'Does she still love me?'

'Oh my God, so, so much, Tim,' Gavin replied earnestly.
'Don't ever doubt that.'

'Then why isn't she here?' he asked, pushing Gavin off him
and turning his back, pulling his duvet tightly around him.

The next morning, Gavin found Tim sitting up in his bed,
nervously clutching one of his teddy bears to his chest.

'I've wet the bed,' he said quietly.

'Don't worry, sweet boy,' Gavin said, kissing Tim firmly on
the forehead. 'Jump in the shower and I'll get this all stripped
and in the wash.'

'I'm sorry, Daddy, I didn't know, I just woke up and I was
wet...'

'It doesn't matter, have a shower and we'll go and get some
breakfast, shall we?'

Tim managed the smallest of smiles and walked out of the
bedroom towards the bathroom as Gavin stripped his wet
bedsheets and put them in the washing machine. Ten minutes
later, Tim appeared in the kitchen doorway, bath towel around
his waist.

'Mummy isn't coming home, is she?' he said quietly.

'Not at the moment,' Gavin said slowly. 'But you'll go and
see her for a few days at Louise's tomorrow and we'll work all
of this out, I promise.'

'At Louise's?' Tim said, eyes brightening up a little.

'It'll be all right, big man,' Gavin said, hugging Tim close. 'I
know there's a lot going on up there.'

He tapped Tim lightly on the temple.

'I'm here anytime you want to talk, okay?'

Tim nodded, putting the hood of his poncho towel up and
lowering his head. As he walked away from Gavin, he paused,
turning back and asking:

'Are *you* okay, Dad?' his voice was small, wavering with
panic.

'Hey,' Gavin said, tears springing to his eyes immediately. He swallowed, controlling his voice and using the calmest whisper he could manage as he rushed towards Tim and grabbed him for another cuddle. 'I'm absolutely fine,' he continued, kneeling down to make eye contact. 'It's not your job to worry about me and Mum, okay? It's our job to worry about you.'

'Okay.'

Tim nodded sadly, turning his back on Gavin and walking towards the stairs again.

'Don't be afraid to let the emotion out, Tim,' Gavin called after him. 'Whenever you need to, let it out. Shout and scream, cry. Whatever you need.'

'You tell me not to shout,' Tim said, looking back with a small smile.

'Well, I'm giving you a free pass for a while, okay?' Gavin replied, heart aching.

'Okay,' Tim wrestled himself out of his towel. 'Can you find me some pants and socks?'

'Find them yourself,' Gavin said, standing back up to his full height. 'They're in your drawers where they always are.'

* * *

'Tim's going to be okay, isn't he?' Gavin asked, refocusing on Imogen as she sat in Louise's spare room on the other end of their Zoom call. 'I worry about him, with all this. We're doing okay with him, aren't we?'

'He'll be okay,' Imogen said, pausing and looking down at the dressing table before her. If Gavin hadn't known better, he'd have thought she was embarrassed or ashamed. 'I know I didn't always make things easy for you,' she continued, glancing up to make eye contact through the screen. 'With Tim, I mean.'

Gavin took a sharp intake of breath. This wasn't what he'd been expecting. Imogen wasn't the self-reflective type, she blamed, she judged, she projected. Was it some kind of trick?

'I didn't make things easy for you either,' he said warily.

'No, you bloody didn't,' Imogen replied, a small laugh escaping.

'Look at us,' Gavin said. 'Talking like proper grown-ups.'

'About time I suppose.'

'I do love you, Imogen,' Gavin said without meaning to. 'I'm not sure it's enough though, for either of us.'

'It's okay,' Imogen said calmly. 'I get it, I do. I'll never be Steve, will I?'

Gavin winced.

'It's not about him, it's about us.'

'Stop lying to yourself, Gavin.

'I'm not, I...' Gavin said, trailing off, unsure how to answer.

'What's happening with him?' Imogen persevered.

'What do you mean?' Gavin stuttered defensively. 'We're in lockdown, I'm not seeing him or anything. I'm not seeing anyone but Tim, am I?'

'I assume you're speaking to him, though? By the looks of it, you're still the best of Facebook friends.'

'Still Facebook stalking me?'

'Are you in contact with him?' Imogen continued, pursing her lips together.

'Yes,' Gavin replied as gently as he could. 'We're talking again, is that what you want to hear?'

'Not really,' she said quietly. 'But I can't fight it forever, can I? He's an itch you haven't scratched. I can't beat him, God knows I've tried. I keep thinking about the two of you. I always knew you loved him, after I caught you both that night in the pub. Do you remember? But I blocked it out. Told myself it was just a teenage thing. But it never went away for you, did it?'

'No,' Gavin said slowly, leaning forward, both elbows on the kitchen table in front of him, face close to his computer screen. 'Do you really want to do this?'

'I just need the truth, Gavin.'

They held each other in eye contact through their respective screens for what seemed like hours.

'I fucking hate having to talk through a screen, don't you?' Gavin said eventually.

'Don't change the subject,' Imogen said sternly. 'You owe me this. I need the truth, Gavin. Are you gay?'

'Christ, Imogen,' Gavin said, pressing his palms into his eyes before pushing his hands back through his hair, skin bristling in discomfort at the word gay on her lips. 'It's not that simple.'

'Stop trying to make it mystical, Gavin, it's a yes or no question.'

'That's just it, it's not, it's really not. Steve's… I don't know. I just…'

'You just what?'

'I love him, okay?' Is that what you want to hear? You're right, I never got him out of my system. None of this is going to make you feel better, Imogen, I don't know why you want to hear it.'

'Was everything about us a lie?'

Gavin had expected anger or hurt but Imogen was remarkably calm. Too calm.

'I need to know, Gavin,' she repeated. 'Please.'

'I love you, Imogen, you know I do.'

'I don't understand how you can if you still love him? Are you bisexual?'

'I don't know!' Gavin shouted, squeezing his arms tightly against his body, as if the walls were closing in around him. 'Does it matter?'

'Yes!' Imogen shouted back. 'If you don't get that, you're more fucked up than I thought.'

'Do we have to have this conversation?' Gavin said, looking away from the screen.

'I need to know if we've got a chance?' she said, surprising him. Was she toying with him? One look at her face told him she wasn't. It was like the hard Imogen exterior she'd wrapped herself in for all these years had begun to crack and the old Imogen, younger, filled with endless possibility, was clawing her way free. 'I mean, can we find a way back from this?'

'I hurt you,' Gavin said eventually. 'I lied and lied, fucked everything up.'

'Yes,' she said. This time it was her turn to look away from him. 'But do you still want to work it out? With me, I mean?'

'We didn't end because of Steve, Imogen. We ended because we made each other miserable.'

'He's always been there in the background though,' she mused. 'I wonder if all of our problems aren't because of him, really.'

'That's not fair, he hasn't done anything, he...'

'I don't mean him in reality. The *idea* of him. How can I ever compete with this perfect spectre you carry around with you?'

'It's not like that.'

'I think it is,' she continued, scratching her nail in a circle on the bedroom table as she spoke. 'Do you blame me?'

'Blame you? For what?' Gavin frowned.

'For coming between you and Steve all those years ago?'

'Can't we move on from this? We were getting on well a minute ago,' Gavin said, heart speeding up again. Imogen took a deep breath before replying.

'We can only move on if we're honest with each other,' she paused, as if unsure of herself. 'Are you two... Is he back in the picture?'

'I wouldn't go that far,' Gavin started. 'I mean, we're talking again but...'

'Gavin,' Imogen said. 'You don't have to lie. We've got to be open if we're going to have a chance.'

'I never blamed you,' Gavin said. 'Steve and I were over long before I met you. It wasn't your fault.'

'You weren't over,' Imogen started. 'I wanted to believe that, maybe you wanted to believe it yourself, but you weren't over. You're still not over.'

'I wasn't ready,' Gavin said. 'I don't regret marrying you, though. We've got Tim, haven't we? Whatever we've done to each other since, we created an amazing little boy. How could we regret that?'

'He is amazing,' she said, smiling sadly. 'But marriage is about more than kids, isn't it? Was it ever real love? Me and you?'

'Maybe it wasn't the fairy tale but...'

'I never wanted the fairy tale, but I wanted something more than we had, so did you.'

'So, what are we saying? Do you want to try again?'

'I don't know. Do you?'

'Honestly?' Gavin rested his chin on his hand, staring through his laptop screen at his wife, sitting in her best friend's spare room. 'I don't know either.'

A softness descended over them, a comfort in each other's honesty that Gavin hadn't experienced for many years.

'Have you noticed we're more comfortable talking now than we were before we separated?' Gavin said.

'Yeah,' Imogen said. 'No game play, no pretence. Just the two of us pretending to be adults.'

'We're doing okay with that, though, aren't we? Pretending to be adults, I mean.'

'Yeah, I think we are. But you've still got a lot of shit to sort out, up here, I mean,' Imogen said, tapping her temple. 'I'm only willing to try again if you think it can be something real. Steve's ghost can't be in the background.'

'I know,' Gavin said, swallowing, not sure how to respond.

'Right, got to go,' Imogen said brusquely, her tolerance for exposing her vulnerabilities clearly at its peak. 'I promised Louise I'd watch a film with her. You'll drop Tim off in the morning?'

Gavin nodded, a gesture Imogen mirrored before waving at her screen and clicking 'leave meeting'. After a few more seconds of awkwardness and another click, she was gone and Gavin sat alone in his kitchen, the dull hum of the dishwasher filling his ears.

~ Chapter 27 ~

Zoom calls, endless Zoom calls. Lockdown had moved beyond the banana bread stage and people had stopped pretending they were using the time to learn foreign languages but Zoom calls were still a necessity.

'How are things with whatshisname?' Gavin asked, staring at Steve through his laptop screen.

'He's doing my fucking head in,' Steve said in a tone halfway between serious and joking. 'The idea of personal space is an anathema to him.'

'Anathema,' Gavin laughed. 'Who uses words like anathema. You read too many books.'

'Impossible!'

'Things aren't going well?' Gavin said, ashamed to find himself feeling a little lighter at the prospect.

'He thinks if we aren't together *all* the time there's something wrong.'

'Dump him,' Gavin joked. Half joked. Didn't really joke.

'Fuck off,' Steve said, smiling. 'I'm serious.'

'Okay, okay,' Gavin held his hands up in submission, pursing his lips and staring at Steve's face on his laptop. 'It'll be lovely to see you, though, as soon as we're able.'

'Yeah,' Steve said quietly. 'It's a hell of a time, isn't it?'

'It really is,' Gavin replied. 'Some days, I like lockdown, you know? I know it seems awful to say, but I've got room to breathe. I hadn't realised how much I needed that. Does that sound selfish?'

'No, I think a lot of people feel like you,' Steve said, lowering his voice before continuing. 'Although, I'd give anything for a bit of peace and quiet.'

'Whatsisface?' Gavin said, his heart speeding up a little again. 'Is he really that clingy?'

'We weren't ready to move in together,' Steve said. 'We only did it because of lockdown, because we'd have been on our own otherwise.'

'The isolation would have been hard though,' Gavin said slowly. 'I've got Tim for cuddles. And I get to see Imogen because we're bubbled.'

'I like my own company, always have done. I don't need people that much.'

'Yeah, true,' Gavin said. 'They asked me to look after you when you joined school, d'you remember? What a joke, you didn't need looking after, you never have.'

'I wouldn't go that far,' Steve said quietly. 'It meant a lot to me... having you around.'

Gavin could still picture Steve's mum in a stupor on the sofa surrounded by wine bottles, dog shit wafting in from the dirty kitchen.

'Whereas he,' Steve said, his voice still a whisper, indicating with his thumb over his shoulder. 'He's like a leech.'

'He's letting you have this call with me, he can't be that bad.'

'Nah, I snuck off. We'll argue about it later, trust me. He's in the other room watching TV. Probably with his arms crossed, waiting to shout at me.'

'He can't be that bad?'

'He's fine, I'm being unkind. He's just a bit intense, that's all.'

'How are things with you? After the split?'

'I think Imogen wants us to try again,' Gavin said slowly.

'Does she?' Steve said, visibly winded. 'Wow.'

'And you?'

'I don't know,' he said honestly. 'I mean, it'd be great for Tim, he hates us living apart. And we're communicating properly for the first time in years.'

'Right,' Steve said tersely. 'Well, that's great then.'

'You don't sound convinced.'

'I don't know,' Steve shrugged. 'What do you want me to say?'

'I don't know,' Gavin mirrored his shrug, wishing Steve was sitting next to him and not hundreds of miles away.

'You know how I feel about you,' Steve replied suddenly, as if it were nothing. Gavin's heart lodged in his throat and he swallowed sandpaper, not sure how to respond.

'You can't say things like that,' Gavin started. 'It's not fair.'

'I don't think you can lecture me on fairness, do you?'

Gavin was about to answer when his mobile rang. Glancing down, he saw his mum and dad's number flashing.

'Hold on Steve, it's my mum,' Gavin said, grabbing his mobile from the table in front of him and answering, heart speeding up.

'Mum, everything okay?'

Had one of them caught the coronavirus? His mum wouldn't stop going to supermarkets, day in day out, because it was the only place she was allowed to go. She didn't need to go every day and Gavin had tried to warn her it wasn't safe, that she was putting them both at risk, but it fell on deaf ears.

'We're fine, don't worry,' his mum said. 'Just ringing to say hi.'

'My heart stops every time you call,' he said. 'Thinking it's bad news.'

'Don't start, Gavin. I have to go shopping, we can't starve ourselves.'

'You could get deliveries, you're on the priority list.'

'I didn't ring for an argument.'

'I'm not... I didn't... anyway. How are you?'

'We're fine, I just told you.'

'I'm just in the middle of another call, Mum, can I call you back?'

'How can you be in the middle of another call? You're on the phone to me.'

'A Zoom call, I mean.'

'Oh, right. I know you said I should set that up but me and your dad can't work it out, you know what we're like with technology. We'll have to wait until you can come and visit us again to sort it.'

'Okay, can I give you a call back in a bit?'

'You never call, Gavin. I just wanted to see how you were, that's all.'

'I'm in the middle of another call, that's all.'

'Besides, I wanted to tell you, me and Dad were thinking of booking a holiday. One of those all inclusives somewhere on the Mediterranean.'

'We're in the middle of a pandemic, Mum.'

'Not now, obviously,' she said. 'In the summer. You can get some brilliant deals at the minute.'

'I don't think...'

'I need something to look forward to, Gavin, don't spoil things. You always spoil things, do you know that? This is very hard on me and Dad, I don't think you realise.'

'People are dying, Mum,' Gavin said. 'I just think you should hold off on booking a holiday because this might not be over as quickly as you think.'

'It'll be over in a few weeks, you mark my words.'

'Look, Mum...' Gavin said, covering his eyes with the palm of his hand. 'Can we talk later? I'm in the middle of a Zoom.'

'Yes, don't worry about your old mum and dad,' she said in a tone that suggested he really should worry about his old mum and dad. 'We're fine.'

'Mum!' Gavin said. 'I'll call you in a bit, okay?'

'Don't call too late. You know me and Dad like to go to bed early and watch television nowadays. Not much else to do is there? Not much to get up for either, mind. The days do drag, don't they? That's why we're booking this holiday, something to look forward to, see?'

'Okay, Mum,' Gavin said. 'How about I give you a call in the morning after I've picked Tim up from Imogen? Then you can say hi to him, too?'

'Terrible thing, your breakup, Gavin. Can't you talk to Imogen? Do something about it? I'll never understand it, you're such a lovely couple.'

'Mum, can we not do this now? I'm on another Zoom.'

'Okay, Gavin, no need to take that tone with me. I told you not to worry about us. You call us tomorrow, or whenever you've got time. I know you're busy.'

'Jesus Christ.'

'What's he got to do with it?'

'Mum, I'll call you in the morning after I've picked Tim up. Love you – give my love to Dad.'

'All right, love. You sure you're okay? You seem a bit stressed out?'

'I'm fine. I'm just on another call.'

'A Zoom, you said.'

'Yes! A Zoom.'

'Okay, love. Speak tomorrow then?'

'Yes! And Mum? Maybe hold off on booking that holiday, okay?' Gavin said, hanging up before his mum could get another word in.

'How are they?' Steve said, laughing quietly to himself.

'Same as ever,' Gavin said, smiling. 'Where were we?'

'You were talking about Imogen wanting to get back together,' Steve said evasively. 'For Tim, if nothing else.'

'You were saying something else, I think,' Gavin said slowly. 'About how you feel?'

'Don't think so,' Steve said, shaking his head. 'How is Tim doing? After your split?'

For a moment, Gavin didn't answer, he simply stared at Steve through his screen. He didn't imagine it, did he? Steve had said 'you know how I feel about you.' What was Gavin supposed to do with that? They couldn't just leave it hanging in the air like that, undiscussed, could they?

'He spends half the week here and half at Louise's with Imogen,' he replied, studying Steve intently.

'Is that allowed? With lockdown, I mean?' Steve said, avoiding eye contact.

'Yeah, we're in a bubble together, Tim goes back and forth.'

'And he's okay with that?'

'He has to be,' Gavin said, pursing his lips. 'He's getting used to it and he's got Matthew and Maria there.'

'Yeah, I guess he's with his mates.'

'He'd still prefer to be with both his parents, though.'

'I'm sure you're doing a great job,' Steve said gently.

'I pretend I'm okay for him,' Gavin said quietly. 'Some days, that has to be enough. Tim is… I don't know, sometimes I can't quite reach him, there's a distance. I think he blames me for it all and he's right to.'

'I'm sure you and Imogen both played your parts, Gavin. Nothing is one sided. You're allowed to try and find happiness.'

'That'd be fine if that's what I was doing but I'm not, am I? I'm just sitting in this house day after day.'

'We all are.'

On the other side of the screen, Steve got up and filled his kettle at his kitchen sink and stood with his back to the laptop camera for a moment as he put a teabag in and waited.

'I'm sure Tim doesn't really blame you,' he said loudly without turning. 'It's probably that he hasn't got anyone else *to* blame. That's your job, isn't it? To take the shit from him for a while? I'm sure he makes Imogen feel the same when he's with her.'

'When did you get so wise?' Gavin said, raising his voice so that it would carry across Steve's kitchen sufficiently.

'Didn't you notice?' Steve said, turning around with a new cup of tea in hand and walking back to his table, putting his face close to the screen and grinning. 'I've always been wise.'

'Maybe you have.'

'And how's Imogen?' Steve asked more seriously.

'I see remnants of the woman she used to be coming back, the woman I took from her.'

'Everything isn't about you,' Steve said. 'She's a grown woman, you can't shoulder all the blame.'

'She wants to get back in the house, of course,' Gavin continued, ignoring Steve. 'Maybe that's why she wants to get back with me? I've told her when lockdown is over, I'll get a flat or something.'

'Don't you have any friends you can stay with?' Steve said, frowning.

'Not really, how fucked is that? Besides, it's lockdown, I couldn't stay with anyone if I wanted to.'

They stared at each other silently through the screen for a while.

'I have you,' Gavin said finally. 'You're probably my only friend. How sad is that?'

'Pretty sad,' Steve said, shrugging his shoulders and leaning closer to the screen. 'But we're not friends, are we? We're unfinished business.'

'Stop fucking around with me,' Gavin burst out before he could stop himself. His entire body began to beat. It was clammy, an open wound, moist and bloody, filled instantly with life.

'Ignore me,' Steve said quickly, 'I'm being stupid. Imogen wants you back and I'm in a relationship and...'

'You can't do that. You can't tell me you have feelings for me, you can't say we're unfinished business, then just say "forget it".'

'I'm being stupid,' Steve repeated, falling over his words, jittery, unsure.

'Stupid? Stupid is wasting so many years. What do you want Steve? Just say it.'

'It doesn't matter what I want, does it?' Steve replied. 'It never has done.'

'That's not fair!'

'Isn't it? Come on, you're the king of fucking people around. Fucking me around at least.'

'Christ, we were teenagers, Steve!' Gavin said.

'And now we're not and I still have no idea where I stand with you!' Steve shouted.

'You're in a relationship!'

'And I'd dump him in a heartbeat if I thought there was a chance for us. It's you, Gavin. It's always been you, you know that.'

Silence put its hands around Gavin's throat, squeezing gently at first, then more tightly until no words could escape.

'Teenage infatuation is different to an adult relationship, though,' Gavin managed to say eventually.

'Don't do that. Don't diminish it. It wasn't infatuation,' Steve said, taking a deep breath and blowing it out slowly and deliberately.

'What was it then?'

'You know what it was. Love.'

'But we're grown men now,' Gavin said desperately. 'I've got a son, it's a big deal for me. We've no way of knowing how it would work out.'

'That's life, Gavin! Nobody knows how things will work out, you just have to give things a try, work at them and hope for the best. What do you expect, a written guarantee? You can't always run away. At some point, you've got to stop and face up to things.'

'I've got a son.'

'So you keep saying.'

'It makes a difference.'

'I'm not saying it doesn't but if you and Imogen do split, you'll both meet other people at some point, you can't avoid it.'

'Maybe, but it's too soon,' Gavin said, feeling deflated, exhausted from the conversation.

'I'm not saying we should rush anything; I'm not asking you to introduce me to him as his new step-dad tomorrow... all I'm doing is asking you to think about it? Give us a chance? Give yourself a chance at happiness.'

'You'd dump Whatsisface for me? I don't want to be a homewrecker, that's not who I am.'

'I'm dumping him anyway, it's nothing to do with you, he does my head in.'

'What if we're both on the rebound? What then?'

'Then it won't work out and we move on. Fuck's sake, Gavin, how do you think life works? You make choices, you see how they work out. Some of them are shit, but guess what, some of them are bloody wonderful.'

'And Imogen? She wants to give us another go,' Gavin said. 'We're Tim's parents, we owe him it to make an effort...'

'Look, Gavin,' Steve said, raising his voice. 'I can't make the decision for you. You need to do what *you* want. Not me, not Imogen, not even Tim. You! All I can do is sit here and lay myself bare and hope you'll do the same.'

'It's complicated!' Gavin said, putting his head into his hands, fingers gently massaging his eyeballs through his eyelids.

'Only because you make it complicated!' Steve said, hand reaching out and touching the screen in front of him, as if caressing Gavin's face.

'I know one thing,' Gavin said quietly. 'I'm tired of running.'

'Then stop,' Steve replied, resignation and hope and trepidation fusing in his voice. 'Just stop running and be with me. We can make it work.'

~ Chapter 28 ~

'Don't know what they both see in you, myself,' Jackie smiles, chuckling to herself. 'Quite the Don Juan on the sly, aren't you?'

Gavin bursts out laughing at that, a beautiful, heartfelt sound that echoes around them for a moment, stunning Jackie into silence.

'Hardly,' he replies, leaning back on the pond railings. He's so much more than the man he's describing, so much more... *himself*. Whatever decision he made, it was clearly the right one. He's sitting so comfortably in his skin.

'So? Who did you choose?' she asks. 'You look happy.'

'Thanks, Jackie,' he replies, smiling. 'I am happy... you're good company.'

'I've let you talk about yourself for hours,' she counters, an impish smile crossing her own features. 'What's not to like.'

'You did quite a lot of talking yourself Stalky Shirley,' he laughs, leaning forward with clear mischief on his mind.

'Ha!' Jackie laughs out loud, her nervousness from earlier all but gone as a strange feeling overcomes her, one she doesn't recognise.

'I like spending time with you, Gavin,' she says eventually.

'Yeah, I think we're friends now,' he says, smiling.

'Friends? We've only just met. We're hardly friends.'

'We've told each other more about each other in the past few hours than I told my wife in our entire marriage,' Gavin says. 'I think that makes us friends.'

'I don't do that... I don't make friends.'

'What's that supposed to mean?'

'I've never had a friend before.'

'Shit, Jackie. You're really fucked up, aren't you?'

'That doesn't feel that supportive, Gavin,' Jackie says, smiling.

'No more following people around pretending they're your friends, okay? Actually make some. Meet me at the pub later?'

'It's all topsy turvy with you,' Jackie says thoughtfully.

'What do you mean?' Gavin asks, frowning.

'Like I said, I look for people. Broken people, people in need of help and advice. Every day I go looking, here in the park, down at the seafront, in cafés. Doesn't matter as long as I find someone. I strike up a conversation with them, try to get an insight into what's going on with them. I try to help them.'

'I know, you said. On one side, that's lovely,' Gavin says, staring directly at her face, holding her with his eyes, corners of his mouth gently turning up at the edges. 'But on the other side... bit creepy, right? You know it's got to stop?'

'But with you,' Jackie continues, ignoring him. 'It's all back to front. You started talking to me, I didn't have to find a way to introduce myself. And it's become evident you don't need my help at all, you've got it all sorted already. In fact, somehow with you, I feel like I'm the one on the couch.'

'It's more of a bench,' Gavin says, smiling broadly.

'Bench,' she repeats, mirroring his smile.

'I'm in a much better place now,' Gavin says. 'That's true. But it's not all sorted, far from it. Life is messy, Jackie.'

'But you got through it all? You sorted yourself out, even with all the mistakes?'

'Not on my own, I didn't. When I tried to do it alone, I nearly had a breakdown. Things only got better when I started talking to people, to Steve, to Imogen. Even connecting with Tim properly played its part. It's hard to make progress if you don't let people help you, Jackie.'

'What makes you think I need help?' Jackie asks, breaking contact with him and staring down at the dirty flagstones beneath her feet.

'We all need help, Jackie. Maybe your incessant need to help other people is a cry for help?'

'It's a selfish drive, you mean?'

'I didn't say that. Christ you're good at finding a negative.'

'I'm my mother's daughter,' Jackie responds flippantly.

'I'm sorry you had to grow up like you did,' Gavin says solemnly, with real compassion in his eyes.

'It's not your fault,' she replies quietly, leaning back and holding onto the fence railings, allowing her head to loll back so she can stare at the sky.

'Why do you still call yourself Jackie?' Gavin asks.

She swallows deeply, eyes trained on small white clouds moving slowly across the blue grey sky.

'Aren't you tired of the whole "call me Jackie" schtick.'

'Schtick?'

'Schtick.'

'It gives me an air of mystery, doesn't it? *Call me Jackie...* I've always been rather fond of it as an introduction.'

Gavin walks over to Christopher and Elsie's bench to sit down again. Jackie closes her eyes before looking directly at Gavin, a warm feeling flooding over her. She isn't used to feeling like this. Nobody ever asks anything about her, that isn't the point of Jackie. Jackie is there to do the asking, to keep her real self hidden from view, safe and protected.

Okay,' he says sensitively. 'Jackie it is.'

She smiles, hoping it will hide the shadow of sadness dancing under her skin. It's getting late, they've been sitting chatting for hours which means their time is nearly over. Which means Jackie's time is nearly over. She understands what she has to do now.

'Sometimes I wonder if I exist at all,' she says wistfully, leaning back into Elsie and Christopher's epitaph, surveying the enclosure around her. Overgrown, dappled sunlight breaking through the bamboo branches, birds splashing in the birdbath behind the pond. Nothing like the dark, shadowy space in her dream where she drowns each night.

'What do you mean?' Gavin asks, staring at her intently, making her wish she hadn't taken her sunglasses off.

'I live life in the cracks,' Jackie mutters, feeling the cool rectangular edges of a brass plaque push into her back. 'In the shade of other people's stories, other people's lives. Like yours.'

'You don't have to,' he prompts gently.

She waves him off, shrugging.

'I mean it,' he perseveres. 'There's a whole world out there waiting for you.'

'I think I like past-you more, He's less *self-helpy*,' Jackie says, a tiny smile on her lips. 'Just because *you've* been on a journey, doesn't mean everyone else has to be.'

'You can't hide your kind of light,' he continues, ignoring her shade. 'It escapes whether you like it or not.'

'Oh stop,' she replies, feeling a blush warm her cheeks in spite of herself. 'Just leave it, will you?'

'You had a terrible childhood. You lost your way after your mum died but you're not dead, you're not even old. You've got half a lifetime or more left to live, Jackie. But you have to make a decision to live it.'

'It's getting late,' she says quietly, aware that she doesn't have a lifetime left at all, she only has hours.

'Meet me in the pub later?' Gavin says.

'I don't do that.'

'Do what?'

'Meet strangers.'

'That's exactly what you do. What you don't do is make friends. Well, I'm your friend now whether you like it or not. But I can't do it all on my own. You've got to make the first step with me.'

'We're not friends, Gavin. We chatted, that's all.'

'It was more than a chat, Jackie, we both know that.'

Silence. Breeze rustling bamboo.

'Do you want to know what I've learned from all of my

mistakes, Jackie?' Gavin continues, standing up suddenly.

'I've got a feeling you're going to tell me,' Jackie replies wryly.

'You can't live life slightly. You can't lock big chunks of it away and expect to be happy. You've got to embrace all of it, even the bits that terrify you.'

'Easier said than done, remember?' Jackie replies quietly, searching his face as if the answer might be written there.

'All the important things are difficult,' he says, smiling. 'Life's shit like that.'

'And what if I can't?' Jackie asks. 'What if I can never embrace her? She doesn't want to embrace me so why should I show *her* kindness?'

'Her?' Gavin asks gently, frowning a little.

'Doesn't matter,' Jackie replies, squeezing her eyes shut and massaging her eyebrows with both hands. 'I'm talking rubbish, ignore me.'

'Jackie,' Gavin continues. 'It matters. Whatever – whoever – it is you're shutting away, it matters.'

Her heart is angry in her chest, wrestling from its straitjacket, frenzied, furious for freedom. She opens her eyes again to find Gavin staring at her compassionately.

'We all have *visible* lives, the parts we put on display,' Gavin says. 'But what about our *invisible* lives, the bits we pack away because we can't face them?'

Jackie stares silently at Gavin, opening her mouth to find no words will come out.

'Thing is,' Gavin continues, '*my* invisible life wasn't only hidden from everyone else, I hid it from myself, too. But keeping it buried was killing me, Jackie.'

He stares at her, eyes penetrating her, searching, uncomfortable. She closes her mouth and swallows, raising her hand to cover her lips as she does so, aware fresh tears are already pouring down her cheeks.

'There's more you've buried, more you're hiding from,' he says gently, reaching out his hand to squeeze hers. 'You need to set it free.'

'Just because you couldn't accept yourself, doesn't mean everyone else is the same,' she snaps defensively, pulling her hand away. 'Some people's visible lives are just their lives. There aren't hidden layers, there aren't things lurking underneath.'

'Nobody said anything about lurking,' Gavin replies calmly.

Jackie takes a deep breath, slows her heart rate.

'Sorry,' she says eventually. 'I didn't mean to snap, I just...'

'It's okay. I didn't mean to push.'

'You weren't pushing, I'm just... I'm not used to this, that's all.'

'What?'

'Kindness.'

Gavin pauses, shoving his hands in his pockets and shrugging.

'You don't have to do everything alone, Jackie.'

'I know,' she begins, taking a deep breath and holding it, trying to slow her heart, to remain grounded.

'I don't think you do,' he replies quietly. 'I know we've just met but... I don't know. Let me be your friend, Jackie.'

She swallows, gritting her teeth and trying to control the tears.

'Who did you choose?' she asks. 'At least tell me that before we part company.'

'We don't have to part company, that's what I'm saying. Come to the pub later?' he replies.

'I'm not...' she stutters uncomfortably. 'I told you, I don't do that. I don't meet people in the real world, I...'

'If you don't come, you'll never know if I chose Imogen or Steve, will you?'

'I could make a pretty good guess,' Jackie says, wiping her eyes.

'But you'd never know for sure,' Gavin says.

Jackie falls silent, pulling her rain mac closer around her. The afternoon air is cooler now, she's shivering.

'If you want to feel like you exist,' Gavin says, his voice more serious, 'you need to make a choice. Get off your bench and join the real world.'

'I'm not always on my bench.'

'Your metaphorical bench.'

'Just tell me who you chose for God's sake!'

'No!' Gavin laughs. 'If you want to find out, I'll see you in the Good Companions at eight o'clock.'

'I told you...'

'I know what you told me. I'm choosing to ignore you. You're going to choose to come.'

He walks away from her, pushing open the low metal gate separating the pond enclosure from the wider park.

'Don't be late!' he shouts over his shoulder.

~ Chapter 29 ~

Back at her tiny flat, she slams the door behind her and throws herself on her bed, putting a pillow over her head. She isn't sure what she's feeling. Nervous? Excited? Scared? All of those things. More. But she's *feeling*! She's feeling in a way she can't remember feeling before.

At some point, she makes herself a microwave meal, glancing unconsciously at the clock endlessly, incapable of focusing on anything other than his voice.

'Eight o'clock. If you want to know who I chose, come along and have a drink with us.'

She can guess who he's chosen. She doesn't need to go to find that out. Even if she's wrong, she's bound to see him out and about on the streets of Seven Dials sometimes, she'll be able to work it out. He can't blackmail her into facing things she doesn't want to face. Besides, he's a stranger, what does she care? He told her his story and didn't even need help. What was the point of spending the day with him? He didn't even need her.

That's exactly the point, Jackie.
What is?
You needed him, not the other way around.
I don't need anyone, never have done.
But I do, Jackie. I need other people very much. Let him in.
I can't, I don't...
You said you understood?
I do, but...
I need a friend, Jackie. Please, for me?

A friend. Jackie paces, pottering around with purpose, washing up, tidying and clearing things away. She showers and lays back on her bed, towel still wrapped around her as she stares at the ceiling, closing her eyes and breathing deeply.

'You haven't got long,' dream voice whispers, barely audible. 'Things are different this time.'

The sun is shining in the pond enclosure as Jackie enters the dream. She can hear the dream woman singing Nina Simone's 'My Baby Just Cares For Me' quietly, beautifully.

'Nice voice,' Gavin says, making her dream-self jump. What's he doing here? She turns around to see him glowing before her, handsome, happy.

'I didn't ask,' she replies, flustered.

'What happened to the fish?' he says absently.

'It's teeming with them,' she replies, staring at the fishpond. 'Just look below the surface.'

'I'm Gavin, by the way.'

'I know who you are,' she says quietly as a cloud covers the sun and he melts away into shadow, his skin becoming translucent before he finally disappears before her eyes, white smoke into the breeze.

'Say my name,' the familiar dream voice whispers in her ear. Jackie glances at the pond water and shudders.

'You don't have to push me in,' Jackie says. 'You don't have to kill me.'

'I need you to go, Jackie.'

'But you don't need to kill me.'

Silence. Still waters. Her breathing is synchronising with the breath of the dream figure in her ear. In, out, in, out until their breathe is a unit, one indistinguishable from the other.

'You're my dream, Jackie,' the voice says eventually. 'Not the other way around. I wear you like you wear Mum's damn rain mac.'

Jackie swallows, dry throat, as if pieces of broken glass are lodged there.

'Say my name,' the voice repeats urgently. 'I need to hear

you say it.'

'Shirley,' Jackie acquiesces quietly. 'You're Shirley.'

'I have to be *myself* again,' Shirley continues. 'You see that, don't you?'

'I was only ever trying to help.'

'And you did,' Shirley says in soothing, softer tones. 'More than you can ever know. But I need my life back.'

'I'm scared, Shirley.'

'You don't need to be,' whispers like a lullaby. 'I won't try to kill you again, I was wrong to try, but I didn't know what else to do.'

'Do you blame me?' Jackie asks her original self, tearful.

'For what?'

'For burying you.'

'I used to.'

'I blamed you, too.'

'Blamed me?'

'For letting Mum treat us like she did, for the librarian. I've spent a long time hating you for being weak. But you weren't weak, Shirley. You were strong, stronger than I've ever been. You got us through all that.'

'And you got us through after Mum died, Jackie. I'm grateful for that.' Shirley replies. 'You blamed me because I blamed myself. That's why I created you, I suppose? A persona to hide behind, someone with confidence and purpose. But I can't do it anymore. You see that don't you? I've lost so much by hiding in your shadow. I'll never have children, a family, I've let all that slip away. But I could still have friendships. A relationship, even? I need to salvage something for myself from this life.'

Jackie nods, tucking her hair behind her ear as it blows in the warm summer breeze.

'I'm sorry,' Jackie says sadly. 'I didn't mean to take so much from you.'

'You don't ever need to apologise,' Shirley says. 'You did

what I needed you to do *when* I needed you to. But you can rest now. I promise I'll look after you, just like you've looked after me.'

'Will you be okay without me?' Jackie asks.

'I won't be without you, not really. You just have to let me be in charge again.'

The dream pond shimmers around them, more beautiful than it has ever been in real life, an array of blues and greens and silvers and golds. The sun is brighter, warmer. As Jackie stares at Shirley's face, it is bathed in light and the two women stand face to face, identical yet different, illuminated to each other for the very first time.

'You're beautiful,' Jackie says, reaching out and touching Shirley's cheek lightly. 'Have I ever told you that before?'

'No,' Shirley says, a tear welling in her brown eyes. 'Thank you, I appreciate it.'

'And your hair,' Jackie says, rubbing it between her fingers. 'It's not like straw at all. I'm too hard on you. I've always been too hard on you.'

'Likewise, Jackie,' Shirley says, smiling. 'Thanks for all you've done for me.'

For a timeless moment, they embrace, holding each other tightly as sunlight and breeze and birds shimmer around them.

'Okay,' Jackie says eventually. 'I'm ready now. You've got a date with a friend to keep. How do we do this?'

'I don't know? Why don't you walk out of the pond enclosure and into the park?' Shirley says, shrugging.

'Okay,' Jackie says. 'But remember, I'll still be here if you need me.'

'You'll always be with me, I know that now,' Shirley says, touching her chest. 'Safe in here.'

'Thanks for not drowning me,' Jackie says quietly, a small smile crossing her lips.

'Not for want of trying. You never drowned anyway,' Shirley replies, returning Jackie's smile. 'Too stubborn.'

'Right, I'm ready,' Jackie says, reaching out and grabbing Shirley's hand. 'Wake up, go meet Gavin. Enjoy our life!'

With that, she turns her back and walks away from Shirley, slowly dispersing into the light, into the perfect birdsong of the park, into the glistening flamelike reflections bouncing endlessly off the water of the pond.

When Shirley wakes, she isn't drenched in sweat and her heart isn't racing. She sits up calmly, glancing at the clock on her wall. It's still a little early for her meeting with Gavin but she decides to get ready and head to the pub anyway. She stands up, dropping her damp towel and standing naked by her wardrobe, grabbing Jackie's rain mac and rushing over to the kitchen, opening the bin lid and shoving it in, squishing it down and turning away with a massive smile on her face. There, on the bedside table, her mother's sunglasses. Jackie O's sunglasses. Not hers. She rushes towards them and grabs then, snapping them in two and flinging them across the room, making a mental note to go shopping for new clothes first thing in the morning. For now, though, she'll have to make do with Jackie's clothes.

Jackie never went into pubs; she didn't drink and didn't like being around drunk people. They unsettled her because they were unpredictable and unpredictability was a dangerous trait in her opinion. It wasn't that she had no sympathy for the drinkers, even the maudlin, over-the-edge ones, it was simply that she didn't know how to help them because she didn't understand alcohol.

Shirley is going to do things differently, though. Rewrite the rules and change her processes. Shirley will make genuine connections rather than one-offs; she will meet people properly. Gavin has invited her, he's promised he'll be there with Imogen or Steve and that's enough for her. He won't let her down.

She feels nervous as she orders at the bar, asking for a small red wine as she knows she'll be able to drink it slowly without seeming odd. Taking a sip of wine, she winces slightly at the taste and surveys the pub warily. New territory, terrifying and exciting at the same time. There are two men sitting at the bar, drinking in solitude near to one another. Across the bar, sitting at a corner table near the Ladies, sits a late-middle-aged man with a pint of lager clutched in his hand. There is no obvious turmoil hiding beneath his features, no dark bags under his eyes, no obvious signs this man is broken. In short, not her usual type at all. For a moment, she pauses, unsure of herself. Perhaps she should simply sit with her wine and people-watch, waiting for Gavin and his mystery love. She saunters slowly across the room, more self-conscious than she's ever been as Jackie, despite the fact nobody is even looking at her. She sits down at the table next to the middle-aged man, unsure what a genuine approach looks like if you want to start a conversation with someone. She's used to Jackie singing or making extravagant displays to garner attention. None of these things are appropriate for a woman who is trying to actually meet someone.

'I'm Shirley,' she says eventually, the name falling off her tongue more easily than she imagined it would. How many years since she's used it? Too many, wasted years, hidden years, where she locked herself in fantasies and created narratives. No more. She will embrace reality, life in all its glory and stench and perfume and disaster.

'Oh,' the man says nervously, staring at her with confusion, as if waking from his own thoughts. 'Hi.'

'Hi,' Shirley replies as she leans over, extending her hand. 'Can I join you?'

'Um,' the man says, looking over his shoulder as if unsure she's talking to him. 'Yeah, okay.'

'You look like you could use some company,' Jackie says,

immediately correcting herself, realising they're Jackie's words, not hers. 'I mean, well, I could use some company, actually. Although, I'm meeting someone in a bit. At least I think I am. Not a boyfriend or anything, just a friend. But I looked over and...' she pauses, takes a deep breath. This is harder than she thought. 'Sorry, I. Sorry. You have a kind face, that's all. I thought it would be nice to chat.'

'I'm David,' he said, breaking out into a large, welcoming smile and taking Shirley's hand and shaking it warmly. 'It's nice to meet you, Shirley.'

'Sorry for babbling,' she says, sitting down into the seat next to him, heart hopscotching in her chest.

'No need to apologise,' he says kindly, looking down at his pint, stroking the mist on the outside of the glass before looking back at her, a small smile still covering his features.

'It's a pleasure to meet you, too, David.'

This is new. No agenda, no trying to pry inside his mind, to work him out, to help him. Just to be with him, listen and *be listened* to.

'You been married? Had kids?' he asks candidly. She baulks slightly and he's attentive enough to notice as he immediately follows up anxiously with: 'I just... I don't know, at our age, it's always useful to ask, isn't it? To know where the land lies.'

Shirley laughs, reaching her hand over and placing it over his.

'No husband, no ex. No children. Actually, I'm menopausal so there's no chance of kids for me...' she pauses, shaking her head slightly. 'Sorry, oversharing.'

'You overshare all you like, Shirley,' he smiles. 'It's refreshing.'

At that moment, Shirley hears someone walk in through the pub door and knows without looking that it's Gavin.

'Look, my friend has just arrived. Can you hang on a minute?'

'Yes, of course. Look, I don't want to get in the way of you and your friend, it's fine. I only popped in for a quick pint anyway and...'

'No,' Shirley says firmly. 'I'll be back in a minute, that is, I mean, if you want me to?'

He nods eagerly.

'Right,' she says, grabbing her wine glass and drinking the rest of it in one gulp as she heads over to Gavin at the bar.

'You came,' Gavin says warmly, a wide smile on his face.

'Yeah,' she replies. 'We're friends, aren't we? That's what friends do.'

'Don't get ahead of yourself,' Gavin teases. 'I don't like you that much.'

'Stop it,' she says, pushing him lightly, then glancing away before he makes eye contact. With Gavin, she suddenly feels naked without her Jackie sunglasses.

'Drink?' he asks.

'No, it's okay,' she says quietly, indicating to the barman to get his attention. 'I think I'm in a round. That's what you call it, isn't it? A round?'

'A round?' Gavin says, raising his eyebrows. 'The woman with no friends is in a round, is she?'

'Stop it,' she says, turning her attention back to the barman. 'Another red wine, please, a pint of whatever he's drinking,' she says, nodding over to David at his table.

'No problem,' the barman says. 'Anything else?'

'Whatever he's having,' she says, nodding sideways to Gavin.

'Don't be silly, I'll get mine,' Gavin says, side-eyeing David across the room. 'A round, eh?'

'Yes, a round. We got chatting, that's all. He's nice,' Shirley says, smiling coyly.

'Good for you, Jackie,' Gavin says, placing a hand on her shoulder. 'Good for you.'

'Shirley,' she corrects.

'What?'

'Call me Shirley.'

Gavin pauses for a long time, beaming like a child at Christmas.

'It's lovely to meet you, Shirley,' he says finally.

'Anyway,' Shirley says, changing the subject. 'The deal was, if I turned up, you'd tell me who you chose. So?'

'So?' he says, licking his top lip playfully.

'So... who did you choose?'

'You'll see in a minute. Are you going to come and join us?'

'Not just yet,' she says, a glint in her eye. 'Maybe later though, yeah?'

'Okay, tiger,' Gavin grabs her and embraces her tightly. For a moment she stands stock still, not returning his hug, not sure what to do. Then slowly, she lifts her arms up and puts them around Gavin's back, gently squeezes him and holds him back, warmth flooding through her system, a warmth she can't remember feeling before.

'You changed my life you know, Gavin,' she says, still in his embrace. 'I know how ridiculous that sounds, I know we only met this morning, but...'

'I didn't do anything,' he replies, releasing her embrace and holding her away from him, studying her face, her eyes. 'I just wittered on about myself a lot. Whatever changes are happening, you've made them yourself.'

'Maybe you're right,' Shirley replies, blinking back tears. 'Your story was boring anyway.'

'Ha,' Gavin laughs. 'I love you, too!'

They stand holding each other's arms for a moment, half embracing, eyes locked onto one another, nodding empathetically. Then the pub door pushes open behind them and a man walks in.

'There you go,' Gavin says, glancing over his shoulder and

waving a greeting before looking back at Shirley, face bathed in happiness.

Shirley swallows, nodding her head and squeezing her eyes shut, overwhelmed not only by Gavin's happiness, but by her own.

'Good choice, Gavin,' she says, placing her hand on his chest to feel his heartbeat, not racing, not slow, but quickened. Then she takes a deep breath and picks up her drinks and turns her back on Gavin, walking back over to David, shouting over her shoulder as she does so:

'Good choice.'

END

~ More from this author ~

Beat The Rain

Semi-finalist, Best Debut Author, Goodreads Choice Awards.

Louise and Adam are trapped in an unhappy marriage, each on a path of self-destruction, moving towards inevitable tragedy. When they meet the enigmatic Jarvis, both are fixated on him. Can they save their marriage? Should they even try to?

The Pursuit of Ordinary

Finalist, The People's Book Prize for Fiction.
Longlisted, The Guardian's Not The Booker Prize.

Dan saw Natalie's husband Joe die. So why can he still hear him?

Is Dan ill or has he really been possessed by Joe? Homeless and afraid, Dan decides the only way to find out the truth is to track down Joe's widow, Natalie. Can he convince her that Joe lives on inside him? Can they both fight their growing feelings for one another as Joe, trapped inside Dan, grows evermore lonely and afraid?

~ About the Author ~

Nigel was born in London, England, and now lives in Brighton with his partner, their two children, a kitten and insane puppy. He's a lapsed marathon runner, occasional performer and drinker of coffee and wine. Not at the same time.

Find out more about Nigel on his website and social-media pages:

Website
www.nigeljaycooper.com

Facebook
www.facebook.com/nigeljaycooper

Twitter
www.twitter.com/nijay

If you enjoyed Life, Slightly, please recommend it to a friend and post a review – they really make a difference.

~ Acknowledgements ~

Thanks to Andrew, Florence and Louis for your continued love and support. Juggling family life, work and writing isn't always easy and I wouldn't be able to do any of it without you. I love you all more than you'll ever know.

Bodie dog, it's a good job I love you as well, because you're a menace and don't make anything in my life easier. Also, stop chasing Peggy cat, she was here before you.

Laura Pearson, thank you for putting together a group of writers on Twitter who were determined to hit their daily word counts. Without this drive and support, I'd never have finished the first draft of *Life, Slightly* (then called *Other People's Lies*). To all the writers who were in that little support bubble, you have no idea what it meant to me, I was having a difficult time back then and it really helped – thank you all.

Bruce, this book would be a very different beast without our work together, thanks for your continued insight and support.

Judith Kingston, thank you for your perceptive feedback on the first draft, for your grammar pedantry and for convincing me to get rid of those terrible, terrible police officers. Most importantly, thanks for reminding me that 'a cage is always a cage, no matter how you dress it up.' I redrafted a huge part of the novel based on this sound observation.

Awais Kahn, your feedback, endorsement and support has been amazing, thank you so much.

Finally, a huge thankyou to my parents; Roundfire; my readers; book bloggers; the wider online writing community – your support is vital as I continue to navigate this strange and sometimes unsettling literary journey.

**ROUNDFIRE
BOOKS**

FICTION

Put simply, we publish great stories. Whether it's literary or popular, a gentle tale or a pulsating thriller, the connecting theme in all Roundfire fiction titles is that once you pick them up you won't want to put them down.

If you have enjoyed this book, why not tell other readers by posting a review on your preferred book site.

Recent bestsellers from Roundfire are:

The Bookseller's Sonnets
Andi Rosenthal
The Bookseller's Sonnets intertwines three love stories with a tale of
religious identity and mystery spanning five hundred years and
three countries.
Paperback: 978-1-84694-342-3 ebook: 978-184694-626-4

Birds of the Nile
An Egyptian Adventure
N.E. David
Ex-diplomat Michael Blake wanted a quiet birding trip up the Nile
– he wasn't expecting a revolution.
Paperback: 978-1-78279-158-4 ebook: 978-1-78279-157-7

Blood Profit$
The Lithium Conspiracy
J. Victor Tomaszek, James N. Patrick, Sr.
The blood of the many for the profits of the few… *Blood Profit$* will
take you into the cigar-smoke-filled room where American policy
and laws are really made.
Paperback: 978-1-78279-483-7 ebook: 978-1-78279-277-2

The Burden
A Family Saga
N.E. David
Frank will do anything to keep his mother and father apart. But
he's carrying baggage – and it might just weigh him down …
Paperback: 978-1-78279-936-8 ebook: 978-1-78279-937-5

The Cause
Roderick Vincent
The second American Revolution will be a fire lit from an internal spark.
Paperback: 978-1-78279-763-0 ebook: 978-1-78279-762-3

Don't Drink and Fly
The Story of Bernice O'Hanlon: Part One
Cathie Devitt
Bernice is a witch living in Glasgow. She loses her way in her life and wanders off the beaten track looking for the garden of enlightenment.
Paperback: 978-1-78279-016-7 ebook: 978-1-78279-015-0

Gag
Melissa Unger
One rainy afternoon in a Brooklyn diner, Peter Howland punctures an egg with his fork. Repulsed, Peter pushes the plate away and never eats again.
Paperback: 978-1-78279-564-3 ebook: 978-1-78279-563-6

The Master Yeshua
The Undiscovered Gospel of Joseph
Joyce Luck
Jesus is not who you think he is. The year is 75 CE. Joseph ben Jude is frail and ailing, but he has a prophecy to fulfil ...
Paperback: 978-1-78279-974-0 ebook: 978-1-78279-975-7

On the Far Side, There's a Boy
Paula Coston
Martine Haslett, a thirty-something 1980s woman, plays hard on the fringes of the London drag club scene until one night which prompts her to sign up to a charity. She writes to a young Sri Lankan boy, with consequences far and long.
Paperback: 978-1-78279-574-2 ebook: 978-1-78279-573-5

Tuareg
Alberto Vazquez-Figueroa
With over 5 million copies sold worldwide, *Tuareg* is a classic adventure story from best-selling author Alberto Vazquez-Figueroa, about honour, revenge and a clash of cultures.
Paperback: 978-1-84694-192-4

Readers of ebooks can buy or view any of these bestsellers by clicking on the live link in the title. Most titles are published in paperback and as an ebook. Paperbacks are available in traditional bookshops. Both print and ebook formats are available online.

Find more titles and sign up to our readers' newsletter at
http://www.johnhuntpublishing.com/fiction

Follow us on Facebook at https://www.facebook.com/JHPfiction
and Twitter at https://twitter.com/JHPFiction